D1015824

ALSO BY GREG RUCKA

THE QUEEN & COUNTRY SERIES

Private Wars

A Gentleman's Game

THE ATTICUS KODIAK SERIES

Walking Dead

Patriot Acts

Critical Space

Shooting at Midnight

Smoker

Finder

Keeper

STANDALONE

A Fistful of Rain

THE LAST RUN

THE LAST RUN

A QUEEN & COUNTRY NOVEL

GREG RUCKA

BANTAM BOOKS
NEW YORK

The Last Run is a work of fiction. Names, characters, places, and incidents either are the product of the author's imagination or are used fictitiously. Any resemblance to actual persons, living or dead, events, or locales is entirely coincidental.

Published in the United States by Bantam Books,
an imprint of The Random House Publishing Group,
a division of Random House, Inc., New York.

BANTAM BOOKS and the rooster colophon
are registered trademarks of Random House, Inc.

Library of Congress Cataloging-in-Publication Data

Rucka, Greg.
The last run : a queen & country novel / Greg Rucka.
p. cm.
ISBN 978-0-553-80475-1
eBook ISBN 978-0-553-90788-9
1. Women intelligence officers—Fiction. 2. British—Iran—Fiction. 3. Espionage, British—Iran—Fiction. 4. London (England)—Fiction. 5. Iran—Fiction. I. Title.
PS3568.U2968L37 2010
813'.54—dc22 2010010561

Printed in the United States of America on acid-free paper

www.bantamdell.com

2 4 6 8 9 7 5 3 1

First Edition

Design by R. Bull

To Jay
and
to Evan,
With all my love.

THE LAST RUN

PREOPERATIONAL BACKGROUND
CHACE, TARA F.

For Tara Chace, it was the fall that did it, the absurdly long pause that came between missing the handhold and slamming into the ground. Like all falls that are too far, this one lasted long enough for her to realize what had happened, and what, as a result, would inevitably happen next. It was a moment of perfect clarity; not of vision, but of self-awareness, and Chace saw herself then as she had only four other times in her life. She saw herself as the woman she was—frankly, honestly, without self-pity, judgment, or false modesty. Who she was, who she had been, and who she wished to be.

Then she hit the ground, her back impacting first, followed almost immediately by her skull.

The first such moment of clarity had occurred when she was only ten years old, the day her mother, Annika Bodmer-Chace, informed Tara that, come the spring, she would be attending a boarding school in Cheltenham, England, and would no longer be living in Switzerland with her mother and father. The conversation—if it could be called such—had occurred in the sitting room of the Geneva house, with Chace seated in a chair so large it had threatened to swallow her, and her mother on her knees before her, speaking gently and sweetly in French, holding both of her child's hands in her own as she imparted the news. When Chace looked past her mother and out the window, she could see snow falling with a sedate grace.

"For your education," her mother told her with the same, bright smile that made men and women alike wonder what other sweet lies and promises it concealed. "You must be educated like a proper lady."

"Like you?" Chace asked.

The smile broke wide, Annika laughing. At thirty-four, she was a near-perfect mirror for the woman Chace would grow to become, the same golden blond hair and sky blue eyes, strong and fine-boned. The only marked difference were in the first creases of age in her flawless skin, lines made by laughter that Chace would never share.

"No," Annika said. "A *proper* lady."

The understanding had been sudden and complete then. The cascade of dueling infidelities between her mother and father had reached its breaking point. Chace knew they were separating, and understood that divorce would follow, that it would be ugly, that it would be brutal, and that her mother would never, ever change. She saw in her mother a vision of herself as she might be, selfish and spoiled and utterly oblivious to the pain she inflicted upon others, a woman-child who would never grow up.

Which meant Chace was going to have to, and quickly.

The second of such moments occurred when Chace was twenty-two, in her last year at Cambridge but down to London for a long weekend with a group of her peers, amongst them the only one she called a friend, Rachel Beck. This was in the days on the cusp, after the Cold War but before the Global War on Terror, before the Firm had been reduced to advertising openly for new recruits. For two years, Chace had been vetted with deliberation by SIS's talent-spotters at the university until, finally, assured of her loyalties, intelligence, and potential, she had been invited the night before to a discreet—read: *secret*—meeting in a cramped office situated in the basement of one of London's finer hotels. Chace, who had long since developed a strong suspicion of what was really going on, had attended the meeting, in part to assure herself she'd been correct, but mostly because the secrecy and deception involved had appealed to her.

Arriving for the interview precisely at twenty minutes past three in the afternoon, Chace had found an empty room, two chairs, a table, and a tea set on the sideboard. Touching the pot with the back of her hand, she'd found it scalding hot. She'd ignored the refreshment, taken a seat, smoked a cigarette, and had begun contemplating smoking another when a small and rather sad-looking man entered the room. He made no apology for keeping her waiting, and Chace had liked that, because, of course, she'd understood the delay as intentional. She was certain she'd been followed to the meeting, and would've been surprised if she hadn't been under surveillance within the room itself.

The man gave his name as Mr. Smith, and producing a file from his bag, he proceeded to relate a comprehensive and remarkably thorough accounting of her life up to and including that very day. Everything was laid bare in the most clinical fashion: her family, her friendships, her education, her vices, her lovers, her indiscretions, including one or two that Chace herself had tried to forget. It was a recitation of facts, devoid of all judgment but her own.

Then Mr. Smith had said, "There are those who feel you could be of great service to your country, if you chose to dedicate yourself in such a direction. I speak, Miss Chace, of a lifetime of service, of challenge and sacrifice that will be known to only a very few at the highest levels of Government. It is a life without public recognition, without common reward, but it is, at its heart, greater and more vital. A secret life, to be sure, but one where what you do and say can—not to overstate it—alter the course of history."

Mr. Smith had paused, perhaps to give Chace the opportunity to speak, but she didn't take it. After several seconds, with no change of his expression, he continued.

"Very few people are invited to this calling. Of those who answer, even less actually succeed. You could be one of them."

Chace remained silent.

"Certainly, this is not a decision to be made with haste," Mr. Smith said. "By the same token, it is not one that can be indulged. An answer is required before midnight Sunday."

Chace nodded, smiled, whereupon Mr. Smith recited a phone number for her to remember. If she was interested, she was to call the number and say that she was staying in London for the week. If not, she needn't bother to call.

She left Mr. Smith in the basement, making her way on foot to meet Rachel and the others near Sloane Square, struggling with her thoughts. By the time she reached them, though, she had come to a decision: she would forget Mr. Smith and his phone number, along with everything else he'd said. There was an appeal to the offer, to be sure, and it wasn't a fear of failing that restrained her; she had no doubt that, of those few who were called, she would certainly be one to succeed. But it was that same vanity, ultimately, that held her in check.

She loathed, with passion, the idea of being anonymous.

The dinner that evening had been a typically indulgent affair, catty and gossip-laden, lubricated with alcohol, which Chace enjoyed, and a smattering of recreational drugs, which she eschewed. This was followed by dancing and more drinking at a string of clubs, all of them deemed fashionable for one reason or another. Rachel, unlike Chace, was *nouveau riche,* and while her father had substantially more money than any number of them put together, to the Sloanes she was not, and never would be, one of them, try though she might, and try heroically she did. While no one was ever overtly unkind to Rachel's face, as soon as her back was turned the knives promptly emerged to carve out a hundred imaginary faults and sins.

To Chace, who'd met Rachel her first year at boarding school and now had known her for over a decade, it was painful to behold; her friend, desperate to believe that she had been accepted, only to be reminded again and again that she would never belong; while at the same time, Chace herself was welcomed with open arms through no effort of her own, simply an accident of birth.

At two in the morning, stumbling into cabs outside of yet another too dark and too loud dance club, Rachel had doubled over vomiting, apparently sick drunk, much to the amusement and relief of Chace's fellow Sloanes. Chace was urged to send Rachel home in a cab so that the party might roll on to its next port of call.

That was the moment. With one hand on Rachel's back, the other holding her friend's hair out of her face, smelling the petrol and alcohol and vomit, hearing the laughter and mockery of these inbred and overly privileged young women, Chace saw herself as one of them, and she hated herself thoroughly for it.

She spent the next day nursing Rachel through one of the worst bouts of food poisoning Chace ever witnessed. That night, with just under an hour to spare, she dialed the number Mr. Smith had given her.

"I'm thinking I'll be staying in London for the week," Chace said.

The third moment came five years later, as Chace stood on the balcony of Tom Wallace's flat in Gosport, looking out at the lights glimmering on the water, a glass of whiskey in her hand. Wallace stood beside her. They were both a little drunk and very well fed, and surrounded in the warmth of contented, companionable friendship.

Following her entry to SIS, Chace had been sent to the Firm's training facility in Gosport, near Portsmouth, for the requisite sixteen-week induction and education course required of all fledgling spies. The Powers That Be had marked her early on as an analyst, due to several factors, not the least of them being her raw intelligence and the fact that she already spoke four languages fluently, and could pass as native in three of them. Her career trajectory had already been planned by the time she'd unpacked her things in the School dormitory. She would complete her training, be posted as a Number Two to some low-priority theatre to get her legs, and provided she acquitted herself well, would be reposted in due course to a more active theatre. She would serve out her tours and, if all continued as planned, would return to London to a job in the Intelligence Directorate, working for the Director of Intelligence, perhaps heading up one of the Desks herself. If she proved particularly brilliant, she might even find herself named D-Int one day.

No one had bothered to inform Chace about this, however, and it was shortly after the introductory lecture, where the hierarchy and divisions of SIS were broken down for all new recruits, that she began asking questions about the Special Section. About those agents who were tasked directly under the Director of Operations. The Special Operations Officers, the ones who worked out of headquarters in Vauxhall Cross, who were expected to dash around the world at a moment's notice. The agents who, when feces sailed en route to fan, were expected to intercept and leave not a trace behind.

They were called Minders, Chace was told, and she'd be much better off forgetting about them, as their life expectancy was short, their pay was horrible, their new boss was a nightmare, and they hardly did *real* intelligence work, anyway. Minders were to be tolerated, not admired. Minders were an evil and, many argued, not even a necessary one. If she thought they were James Bond, she was sadly mistaken, because James Bond didn't exist, and if he did, he'd have died long ago from terminal stupidity. Wouldn't she much rather continue her studies in cryptography?

Yes, thank you, Chace said, and I'd also like to take the Fast Driving Course, and the Escape and Evasion Course, and Advanced Small Arms Training, please, if you'd be so kind. And Flaps and Seals. And Locks and Safes. And Explosives. And Night Operations. And anything else that you think a Special Operations Officer might need to know.

Right, look, she was told, we can see where you're going with this, and believe us, it's not going to work. First of all, Minders are almost always drawn from the military, understand? Prior experience, prior service, the SAS and Royal Commando blokes, they already know how to kill a man with a set of bicycle clips and a banana, they're halfway there, you see? That's one. And two, forgive us for saying it, but you're a woman. And there's never been a woman in the Special Section, and the new D-Ops, Paul Crocker, sure as hell isn't going to make you the first. And third, did we mention the part about Minders dying? Because they do that, quite a lot, actually.

So just forget about all this Minder nonsense, and if you really dedicate yourself to your Russian studies, why, what would you say to being posted to Moscow as the Station Number Two?

By the fourteenth week of the course, it was clear to all who were paying attention that Tara Chace was on her way to being one of the most brilliant agents to ever pass through the School. Her test scores, across the board, were stellar, as were her learning curve and her retention. She went from having never fired a gun to rating as an expert in both small arms and rifles. She became so vicious in hand-to-hand training that her fellow students first loathed, then actively avoided, sparring with her. When she was sent into Portsmouth on a practical to acquire an asset, given four hours to get from that asset not solely personal details, but also their passport and bank account numbers, Chace not only returned in three with all of the aforementioned information, but with her target's Jaguar, as well. That she'd targeted a lieutenant in the Royal Navy who should have damn well known better was simply the icing on the cake.

So it was that, when Paul Crocker, less than six months in as D-Ops and suddenly down to two Minders because of an unfortunate turn of events in Sudan, saw Tara Chace's file, there was really no decision for him to make. Contrary to what had been said to Chace at the School, Crocker didn't give a rat's ass that she was female; she could do the job, and he needed a warm body. But it wasn't enough that she looked brilliant on paper, and the last thing Crocker could afford in the Section was anyone—man or woman—who fancied himself the star of his own action film.

Chace was summoned to London for an interview, and by the time it was over, the School had received a call saying that she would not be returning, but instead was being posted to the Special Section immediately as Minder Three. Could they please send along her things?

It was as the new Minder Three that Paul Crocker walked her

into the Pit, the basement office where the Special Section made its home, and introduced her to Tom Wallace, Minder One, her Head of Section.

For almost five years, Chace worked with Wallace, initially as Minder Three to his One, then as Minder Two when the Desk was vacated. He took her under his wing, taught her everything he knew. He led her by example, both in the field and in the office, and it was from Wallace that Chace learned that her most dangerous enemies, her most vicious battles, would be fought in the corridors of Vauxhall Cross and Whitehall, not in Mozambique or Vietnam. They fought together and suffered together and laughed together and worked together and the friendship that grew between them was the most precious and sincere that Chace ever had in her life. It was a friendship of equals, and in a world of secrets, bound by equal parts honesty and trust. They came to know each other at their worst, and at their best.

When Wallace left the Section to teach at the School, it nearly broke her heart, and Chace didn't understand why.

Then she stood on his little balcony in Gosport, watching as he stepped over the windowsill to join her, and all the illusions were swept away. She saw him as he was, herself as she was, and she knew she loved him beyond friendship, beyond anything she had ever imagined herself capable of feeling. She loved him absolutely and completely, and she understood that love was returned in full measure, and she saw how frail a thing it was, and how precious.

The fourth time was when the nurse at the hospital in Keyleigh put her newborn daughter in her arms, the baby girl she named Tamsin, after her father.

The daughter that she and Tom Wallace had conceived less than a week before he was murdered in Saudi Arabia.

Lying in the mud at the base of the climbing wall, pelted with rain and soaked with sweat, Chace came back into herself, her head still ringing. Atop the wall, Minder Two, Nicky Poole, was shouting down at her, asking if she was all right. Chris Lankford, Minder Three, was already on his way down, and the drill sergeant who oversaw the obstacle course was sprinting towards her, telling her not to move for God's sake, carrying his first-aid kit.

Chace closed her eyes. She saw again what had been so obvious, so clear to her, as she'd fallen. It wasn't simply that she'd missed the handhold. It was that her left arm hadn't been able to fully extend to reach it, locking suddenly with the memory of the pain a man in Uzbekistan had caused her almost three years before. Things had gone wrong in Uzbekistan, and she'd ended up in a basement room at the Ministry of the Interior, where she'd been stripped, beaten, tortured, and nearly raped.

Now the pain was gone, only exhaustion remaining, and that, too, was being replaced by something else, the sense of a burden being lifted; the flooding relaxation that follows when a struggle has reached its end.

Three times a year, Paul Crocker sent the Minders back to the School for a refresher course. Three times a year, the Minders would spend two days going over what they already knew, acquainting themselves with new techniques and equipment. Three times a year, they would recertify in weapons and hand-to-hand, in cars and explosives and all other manner of tradecraft. Three times a year, they would run the obstacle course, crawling beneath barbed wire through mud and climbing the wall.

She couldn't count the number of times she'd run the course as a recruit. As a Minder, this had been her twenty-ninth.

This was the first time she had ever fallen.

With a smile, Tara Chace resolved that it would never happen again.

CHAPTER ONE

IRAN—TEHRAN, MINISTRY OF INTELLIGENCE AND SECURITY (MOIS)
29 NOVEMBER 1803 HOURS (GMT +3.30)

If it went wrong, it would cost Youness Shirazi his life; and the ways in which it could go wrong were too numerous to count.

He was alone, for the first time all day, standing at the window and looking past his partial reflection down at Sepah Street, at the Foreign Aliens Office opposite his own. On this side of the city, at this hour, Tehran's traffic was thin, but still the Foreign Aliens Office was bustling, just as it had been ever since the unrest had begun so many months ago.

The plan, Shirazi reassured himself, was a good one, certainly the best that he could manage given the current climate, the present moment. Pressure had been building from on-high for months to deliver something, anything that could be presented as a decisive victory; anything that would hurt the enemies of the Revolution, and serve as a propaganda coup, besides. The Americans, the French, the Israelis, or the British—an embarrassment to any of them would do, and as the Americans had little-to-nothing by way of assets on the ground, as the French had been almost thoroughly neutralized in Iran, and as the Israelis were hiding deep in their holes, it only made sense that the British should be the target.

On the street below, he noted the arrival of the black SUV. Farzan Zahabzeh would be inside, along with their old prisoner. Not that old, Shirazi corrected himself, because if their guest, in his late-fifties, was to be called old, Shirazi himself would be closer to the designation than he cared to admit. He turned from the window, catching his reflection, stopped, gazing at himself. Forty-four, balding, beard and mustache neatly trimmed, his spectacles failing to hide the heavy bags beneath his eyes. He'd managed three hours of sleep last night, up from the hour he'd been averaging the week prior. Insomnia, he reflected, was part of the job.

But it wasn't insomnia that had been keeping him up these past nights, and he knew that.

Shirazi moved to his desk, carefully shifted the stack of old surveillance photos Farzan had compiled to the side, then settled himself at the computer. He typed in his password, Farsi flashing quickly onto the screen, then entered a second password before the system permitted him to bring up the foreign operatives database. As Head of Counterintelligence for VEVAK, Iran's Ministry of Intelligence and Security, the database was part of Shirazi's bread and butter, a listing of all suspected or known opposition agents around the world, of spies, real and, in many cases, imagined, who had or might one day work against Iran's interests. The list itself was by no means comprehensive—in intelligence, Shirazi reflected, such things never were—and much of its information was suspect. But there were gems to be found, hard intelligence that had been bought dearly.

It was one of these gems that Shirazi went to, within the British section, under the SIS subheading. He scanned quickly until he found the name he wanted, then opened the associated file. A photograph bloomed on the monitor, four years out-of-date according to the reference, but Shirazi doubted that the woman had changed very much. The picture had been taken at the border between Uzbekistan and Afghanistan, from the Afghan side. The woman was wearing sunglasses, but the file claimed her eyes were blue, the same way it claimed that she was blond, and five feet eleven inches tall, both facts evident in the photograph. According to Shirazi's information, the woman had no less than twelve different documented work-names, but the only one that mattered to him was her real one: Chace, Tara; and her job, that of Head of Section for the Special Operations Division of SIS, under the supervision of SIS Director of Operations Crocker, Paul.

Shirazi studied the face of Tara Chace impassively, trying to discern the woman who wore it. He didn't know her, he had never met her, all he had was speculation. He knew something of the job in Uzbekistan, and before that the one in Iraq, and another in Georgia. But no details, only guesswork, what SIS had accomplished. What this woman had accomplished.

They would have to send her. The prize was too great, the target too high-value to risk sending anyone else, anyone less subordinate. Neither the British government nor the Americans—and there was no doubt the Americans would become involved—would settle for less. The CIA would demand the British send their best, though how Paul Crocker would get his tall, blond, female Special Operations Officer into Iran without everyone from the Quds Force to the Guardian Council knowing about it, Shirazi had no idea. Nonetheless, he had no doubt that Crocker would accomplish the task; as an adversary, Paul Crocker had long ago earned Shirazi's respect, if not admiration.

There was a knock at the door, and Shirazi quit the files on the monitor as his deputy entered.

"He's in the building," Farzan Zahabzeh said, shutting the door behind him. "I'm having him processed right now."

"How did he take it?"

"The pickup scared him, the way it always does, no matter who. Now he's decided to be indignant." Zahabzeh's grin flickered with malice. "He already asked me if I know who he is."

Shirazi laughed. "And you said nothing?"

"Only that we had questions for him."

"Good, very good."

There was a pause, and Shirazi saw the younger man's attitude change, the pride of power knocked akimbo by a long-ingrained sense of self-preservation. He understood it, and knew what Zahabzeh was thinking, and knew he would have to reassure him; Shirazi could entertain his own doubts, but it was vital that Zahabzeh have none, that he be as committed, in his way, to their course as Shirazi already was.

"There's still time."

Shirazi shook his head. "No. Once he entered the building, there was no going back."

"We could simply question him about anything, about the Greens, say, then let him go. That would do it, that would be all it takes."

"And how would that help defend the Revolution? We must see this through. Think about the result, think about what we will gain. For months we've been pressured to strike back against those who have struck us. This is how we do it. The result will more than justify the means."

Farzan Zahabzeh grimaced, scratched his chin beneath his beard. He was ten years Shirazi's junior, still carrying enough of his youth that the job hadn't begun to show on him. Full of energy and strength, not much taller than Shirazi, but larger, clearly stronger. But his junior nonetheless, and with a lot left to learn.

Another knock, this one more forceful and somehow more formal, the hand of one of the guards, leading the prisoner into their trap.

"It's all or nothing," Shirazi said.

"All or nothing," Zahabzeh agreed, and went to answer the door.

The prisoner drew himself up in his chair, cast an angry glance at Zahabzeh standing beside him, then glared at Youness Shirazi.

"Do you know who I am?" the man demanded.

Shirazi considered the question, taking the man in. He certainly looked old, or, at the least, older, though Shirazi thought that might simply be the result of seeing him here and now, rather than as he appeared in photographs taken over thirty years before. Beard and hair both more gray than black, small eyes. None of the clothes of the *ulema,* the learned Shi'a scholars, but instead a simple buttoned shirt, tan, and even simpler black trousers. While he watched, the man began scratching at the back of his right hand with the nails of his left, an unconscious gesture that persisted for several seconds before stopping.

Shirazi met the prisoner's eyes, returned the stare with the practiced patience he had learned from twenty years in counterintelligence, unwavering, until the man's indignation faded and the fear reasserted itself. Then, satisfied, Shirazi looked to Zahabzeh, and gave him a small, almost inconsequential, nod.

Zahabzeh took up the stack of photographs and began laying them out in a roughly chronological line along the desktop, facing away from Shirazi, towards their prisoner. Some of the photographs had suffered with age, their edges yellowing and beginning to curl, and in the few of them that had been taken in color, that same color had begun to wash away, rendering the figures insubstantial, almost fictional, and dreamlike.

Or nightmarish, Shirazi thought, as he gauged the man's reaction. At first there had been nothing, blank incomprehension, perhaps bewilderment, but when his eyes fell upon the third photograph, the one with the two young men in the back of the car, everything changed, the reaction inescapable. The prisoner started in his chair, stifling an exclamation. He looked up and then, meeting Shirazi's eyes, quickly away, to the side and down, as if hoping to find refuge somewhere between the cracks of the linoleum floor. Zahabzeh ran out of room on the desk, went back to the beginning, now laying the photos one atop the other. Somewhere, outside Shirazi's office, a phone rang and was quickly answered.

"That was a long time ago," the man said. He brought his head up, looking at Shirazi again, and his voice touched on plaintive. "I was young. Very foolish. It was thirty years ago."

Zahabzeh finished placing the last of the photographs. Some of them were now stacked four-deep. Shirazi adjusted his glasses, rotated his chair to face the wall on his left, where a portrait of the Ayatollah hung. He pretended to contemplate it.

"I was foolish," the man said, softly.

"You are a spy," Zahabzeh spat, and Shirazi had to fight a smile at the savagery of the declaration. "A spy in service of the British."

"What? No!" The man twisted, unsure who to address, finally settling on Zahabzeh. "No, I swear!"

Zahabzeh plucked one of the pictures from the desk, a black-and-white surveillance shot of their prisoner at twenty-five, seated outside a Tehran café, his head bent to the ear of a handsome European. He shoved it angrily in the man's face.

"This!"

"No, I don't—"

Zahabzeh scooped up a handful of the photographs, began dropping them into the old man's lap. "This one. This man, we know him, SIS. This one, his cover was as a trade representative. This woman, a known British whore. Did you sleep with her, too? Or was it only the boys? Is that how they paid you? With sex? Sex and money? This one, do you remember this party? This one, what are you handing him, the so-called trade representative? What secrets did you sell? You were in the Army, you were a soldier. How many men died because of you? How many men died because of secrets the British gave to Saddam? This one. This one. This one."

Zahabzeh continued to assault him with the photos, one after the other, and the prisoner was cringing, drawing back further against his chair, until, with no place to go, he lashed out with an arm. His hand caught the remaining stack in Zahabzeh's hand, sent it flying. They hit the floor with a slap, sliding over one another like an opening fan.

"I'm not a spy!" The old man pushed himself out of his chair, past Zahabzeh, grabbing the edge of the desk. He appealed to Shirazi. "These are the mistakes of a young man, a stupid, foolish boy! Why are you doing this? Why now? I swear to you, I swear by the Prophet's name, it ended thirty years ago!"

Shirazi, his eyes still on the portrait, replied, "Things have changed."

The prisoner shook his head, and then, at last, followed Shirazi's gaze to the picture hanging on the wall. He groaned softly, pained, then sank back into his chair. It took him two attempts before he could get out his next words.

"My uncle . . . he knows?"

"Of course he knows," Shirazi lied, turning his chair back to face his prisoner directly. "Would you be here otherwise if he didn't?"

"It was so long ago." He spoke in a whisper, to himself, then raised his voice again, speaking to Shirazi. "It ended thirty years ago, thirty-two years ago now. You must tell him that. I beg you, tell him that."

"We did tell him that," Shirazi lied. "But after the last election, after all the unrest, with so many counterrevolutionaries and spies suddenly emboldened, things, as I said, have changed. What we were once obliged to describe as the indiscretion of youth we must now, by order of the Supreme Leader himself, view as crimes against the State. You understand? We did tell him, I assure you."

The man hung his head. "God help me."

Shirazi caught Zahabzeh's look of triumph.

"Not God," Shirazi said. "Not God. We will help you."

The despair that had taken the man near to tears broke with the possibility of renewed hope.

"There is a way out of this for you. There is a way to remove the stain and save yourself. If you help us, then we can help you."

"I will!" the prisoner said. "I will do anything!"

"The first thing you must do," Shirazi said, "is remember."

Then, with the patience of a hunter, Youness Shirazi began walking Hossein Khamenei, the eldest nephew of the Ayatollah Khamenei, of the Supreme Leader of the Islamic Republic of Iran, back through memory.

As it turned out, Hossein Khamenei's memory was surprisingly good.

CHAPTER TWO

IRAN—TEHRAN, PARK-E SHAHR

4 DECEMBER 0651 HOURS (GMT +3.30)

At the School, the instructors had talked a lot about fear, and even though Caleb Lewis had listened to their every word and believed each one that was uttered, he still found himself entirely unprepared for the real thing. It was, without question, awful, purely, completely, clawingly awful. It was a fear that had its own feel, its own scent, even its own taste. Nothing anyone had ever told him, nothing that he had ever experienced growing up, had proved an adequate preparation for its constant presence.

For three and a half weeks, since first setting foot in Iran, fear had been with him, and it showed no signs of leaving anytime soon.

He hadn't wanted the post as the Tehran Number Two. What Caleb Lewis had wanted, what he had trained for, was a desk job, in the Intelligence Directorate, preferably on the Iran Desk. He had wanted to work for D-Int Daniel Szurko, who was by all accounts both a quite brilliant and very pleasant gentleman who demanded the best from his staff. That was why Caleb Lewis had worked so very hard at mastering his Farsi as well as his Arabic, and it hadn't ever occurred to him that doing so would lead to his downfall, the same way it had never occurred to him that doing less than his best in his other coursework at the School might propel his life on an entirely different trajectory.

Then, at the beginning of November, ten members of the embassy staff in Tehran had been arrested, all of them accused of espionage, and after almost two weeks of diplomatic wrangling between Her Majesty's Government and the Islamic Republic of Iran, all ten had been released, declared persona non grata, and sent packing back to England. It wasn't the first time such a thing had happened, and it certainly wouldn't be the last, but what had made this particular instance exceptional was that, of the ten, two actually *were* working for SIS. In the mad scramble to fill the post, Lee Barnett had been pulled from Istanbul and named the new Tehran Number One, but nowhere in the field had D-Ops been able to find an able Number Two.

Which was why, only one week before completing the School, Caleb Lewis had been called out of class by James Chester and directed to report to Paul Crocker in London for immediate briefing by D-Ops. Chester had added, ominously, that Lewis might want to pack up his belongings before he left. Forty-seven hours later, he was getting off a plane in Tehran, his heart trying to climb its way out of his mouth, and his head still reeling with the nearly absurd amount of operational data the Ops Room staff had pumped into it.

Ever since that moment, Caleb Lewis had been desperately pretending he was a spy, and was just as desperately certain he wasn't any damn good at it.

The Ops Room had done their best by him, and, in fact, Lewis was doing a far better job of things than he imagined. The briefing, while hasty, had been thorough, comprehensive, overseen not only by D-Ops, but by Terry Ricks, the previous Tehran Number Two. It was Ricks who had done most of the talking.

"First priority on hitting the ground, Caleb, is to figure out what that bastard Shirazi's done to us since we've been on holiday," Ricks said. "Those VEVAK bastards move quick, damn quick, and they'll be looking to make you as one of ours as soon as you land."

"Understood," Caleb said, nodding, head already starting to swim in confusion.

"Play the rulebook, understand? Take your time, identify the opposition, don't do anything—not a bloody goddamn thing—until you're certain you know when you're being followed and when you're not."

"Yes." Caleb spoke with such emphasis that D-Ops, sitting alone along one side of the briefing table, shot him a glare, and Lewis didn't need telepathy to read the man's thoughts. Crocker was nervous about him, and with good reason. Lewis was being sent into a hostile theatre, green as a new shoot. Everyone present for the briefing—hell, everyone in the Ops Room, if not in Vauxhall Cross itself—knew the importance of Tehran.

Ever since the Revolution, Iran had been, as they said in the old days, a tough nut to crack. But following the last election and the suppression of the Green Revolution that followed in its wake, SIS had seen an opportunity and seized it. It had taken Ricks the better part of a year, but somehow he'd cobbled together the beginnings of a new network, consisting mostly of students and counterrevolutionaries, with a few, precious members of the clergy and low-level government officials. The nascent cell was of paramount importance to SIS, and one needn't be an expert in Farsi to understand why; since the Revolution, reliable human intelligence out of Iran had been near-impossible to obtain. The Americans were widely known to be both deaf and blind in the country, and Britain, even after thirty years of effort, had met with nothing but repeated failure in the face of VEVAK's aggressive counterintelligence program. Israel's operations, while perhaps more successful, had always been jealously guarded and its fruits rarely shared, now even more so with the possibility of a nuclear Iran.

There was no margin for error. If there was a failure in Iran, it would be laid first at Caleb's feet, then at Barnett's, and of the two of them, Barnett, with his years of service to the Firm, had political cover. If Caleb screwed this, his would go down in the record books as one of the shortest careers in SIS history.

"Used cars for code names," Ricks said. "Code words and phrases for all of them, using Farsi only, to avoid suspicion. The lexicon's here, you'll need to memorize it. Newest one recruited, code name Mini, works for one of the *mujtahids* appointed to the Guardian Council. Ideological asset, has refused funds. Very, very skittish, Lewis, and with good reason. His dead drop is in the Park-e Shahr, beneath the eastern footbridge, north side. Checks Wednesday and Saturday. Eleventh brick up, sixth in as you face it on the left. The masonry looks solid, but the brick is loose. Drop-loaded sign is an empty pack of cigarettes on the ground at the foot of the trashcan, to your right as you enter the park from Fayyaz-bakkah Street, facing south. Your drop-cleared is a yellow chalk mark on the front of the south gatepost, at the east entrance to the park. Repeat it back."

Caleb repeated it back without error. He thought Crocker looked surprised he'd managed it.

"Good," Ricks said. "Next one, code name is Phantom, she's a student at Tehran University. Ideological, but is taking payment. . . "

The first Saturday in December, and Caleb woke cold and immediately scared, eyes coming open to find himself staring into his pillow. He sat himself up with a start, certain he'd overslept, checked the clock and saw he hadn't, and fought off the near-overpowering urge to collapse back beneath the warmth of his blankets. Tehran had turned surprisingly cold in the last three weeks, never rising above ten degrees Celsius. Rain had started falling the night before. Sitting on the side of his bed, he could hear it spattering against the windows still.

Caleb roused himself, showered and dressed, took his backpack from its peg, and then, with a moment's hesitation to gather himself and marshal his courage, stepped out of his apartment. He made his way down the two flights onto Mellat Street and into the rain. A car sped past him as he emerged, an old Fiat, and he avoided the spray it kicked up, only to be rewarded twenty yards to the south with a soaking from a speeding Khodro as he crossed Amir Kabir. He shook himself off, continuing towards the Tehran Bazaar, most of the shops not yet open. It wasn't yet six in the morning. He ducked into the first open café he found for a quick cup of coffee, exchanging pleasantries with the owner, and used the opportunity to again try and spot anyone who might be following him.

That he didn't see any surveillance did nothing to ease his fears. In its own way, it made things worse.

There were three drops for him to check, Mini, Cayman, and Quattro, and Caleb took them in reverse order this morning, in an effort to continually vary his routine. No signs set for Quattro or Cayman, and he was beginning to think that maybe he might be home and warm and dry before eight, when, at the entrance to the Park-e Shahr, at the foot of the trashcan, he saw a crushed pack of 57s. The cigarettes were manufactured by the Iranian Tobacco Company, named 57 after the year 1357 in the Iranian calendar, 1979 in the Gregorian, the year of the Revolution.

Without stopping, Caleb continued into the park. The rain began pelting him with thicker drops, and he struggled with the sudden desire to look back over his shoulder, to check, once again, for anyone who might be following him. Thus far he'd seen no one who raised undue suspicion, had seen nothing out of the ordinary, but that gave him no confidence. His contact with Mini since arriving in-country had been limited, only one message two weeks earlier, marginal value about movement on the Guardian Council and a statement that he had to be careful, that he was afraid he was under suspicion. Given everything Ricks had told him about Mini, Caleb had expected a longer silence.

He trudged his way deeper into the park, along the broad central main path, stepping over piles of scattered, sodden leaves. A bicyclist swooped past him, continued on, speeding towards the central fountain. Caleb turned west, onto a thinner trail, overhung with branches, the sound of the rainfall louder on their leaves. The near-constant noise of Tehran's automobile traffic had faded, and now he could hear his own footsteps. There was a bench on his right, ahead of him, and he stopped at it, propping up his left foot and bending to fix the laces on his trainers. He straightened, wiped water out of his hair, and still he saw nobody who might be following him. He turned south, switching paths, then east again, and twice more he stopped to admire the trees, or to look north, as if trying to spot the Alborz Mountains behind the rain.

Finally, his route took him towards the footbridge, fifty meters away now, and he saw the bicyclist who'd passed him earlier, still perched on his seat, one leg down to hold his balance, peering about, and Caleb was slowing his approach when the rider pushed off once more, speeding away, down the trail. Caleb waited until he was out of sight. Then he followed the narrow pathway down the embankment, to where it joined the walkway beneath the bridge.

The sound of the falling rain was louder beneath the bridge, but Caleb didn't idle to enjoy the shelter. He located the brick, shifted it, and inside there was, indeed, a scrap of paper. He pocketed it, replaced the brick, then continued down the path. It had taken him two, perhaps three seconds total to clear the drop.

He used the east entrance to leave the park, marking the south post as he passed it with the chalk he carried in his pocket.

His Number One, Lee Barnett, was in their office when Caleb reached the embassy.

"Drowned rat," Barnett said.

"Pardon?"

"As in what you look like."

Caleb peeled off his jacket, nodding, then took a seat at his desk. For a moment he relished the modest relief in the safety of his surroundings. Their office was buried deep within the embassy itself, unmarked, and always locked, the only keys possessed by Caleb and Barnett. According to Barnett, they indeed had "posh digs," at least compared to other Stations the Number One had experienced. Most often SIS was stuck in something more akin to a closet, with barely enough room to allow a man to change his mind, let alone his shirt. Here, there was space for the two of them to have their own desks, with enough to spare for an ample cabinet that held the secure communications array used to speak with London. Opposite Caleb's desk was the office safe, large and ancient and impenetrable, flanked on either side by floor-to-ceiling bookcases. The room had no windows, not even ceiling lights, but was instead illuminated by two standing lamps, positioned at opposite corners. Instead of being dim, however, that gave the room a feeling of warmth, something Lewis was more than a little grateful for at the moment.

Barnett moved to their little tea table and plugged in the kettle. "Long walk this morning?"

"Had to check the flags on Mini, Cayman, and Quattro," Caleb answered, digging into his pocket. "Mini had loaded the drop, so I took an extra hour before moving to clear it, just to be sure I was clean."

"I thought Mini was keeping his head down?"

"That's what I thought." He unfolded the note. There was a pause, only the sound of the kettle beginning to chatter. "Sir?"

"Hmm?"

Caleb smoothed the note out on his desk, looked at Barnett. "Mini uses code words."

"Is that a question?"

"No. Mini uses code words, the lexicon that Ricks worked up before he got PNG'ed."

"If you need the lexicon, it's in the safe, I—"

"No, this is a number code," Caleb said. "Mini's drop, but it's not Mini's code. This one's different, in English, not Farsi. Looks like a substitution code."

"Give here."

Caleb handed the note over, watched as Barnett's thin face seemed to stretch in confusion, the normally cheerful smile absent. Caleb liked Barnett; it was, in fact, Barnett who had made him feel that his fear was both to be expected and to be managed, and there was something paternal about the man that appealed greatly to Caleb. He was a tall man, veering close to gangly, with a thick head of black hair that had begun showing the gray of distinction at his temples. If Caleb had any problems with Barnett at all, it was that the man smoked like a refinery, and had no qualms about doing so in their office, official embassy no-smoking policy be damned.

Barnett had lowered the note, was staring at the wall, deep in thought. The kettle rattled to crescendo, then shut itself off with a click.

"You weren't followed?" Barnett asked him.

"If they were on me, I never saw them."

The Number One handed the note back to Caleb, reached for the pack of Silk Cut Blue resting on his desk beside his lighter. He shook one free and set fire to it. After another moment he left his cigarette to dangle on his lip, moved to the kettle, and fixed each of them a cup of tea.

"Doesn't make any fucking sense." Barnett handed one mug to Caleb. "If they know the drop, why the hell didn't they nab you when you went to clear it?"

"Not following, sir."

"Mini uses the lexicon, Caleb. This isn't the lexicon. Ergo, Mini didn't load the drop."

"Oh, Jesus," Caleb said. "Mini gave up the drop."

"No, lad, you're not thinking it through. If Mini gave up the drop, why wouldn't he have given up the lexicon, too? And if the drop's been blown, then why didn't Shirazi's goon squad just pin you to the ground the moment you came to clear it? Or, better yet, after you'd cleared it? Did you see anyone else around, anyone at all?"

"There was a bicyclist, just before I got to the bridge, but he was gone before I moved in." Caleb examined the note again, all the more certain that he was looking at two different codes, a primary number key, followed by a rudimentary substitution code, reading:

E N M S A E K H
N H MH A K A SM

Caleb counted up the figures in the first part, fourteen numbers, apparently grouped in twos. "The second part is definitely substitution, but I think this first part is a book code."

"Could be he's waiting until you return." The ash on the end of

Barnett's cigarette dropped onto the back of his hand, narrowly missing his mug of tea. He wiped his hand against his pants, leaning forward to examine the note again. "First time to see if the drop is real. Now that it's confirmed, they'll grab you on the next trip. PNG express, if you're lucky."

"God." Caleb felt suddenly ill.

"I think you're right, I think it's a book code. Caleb?"

"No one in the network uses a book code, sir."

"Thing is, if VEVAK *does* have Mini, then he certainly gave them the lexicon."

"So it's not VEVAK?"

Barnett straightened up, shrugged. "Guess we won't know that until we decode the bloody thing. By which, of course, I mean until *you* decode the bloody thing." He grinned.

"But I don't know the book." Caleb shook his head, unsure if his Number One was making a joke or not. "It could be any book. And the substitution code—I mean, there's no way to even begin to guess the key."

"Well, the book code at least, if it's a message for this Station, it's going to be found in one of those." Barnett used his cigarette to indicate the two bookcases, filled to bursting with all manner of reference, both technical and cultural. At least three different copies of the Koran, and that many again of the collected Omar Khayyám, anything that any previous resident to the Station had thought of merit, or, at the least, of use. "Can't be more than one hundred and fifty, maybe two hundred books there, tops. Crack part-the-first, maybe that gives you the key to part-the-second."

"You can't be serious," Caleb said, and immediately regretted it. One look told him that, for all Barnett's humor, there was nothing about the current situation he found funny.

"Look, Caleb, either this is Shirazi playing silly buggers with us, or it's someone else who's discovered that we use the footbridge in Park-e Shahr as a dead drop. In either case, the location is compromised."

Caleb got to his feet quickly, suddenly possessed of a different fear, one that had nothing to do with his own well-being. "I've got to set the warning flag for Mini. Jesus, if he hasn't been made and they're watching the drop, he'll walk right into them."

"No, sit. Drink your bloody tea."

"But Mini—"

"I'll do it. If Shirazi's crew has eyes on you, there's a chance I'll draw less attention. He's in Elahiyeh?"

"Yes, in the foothills."

"What's the flag?"

"There's a streetlight at the corner of Razm Ara and Estanbol, on the north side." Caleb searched his pockets, pulled out the piece of yellow chalk. "Two horizontal lines on the east side of the post."

"No school like the old school." Barnett took the chalk. "Right, I'll set the flag, you hit the books. I'd start with the ones in Farsi."

"That's what I was thinking."

"Good. Wish me luck."

"I should go," Caleb said uneasily. "Mini's my agent."

Barnett grinned, opening the door. "You're a good lad, Caleb."

It was midafternoon before Barnett returned, saying the deed was done and that the rain had finally stopped, and that there'd been no sign of any VEVAK interest whatsoever. He noted the growing towers of books surrounding Caleb, fixed two more cups of tea, and turned his attention back to the reports he'd been preparing for delivery to D-Int earlier that morning. Each worked in silence.

As Barnett was preparing to leave for the day, Caleb found the book. A copy of Hakim Abu'l Qasim Ferdowsi's epic poem, *Shahnameh.* Even when he had it, he wasn't sure it was correct. The intervening hours had been filled with so many pieces of nonsense, of what appeared to be the correct match of page and word to meaning, only to fall apart at the last moment. An article where a noun was needed, or a number that went to a page or word that didn't exist. Twice already Caleb had managed to decode the whole message, only to realize the sentence was utter, utter nonsense.

Which was why, even after reading it through three times, he still wasn't certain he'd decoded it correctly.

"The grapes are in the water. Falcon."

Barnett, about to pull on his coat, stopped and stared at him. "What?"

"I'm not sure, sir. I think that's the message. *'The grapes are in the water. Falcon.'* Sounds like a keyword code now, but it still doesn't match the lexicon. And we're not running anybody under the name Falcon, are we?"

"Not in this theatre. You're sure you've got it right?"

"No," Caleb said, with utter sincerity. "I'm not."

"Not really what I wanted to hear." Barnett had the communications cabinet open now, extended a long leg to hook a nearby chair, pulling it closer. He parked himself in front of the keyboard, began typing quickly. In addition to the signals deck, there was a headset, as well as a companion handset, for the secure audio link, but Caleb had yet to see them used. According to Barnett, he didn't want to see them used, either, because if one of them was on the headset here in Iran, the odds were it was Paul Crocker at the other end of it in London.

"Give it to me again," Barnett said. "And the substitution code at the end."

Caleb relayed the message once more, Barnett typing more slowly this time as he took it down. Task completed, Barnett turned the transmit key, then whacked the "send" button with his palm. The machine hummed for an instant, then went utterly silent. Barnett removed the key, scooted himself back in his chair, closed and locked the cabinet.

"London's problem now," he told Caleb Lewis.

CHAPTER THREE

LONDON—VAUXHALL CROSS, OPS ROOM

6 DECEMBER 0910 HOURS (GMT)

Tara Chace rubbed the goose egg on the back of her head gently, still swollen from her fall on the obstacle course, and with her free hand took a sip of the traditionally god-awful coffee the Ops Room seemed to run on. Across from her at the briefing table, William Teagle, from Mission Planning, and Chris Lankford, her Minder Three, were talking about what a grand holiday Chris was about to have in Iraq. Despite the theatre of operations, Chace wasn't overly worried for Lankford's safety; the mission was remarkably mundane, barely worthy of a Minder, in her opinion. As a result she allowed her attention to wander around the room.

Chace adored the Ops Room, with its clean lines and clearly demarcated regions, even this renovated version that was a far cry from the one she'd first come to know nine years earlier. You always knew where you were in the Ops Room; you always knew the state of things. When the world was behaving, as it was apparently doing at the moment, there was a feeling of palpable, controlled efficiency, even self-confidence. Everyone to their duty, everything at its place.

All that would change at the drop of a hat, or, more literally and much more frequently, at the ring of a phone. The word would come, something had happened, was happening, was about to happen, and then the orders would ring out, and the whole of the Ops Room would transform, exploding into motion, and still, everyone to their duty, everything at its place.

Chace thought of the letter she was carrying in her pocket, resting against her heart, and had a moment of hesitation. The Ops

Room was one of the few places in the world where she felt she truly belonged, and the thought of leaving it pained her. She hoped she wouldn't have to.

Architecturally, the space was nothing more than a giant cube, with all workstations oriented to have clear line-of-sight to the wall of linked plasma monitors at the far end that perpetually displayed a map of the world. In the left rear, where she sat with Lankford and Teagle, was the Briefing Table. Left front was the Mission Planning Desk, for the moment empty. Right front was the Main Communications Desk, staffed at the moment by Alexis Ferguson, who'd been in the Ops Room for as long as Chace could remember. Right rear, the Duty Operations Desk, with Ronald Hodgson seated at the raised platform, another old-timer, acting as the shift's Duty Operations Officer. At the moment that was the entire Ops Room complement—with the addition of two runners, who were ferrying paper between the various desks.

Chace noted that Lankford's mission had already gone up on the map. A cherry red dot now pulsed on Mosul, a golden halo around all of Iraq. The mission had been designated "Bagboy," with a callout stating that Minder Three had been allocated.

"MOD estimates some two hundred of the crew-served weapons have gone missing in the last three months," Teagle was telling Lankford, in answer to some question Chace had missed.

"They've done an audit of the base?" Lankford asked. "They've actually tipped the place on its side and looked for them?"

"So we're told. Can't be found anywhere."

"Wonder if they checked behind the sofa cushions," Lankford said to Chace.

"They think they're being sold?" Chace asked Teagle.

"That's the fear. The question is who's doing the buying. Bad headline if British troop is killed with British weapon wielded by Iraqi insurgent."

"And their own internal investigation turned up nothing?"

Teagle nodded, then added, "This is why they are asking for our assistance."

"What's the window?"

"Five days turnaround."

"You're going to have loads of fun on this one," Chace told Lankford, certain that he wouldn't. The investigation would be tedious, and already she suspected that MOD had requested SIS assistance merely to cover their own ass. Five days for Minder Three to uncover what, presumably, they had been working months to resolve. It was a token investigation, and it was already assumed by the MOD that Lankford would fail.

Lankford smiled across the table at her, confident. He wasn't yet thirty, with the kind of face that would hold all signs of aging at bay for at least another twenty years, and his sincerity made him seem all the younger and, consequently, made her feel all the older. "I'm going to solve it."

"You do, you'll get a nice Christmas bonus."

"I will, just you wait, Boss."

Chace grinned, then looked to the multiple clocks positioned on the plasma wall, each giving the time in various zones around the world, and she saw that it was now nearly a quarter past nine. Crocker would have just finished going through the Immediates on his desk, now moving on to the Moderates and then the Routines, the less pressing files and reports that demanded his attention. Unless he hit something that caused outrage or panic, he'd be at his desk for another fifteen minutes or so, before heading to his daily meeting with D-Int and the Deputy Chief.

Chace stretched, feeling her left knee pop with an almost-pleasant pain as her leg extended, then got to her feet. "Don't be stupid, Chris, all right? It may be a base, but it's a base in Iraq, and there are a hell of a lot of guns about."

"No fear," Lankford said.

"Yes, fear—it'll keep you alive. Stop by the Pit when you're finished, all right?"

"Yes'm."

Chace started for the door, saw that Alexis, still wearing her coms headset, leads gathered in one hand, was in consultation with Ronald Hodgson at Duty Ops, standing on her tiptoes to reach the top of the raised desk. Ron had a signals sheet in his hand, reading it with a bemused expression.

"Nah, it's a mistake," he was saying.

"Barnett's asking for a confirmation," Alexis told him. "I've run it twice, it's gibberish."

Ron saw Chace, motioned for her to join them, saying, "Falcon's in Jakarta, I think. There's no one running in Iran under that name. Tara, take a look at this."

He handed down the note for Chace to read.

"Lee Barnett sent it Saturday night, as a routine inquiry," Alexis said, by way of explanation. "He says the first part is a book code and queried if we knew what it meant. The second part he maintains is a substitution code, but they don't have the key. He's asking for instructions how to proceed. I've spent the last hour trying to decipher it, but the computer keeps spitting out 'no known code' for the lot."

"Barnett's Tehran?" Chace asked. "How'd he come by this?"

"He didn't say."

Chace read the message again. *The grapes are in the water. Falcon.* "The substitution, it's a number sequence."

"Agreed."

"You've contacted Jakarta?"

Ron shook his head. "I was about to send it up to D-Ops, see if he knew what it meant."

"I'm on my way up there now, I'll give it to him. Meantime, signal Jakarta, query Falcon's whereabouts. And Lex—send back to Tehran. Ask for details on the message, how they came by it."

Alexis nodded, hopped down off the platform, and headed back to her workstation.

"You have any idea what it means?" Ron asked.

"None," Chace said. "But it certainly doesn't bode well for the grapes."

The door to the inner office was closed. Kate Cooke, Paul Crocker's long-suffering personal assistant, was seated at her desk in the outer, her fingers flying over her keyboard. She paused midkeystroke when Chace entered.

"Minder Three?" Kate asked.

"Still briefing. Operation: Bagboy."

"Bagboy," Kate repeated. "When's he due back?"

"Kate, he hasn't left yet. Should be back Sunday, all goes well."

"It's Iraq."

"He's on-base the entire time."

Kate nodded, then resumed her typing. She and Lankford had been on-again, off-again for the last few years, and from the change in her manner, Chace guessed they were on-again once more. Not that Kate would have cared any less about his well-being if they weren't, but Chace knew that she'd never have dared ask for details otherwise.

For a second, Chace thought about saying something to her about discretion, and that perhaps Kate might want to be more circumspect. But the fact was, Chace knew Kate would never have asked the questions of Crocker or Poole. Even if she disapproved of the relationship—and she wasn't certain that she did—the fact was, Chace didn't have a leg to stand on, and Kate knew that better perhaps than most.

Chace moved to refill the mug she'd brought with her from the Ops Room. "Can I see him?"

"He's on with Seale right now," Kate said. "Should be done in another minute."

"What's the CIA want now?"

Kate managed the rather impressive feat of shrugging without missing a keystroke. Chace tilted her head, trying to listen for Crocker's voice over the sound of the keys and through his closed door and, not hearing anything, concluded that whatever it was Julian Seale wanted, it wasn't worth the raising of a voice. She wasn't particularly fond of the CIA Chief of Station in London, though Crocker seemed to get on with him just fine, certainly maintaining the time-honored "Special Relationship" between the two services. But Chace had found the American to be more political than his predecessors, and she didn't trust him. She wasn't naive; she understood that the intelligence service of any country would always be embroiled in the politics of the same. But she felt, strongly, that agencies like SIS and the CIA should walk a fine line, serving what she admitted was often an ill-defined and long-term "national interest" rather than an administration's politics and polling results of the moment. Seale made her uneasy.

Chace slipped back out from behind Kate's desk, sipping at her refreshed coffee, which was infinitely better than what she'd sampled earlier in the Ops Room but had the detriment of being decaf. Yet another change since Chace had come to work for the Firm; in the beginning, it had seemed that all intelligence work was fueled by caffeine and nicotine, in roughly equal proportions. Chace had given up smoking while pregnant with Tamsin, then again some two years ago, and thus far had managed with only a few stumbles. Crocker, for his part—at least as far as she knew—had gone without a smoke for over a year, quitting at roughly the same time his coffee had become decaffeinated.

The heart attack, when it came, hadn't surprised anyone who knew Paul Crocker; the only shock was that it had taken so long to finally happen. And the irony was that, while the job certainly was a contributing factor, it hadn't been the job, specifically, that had caused it. Crocker, his wife, and their younger daughter had taken a weekend trip to visit his older daughter, who was attending university in York. They'd spent a November Saturday together, retired to their hotel for the night, and, as Crocker told it, an invisible elephant had leapt onto his chest and refused to move.

Technically, Chace thought, D-Ops had actually died. Crocker's heart had stopped beating, and for seven minutes before the paramedics arrived, he survived on his wife's breath, on her repeated compressions of his heart. The medics managed to restart a rhythm before rushing him off to the hospital, and by Sunday noon, Paul Crocker had two stents and a new lease on life, one that the doctors told him he was damn lucky to have at all, and if he wanted to preserve it, some lifestyle changes were in order. No more fags, no more red meat, easy on the caffeine, and—this was a laugh to everyone who heard it—less stress.

Between recovery and rehab, Crocker was out of the office for just over nine weeks, through the holidays and into early February, during which time Chace was named Acting Director of Operations, Poole advanced to Head of Section, Minder One, and Lankford to Minder Two. It wasn't the first time Chace had found herself named Acting Director; on three separate occasions since becoming Minder One, Crocker had been forced out of the office, almost always on official business, and she'd been obliged to step into his place, though never for longer than five days.

This time it was different, and markedly so. The question of whether or not Paul Crocker would actually return to the Firm at all hovered, unasked, throughout the building. There were many who felt he had long since passed his sell-by date, that it was more than time for him to go. His list of allies, both within Vauxhall Cross and over the Thames, in Whitehall, had grown perilously short over the years, while the list of those he'd double-crossed, ignored, abused, or enraged had just as significantly lengthened. In certain quarters, Chace was sure the news of his heart attack had led to celebration.

But if those same people had thought that Tara Chace, as Acting D-Ops, would be easier to manage than her absent predecessor, they had clearly forgotten both her loyalty to Crocker and the fact that everything she knew of the job she'd learned from him. While she was less prone to shouting than Crocker, and perhaps a little more liberal with honey than with vinegar, she was no less fierce in pursuit of the D-Ops mandate. She'd handled the day-to-day bureaucratic chores of running the Operations Directorate with skill born of nearly a decade in SIS, but that had been expected. The real test of a D-Ops, everyone knew, was how they reacted in a crisis. Prior to Crocker's prolonged absence, there'd never been an opportunity to see Chace in action in that role.

The opportunity came on three separate occasions. At each, Chace responded as decisively, as quickly, and as knowledgeably as Crocker ever had done. Two of the situations she'd been able to diffuse from the Ops Room alone, dashing off signals to the Stations in question, once getting on the phone to threaten a recalcitrant Number One in Hong Kong.

The third had been different, and as potentially lethal to Chace's career as anything Crocker had ever faced. The son of a leading MP had been kidnapped in the Philippines, along with his girlfriend, and the political pressure within the Government itself to locate and then effect a successful rescue had been both instant and enormous. It was the first time Chace found herself running a legitimate special operation, designated Operation: Tiretrack, and she'd immediately ended up fighting with both the Deputy Chief and C about who to send for the job.

Gordon-Palmer demanded she send both Minders. Chace refused, allocating Poole for the job, and maintaining that Lankford had to be held in reserve in case another Special Op arose elsewhere. Less than twenty-four hours after Poole hit the ground in Manila, London received the ransom demand, and with it, the ticking clock. Forty-eight hours or the boy would start coming home in pieces, wrapped in what was left of the girlfriend.

For two days, Chace had walked Vauxhall Cross, aware of the whispers, of a looming sense of doom. C pressed again for Lankford to be deployed, and Chace again refused. She was called to Whitehall, to the office of Sir Walter Seccombe, the Permanent Undersecretary to the Foreign Office, certainly the most powerful person in Government she'd ever been made to answer to. He demanded to know the disposition of Tiretrack. He interrogated her at length about each and every decision she'd made, then asked why she wasn't doing more. He informed her that, without question, HMG could not concede to the kidnappers' demands. He then warned her about the acute embarrassment to HMG if the operation failed. He pointed out that the MP in question was of the Opposition, and that a successful operation would have as profound political repercussions as a failure. He sent her back to Vauxhall Cross with the clear knowledge that, should SIS blow this, it would be her head sent to the MP in question.

With just under two hours left on the deadline, at four in the morning London time, Poole contacted Chace via the Ops Room. She hadn't been home since the crisis began, and had even resorted to sending Kate to her home in Camden to look after Tamsin the previous night, when no one else could be found for the task. In the three days since the kidnapping, she'd managed, perhaps, three hours of sleep, and had been forced to send a runner out to buy her clean clothes, just to keep from smelling like the inside of a gym sock. She'd been called a bitch twice to her face, and behind her back so many times she'd lost count.

Poole had a lead on a possible location where the two were being held. Could he get support for a rescue attempt? Lankford, preferably, or at least some CIA assistance?

No, she told him. There isn't time.

You're going to get me killed, Poole said.

At which point Chace told him, in front of God and the Ops Room, to draw arms from the Station and get on with the fucking job, and that if he had wanted things easy, he should have stayed in the fucking SAS.

Two hours and six minutes later, Poole contacted the Ops Room again. He had the boy. He had the girlfriend. Might he come home now, please?

Yes, Chace said. You can come home now, Nicky. Nicely done.

And she could swear she heard the smile over the crackle of the satellite phone, as he said, "Thank you, ma'am."

She'd informed C, the Deputy Chief, and the FCO of the successful completion of the mission. She'd told the Ops Room staff they'd done a damn fine job. Then she'd gone home, hugged her daughter, and managed a full six hours of sleep before returning to the office.

Crocker came back to work a week and a half later. Lankford became Minder Three again, Poole Minder Two, and Chace returned to the Pit as Minder One, with a sense of relief only matched by her sense of regret.

"Minder One to see you," Kate said as the door to the inner office cracked open.

"Is there coffee?"

"You know, even decaf has caffeine in—"

"Shut up." Crocker's head appeared past the doorframe. He glared at Kate, then at Chace. "You can come in if you bring coffee."

Chace took the mug Kate handed her, stepped into Crocker's office to find him standing behind his desk, sorting the folders heaped there. She handed over the coffee, which he set aside without tasting. He continued playing solitaire with the files, so Chace turned and closed the door, then took a seat opposite the desk.

"Make it quick," Crocker said, still searching the paperwork. "I'm already late for the daily with Daniel and Simon."

"Ops Room wanted me to give you this." Chace handed over the copy of Barnett's signal. "There's no Falcon running in the Iran theatre. They can't crack the second sequence, but it looks like a number string."

"Thomas Bay's got a Falcon in Jakarta." Crocker glanced at the paper without taking it, went back to sorting, stopped, and pulled the signal out of Chace's hand. "What the hell does this mean?"

"That was Barnett's question, though phrased more politely. I've already got Lex onto Tehran for more details, and Ron's put a signal in to Bay."

Crocker grunted, thrust the sheet back. "Well in hand, then. Anything else?"

Chace hesitated. "It can wait."

"Is it quick?"

"Depends, really."

He stopped, fixed her with a stare. Crocker had three inches and a dozen years on her, black hair and mean, brown eyes that had seemed to grow meaner since the heart attack. Always lean to the point of thin, he'd lost weight, too. The combined effect now made him look, more than ever, like a malevolent scarecrow dressed in a dark three-piece suit. "What is it?"

"No, we can talk later."

She saw his eyes dart past her, to the door, registering that she'd closed it. Crocker took his chair. "Tell me."

"You heard about what happened at the School?"

"You took a fall."

"Yes."

"I talked with Chester when the scores came in. All of you did exceptionally well, as expected. The fall is nothing, Tara. It happens, could've happened to Nicky or Chris."

Chace shook her head slightly. She'd told herself the same thing. Then she'd told herself that wasn't the point. She set the copy of the signal down on his desk; then, after a moment to commit herself, took the letter she was carrying from her pocket and handed it across to Crocker. She watched his jaw work while he read, imagined the ferocity of his desire for a cigarette. At the moment, she wanted one, too.

"The Ops Room?" Crocker asked.

"I think I'd do well in Mission Planning."

He set the letter on the desk in front of him. "This is because of the fall."

"No."

"Because if it is, I'll tell you again, it happens to everyone. Chester says it was raining. He says you were ahead of Nicky when it happened, you were leading."

"It's not the fall, Boss. I'm nine years in. It's enough, it's time for me to go."

"I did nine years."

"You did eight," Chace corrected. "Four as Minder One, and I'm coming up on my sixth, now. And that's not the point. Tamsin's five, Boss, and I've lost count the number of times she's called the nanny 'Mommy' instead of me. She's starting school, she deserves to know that I'll be there when she gets home. Even if I weren't getting old, even if I weren't slowing down, I long ago outlived my operational usefulness to the Firm."

"If this is about self-esteem—"

"Don't be daft. Nine years in the field, Paul. For Christ's sake, if there's an intelligence agency anywhere in the world that doesn't know who I am at this point, it's because they're not bloody trying."

"I think you may be overstating things a bit."

"Hyperbole for the sake of rhetoric."

"I thought you wanted my job."

"I thought I did, too." Chace grinned at him. "Then I did it."

"You did it very well, by all accounts."

"I'm not a vulture, Boss, I'm not going to sit on a branch and wait for your time to come to an end. Nicky's more than ready to run the Section, and Lankford's learned all that we can teach him."

She went silent, watching as Crocker frowned at her from across his cluttered desk. Now that the deed was done, Chace was all the more certain it was the right thing for her to do. She had expected a twinge of regret, had been afraid of taking the step, but there was no anxiety in her at all, just the same certainty that had come to her at the base of the climbing wall, the knowledge that this was right.

She was done, and from Crocker's expression, she knew he saw it, too.

"I'll need you to stay on as Head of Section until I can find a new Minder Three," Crocker said, finally. "Once that's done, I'll move you to Mission Planning, promote Lankford and Poole in order. Will that work for you?"

"More than fair. I'm not looking to leave you holding the bag, Boss."

"No, I know you're not."

He checked his watch, pushed himself up from his chair, and Chace took the cue, got to her feet, as well. "You've informed Nicky and Chris?"

"I wanted to talk to you first," Chace said.

"I'll have to tell the DC and C."

"Of course."

Crocker glanced back at his desk, grabbed two of the red folders waiting there, then saw the copy of the signal from Tehran and took that, too, handing it back to Chace. "Keep me posted on this. If Jakarta's got an agent on walkabout, I want to know."

"Will do."

He appraised her for a moment, and Chace thought he looked uncharacteristically sad, his many years revealed, with all the ghosts that haunted them, a number of them ghosts they shared. Men like Brian Butler and Edward Kittering and Tom Wallace, all of them Minders at one point or another, all of them taken before their time.

"You had a good run, Tara," Crocker said.

She thought about Tamsin, how she would ask about her Da, who he was, what had happened to him. It had been less than a year ago that Chace had finally explained to her daughter that his name was Tom, and that he had died before she was born. The inevitable question: how did he die?

Chace had lied, she'd had to. She'd said nothing about Saudi Arabia, or the Wadi as-Sirhan, or how SIS had been willing to sell her life for a political convenience. She'd lied. She'd told Tamsin they would talk about it when she was older, and that all she needed to know is that Tom would have loved her every bit as much as Tara herself did, that Tom Wallace had been a good man, an honorable, brave, and honest man, and that Tara loved him still.

"I finished the race, at least," Chace said to Crocker.

CHAPTER FOUR

IRAN—TEHRAN, U.S. DEN OF ESPIONAGE
6 DECEMBER 1428 HOURS (GMT +3.30)

One of the problems Shirazi was now dealing with, certainly, was one of his own making, though he had fought against it at the time. The order to arrest the ten British Embassy workers at the beginning of November had come from on-high—not via the President's office, but rather from the National Security Council, the members of which had all been appointed by the Supreme Leader himself. Such was government in Iran; there was a public face, as embodied by the Office of the President, and then there was the real power, hidden deep and out of sight, controlled by the Supreme Leader and his handpicked cadre of supporters.

Shirazi's place in VEVAK put him deep within the second camp, but his role was as a subordinate, and it had not been an order he could refuse. He'd tried, anyway, fighting to secure a meeting with one of the Council members, where he explained why the idea was, to him, such a bad one.

They all knew how this would end, Shirazi said. It would end with the release of all who are arrested, and the declaration that they are all now persona non grata. It would be for show, nothing more, and the British would have to replace the embassy staff they had lost, and Shirazi and his people would be back where they had started, once again trying to determine who of the new arrivals worked for SIS and who didn't.

We know their people at the embassy, Shirazi said. We have already identified them. We will lose time, time that SIS will capitalize on to strengthen their network.

His argument fell on deaf ears. There were other things afoot, he was told, in particular the Kurdish Hezbollah operations in the north of Iraq, not to mention the situation in Basra, as well as a purchase of heavy weapons from China, all of which required shifting the West's attention for the moment. It had been decided that this was the best way to manage it. Certainly, Shirazi would have no difficulty in identifying any replacements SIS sent into Tehran. Or was he telling them otherwise?

So the British had been arrested, amongst them the man Terry Ricks, who Shirazi had months ago identified as the main player for SIS on the ground. Ricks had been very good, had made things difficult for them, never obvious in what he did, never revealing when or if he knew he was being watched. Some days, the follow teams would have no difficulty at all in keeping eyes on him; others, Ricks would seem to shake his watchers by dint of nothing more than good fortune. It was frustrating, even agonizing, but he was, at least, a known quantity. Shirazi was certain that, with patience and time, the man's secrets would be revealed. They would learn the identity of his agents, they would uncover the extent of the British network, and then they would strike, shutting the whole thing down and putting SIS, once more, out of business in Iran.

As Shirazi had foreseen, Ricks was PNG'ed following his release, and over the next weeks the replacements for the depleted embassy staff had trickled into Iran. At least one of them, if not more, was working for SIS and was Ricks' replacement. But who the man was Shirazi did not know, and he hated that. Not simply that there were spies in his country, on his ground, in his face, but that he knew it and yet had not identified them.

Surveillance had been placed on the new arrivals, but all of them, thus far, seemed to be exactly who they claimed. It would be another month before their routines could be firmly established, mid-January, at least, before he would be able to look at the reports the teams had compiled and try to determine which of the staff wasn't exactly as he appeared. It was, once again, a situation that demanded patience.

But knowing who the British had in Tehran would have made

managing the situation with the dead drop in the Park-e Shahr so much easier.

Shirazi was in his office on Monday morning, looking at the very surveillance reports in question, when Zahabzeh called from the apartment in Karaj, just west of Tehran, where he and another four trusted men were keeping Hossein out of sight. Zahabzeh's absence from the office had yet to be noticed, and even if it had been, Shirazi knew it would be assumed that he was on assignment, which, in fact, he was. The call, consequently, angered Shirazi; his orders had been for Zahabzeh to wait for contact, not to initiate contact himself, and he found the younger man's impatience annoying.

"What?" Shirazi demanded.

"He's getting anxious," Zahabzeh said. "We hadn't heard from you."

"I don't care if he's wetting himself in fear. This is why you called?"

"We hadn't heard from you. Can you meet me? Taleqani? By the museum?"

"Two hours," Shirazi said.

Zahabzeh was waiting for him near what had once been the U.S. Embassy, gazing at one of the many political murals that decorated both sides of the street in the neighborhood. This one was of the Statue of Liberty, her face a skull, standing against a background of the American flag. Further along there was another mural, similar in theme, depicting both the United States and Israel as devils, the Big and Little Satans, attempting to shackle the freedom-loving people of Iran. In case anyone missed the point, there was another section of wall, white letters on baby blue, written in English. DEATH TO U.S.A.

To be honest, Shirazi found it all a little much, as if the neighborhood had been decorated for the benefit of tourists, rather than Tehran's residents. One could travel the entirety of the sprawling city, from the wealthier, newer buildings on the northern side of town in the shadow of the Alborz, where Hossein was now being held, to the southern, older city, and find no such rhetoric. Political, even patriotic murals, yes, normally of the Supreme Leader or his predecessor, Khomeini, each man depicted larger-than-life, gazing down with stern rebuke or paternal affection; and others, a lonely soldier or a weeping wife, pieces done to commemorate the suffering caused by the War of Iraqi Aggression, what was known in the West as the Iran-Iraq War.

Shirazi came alongside Zahabzeh, adjusted his glasses, looking up at the skull. When he spoke, he did nothing to keep the annoyance he was feeling out of his voice.

"Your orders were to stay with Hossein and wait until I contacted you."

"He's being watched," Zahabzeh said. "There are four men with him, he won't go anywhere."

"But he will note your absence."

"I hadn't heard from you, not since Saturday. We've seen nothing at the apartment, no sign that anyone is even looking there. I wanted to be sure that everything was still going as planned."

"He takes his walks as instructed?"

"Twice a day, once in the morning, once in the evening, carrying the book. We wire him each time, but so far he's had no conversations with anyone."

Shirazi grunted, turned away from the mural, began making his way up the block, towards the embassy. Zahabzeh fell in beside him. After the hostages had been released, someone, somewhere, had decided that the building should remain as a reminder, and the chancery had been converted into a museum. Only a couple of the rooms were open to the public, and then for just a few days a year, in February. Shirazi had seen the displays inside, the shredded papers that had been painstakingly reassembled, the Farsi translations of the CIA's activities. Some were quite damning, going all the way back to Operation: Ajax, when the CIA had engineered the coup d'état against Mossadegh's democratically elected government, replacing him with a leader more to both American and British liking, Shah Mohammad Reza.

Only part of the embassy was a museum, however. Now the majority of the space was taken up by the Sepah, the Army of the Guardians of the Islamic Revolution, known in the West as the Republican Guards. The Basij militia was now controlled out of the building, as well, under direct supervision of the Guards.

Shirazi wondered if Zahabzeh's choice of a meeting place wasn't meant to be a message. The Republican Guards were the army within the Army, a private enterprise of their own, as much a part of the Supreme Leader's apparatus of control as the National Security Council. No one rose to power—at least, no one rose very high in power—without some connection to the Guards. Shirazi had served within their ranks for a short time, running operations in Lebanon during the late 80s, and Zahabzeh, too, had been one of their number, though his time had been spent mostly in western Afghanistan, in Herat.

If it was a message, Zahabzeh was displaying a subtlety that Shirazi had been sure he lacked. The fact was, they were blackmailing a member of the Supreme Leader's family into doing their bidding for the sake of an operation that had no official approval or oversight. To some, that would be tantamount to treason, no matter the reason, no matter the goal.

"Everything is still going as planned," Shirazi assured him, as they crossed the street, dodging traffic.

"Did surveillance see anyone clear the drop in the park?"

"There was no surveillance." He saw Zahabzeh's surprise from the corner of his eye. "What if the British had made us watching the park? Their agent would have aborted, he would have known the drop was compromised, and all of this would be for nothing."

"But if Hossein is wrong? If his memory betrayed him? What if they no longer use the drop at all?"

"You know as well as I that a good dead drop is worth gold, and the drop in Park-e Shahr is a very good drop, indeed. You can enter the park from any direction, take as long as you like to reach it, as long as you might need to flush anyone watching you. It was safer this way."

"Then we don't even know if they have the message."

"They have the message. I walked through the park Sunday afternoon, the all-clear had been chalked up on the garbage can, just as Hossein described it. I checked the north entrance on my way out, no drop-loaded signal."

Zahabzeh stopped, and Shirazi was obliged to do the same, turning back to face him. "How much longer do we wait?"

"It won't be long," Shirazi said.

"But how much longer, sir?"

"Hossein did as he was instructed?"

"I was with him when he made the phone call. He told his family that he was in Mashhad for the week, to visit a friend."

"Then we have until this coming Sunday before he will be missed. That is what this is about, isn't it? You're losing your nerve?"

Zahabzeh stiffened. "I am not."

"Then stop worrying about what will happen if we fail, and instead worry about keeping Hossein under control. The British will respond. They will have to. When they do, things will begin to happen very quickly, indeed."

"No, I know that." Zahabzeh struggled with his next words. "You're not trying to get me out of the way, are you, sir? Having me stay with Hossein, I mean."

So that was it, Shirazi realized. Zahabzeh's ambition was at war with this newly discovered subtlety. "You are with Hossein because you're the only person I trust in this, outside of myself."

Zahabzeh studied him, then glanced back across Taleqani, towards the embassy and the Guards. "It's a big prize, that's all."

Shirazi removed his glasses, holding them up to catch the midday sun, checking the lenses. They were clean, but he put a breath to them all the same, thinking that Zahabzeh had revealed much of himself in just a few minutes, and that it could make things difficult later. That the younger man had his eyes on Shirazi's job was a given; his impatience to obtain it was something Shirazi had never considered.

"Big enough for us to share it." Shirazi replaced his glasses. "I promise you, when the time comes, you will be there. Everyone who matters will know your part in the operation. You have my word, Farzan."

"You speak as if we've already succeeded."

"We must succeed," Shirazi said. "If we fail, we'll both be shot."

CHAPTER FIVE

LONDON—VAUXHALL CROSS, OFFICE OF THE CHIEF OF SERVICE, "C"
6 DECEMBER 1007 HOURS (GMT)

The morning meeting with C was normally an informal gathering, with Crocker and his opposite number in the Intelligence Directorate, Daniel Szurko, presenting any new business that had arisen in the last twenty-four hours to C, while the Deputy Chief, Simon Rayburn, offered additional interpretation and comment, as well as any bureaucratic insight that might be needed. The casualness was emphasized by the absence of a desk in the proceedings, the meeting instead conducted in the sitting-room portion of C's ample office, with Crocker and Szurko sharing the couch, Rayburn in a reading chair, and C herself seated in another, at the opposite end of the coffee table from the Deputy Chief. There was coffee and tea and sometimes pastry, and normally it was over within fifteen minutes of commencing.

This morning's business was completed within eight, barely enough time for Szurko to down his customary two cups of tea while relating the latest analysis on suspected terrorist activities across multiple theatres. Crocker presented the after-action on an operation in Venezuela that had concluded late the previous night, and Rayburn shared his planned agenda for the upcoming budget meeting he would be attending early that afternoon.

"Very well," C said, when the Deputy Chief had finished. "If that's everything, I think we can all get back to work."

Szurko sprang up immediately, sending crumbs from the croissant he'd managed between gulps of tea showering onto the couch and, in part, Crocker. "Paul, oh, damn, sorry," he apologized. "Sorry."

"It's nothing, don't worry about it."

"I really am, really am sorry."

Crocker shook his head, dismissing the apology as unnecessary. Szurko was, by far, the oddest figure in the room, and at thirty-eight years old and standing five feet five inches, also the youngest and the shortest. Unlike Crocker and Rayburn, he never wore a suit or a tie, instead dressing, as he called it, "casual Friday," in jeans or slacks, often with a button-down shirt, but sometimes, when it actually was Friday, with a T-shirt. His sense of style, or lack thereof, had begun to infect the rest of his directorate, and more and more often, Crocker felt himself out of place in his three-piece.

It would have been easy for Crocker to resent Szurko, but he didn't. Intelligence had to change with the times, it had to not only keep up, but to get ahead. Szurko, with his BlackBerry and his ever-present laptop, was the face of the new SIS, the next generation coming up through the ranks. While Rayburn and Crocker still brought paper to the daily meetings, Szurko avoided doing so if at all possible. If the technology and the clothing had been an affectation, a performance, it would have been different, but neither were, and the man was decidedly brilliant at his job, something that even Rayburn, who had been D-Int for several years prior to his promotion to Deputy Chief, readily admitted. The only real problem with Szurko, and Crocker had seen it before with other exceptionally gifted analysts, was that the man didn't actually seem to be entirely *with* them in the room at times.

"I did have one more thing," Crocker told C. "This morning Chace submitted her resignation from the Special Section to me. She's asking to be moved to the Ops Room staff, into Mission Planning."

"That'll hurt," Szurko said immediately, more to himself than to the others. "That'll hurt a lot, actually."

C glanced to D-Int, then to Crocker. "Has something happened?"

"She feels it's time. Past time, actually, and she may be right."

"You'll want Poole as Head of Section?"

"And move Lankford to Minder Two, yes."

"When does she plan to leave?"

"She doesn't seem to be in a hurry, said she'll stay on until we find a new Minder Three."

"Is there anyone in the pipeline?" Rayburn asked.

"I haven't had a chance to check with the School as yet," Crocker answered. "She informed me of the decision just before I came up for the meeting."

"There won't be," Szurko said. "I was looking at scores this morning, there's no one in the current class. Or in the previous class. Or the class before that one, actually."

"Thank you, Daniel." C got to her feet, and Crocker and Rayburn followed suit. "I think that's all, gentlemen. Paul, if you'll stay for a moment, please."

Szurko and Rayburn headed out of the office, but not before Crocker heard D-Int say, again, "That'll hurt."

When the door had closed, C said, "How much *will* it hurt us, Paul?"

"It'll depend on how long it takes me to find a replacement for the Section."

"That's not precisely what I'm asking. Can we afford to lose Chace?"

Crocker, who had been asking himself the same question ever since Chace had handed over her letter of resignation, said, "I don't think it's a question of that, ma'am. She's made her decision."

"Again, you're not answering me."

"She's one of the best Special Operations Officers working anywhere in the world today, despite what she may think of herself at the moment. Can we afford to lose her? No. Have we lost her already? In everything but body, yes, I think she's already out the door."

C frowned as she settled behind her desk. "Did you try to argue her out of it?"

"I considered it, but you didn't see her. She's made up her mind.

And, to be honest, she made some very good points, not only that her departure was due, but that it was overdue, perhaps. She's been in the Section since she was twenty-four. That's a long time for anyone to be a Minder. In fact, I think it may be a record."

"Overdue, you say."

"She thinks so."

"Sometimes we stay too long," C said. "She does understand that Mission Planning is technically a step down on the career track? You didn't suggest a position in Whitehall? I should think it would be rather easy to have her assigned a position on the JIC as soon as one opens. That would preserve her prospects for future promotion, at the least."

"I can make the suggestion, but I doubt she'll entertain it. She wants to stay in the Ops Room."

C gazed at him for several seconds, her expression unreadable. Alison Gordon-Palmer—if the rumors about the New Year's Honors List were true, it would soon be Dame Alison—perhaps three years Crocker's senior, with limp brown hair that, like Crocker's own, was beginning to streak with gray. Her attire was always professional and conservative, today the blouse ivory, the long skirt a rich, royal blue, matching the blazer that hung on the stand behind her desk. As usual, she'd eschewed makeup, something she resorted to applying only while being ferried in her Bentley to Downing Street.

Rayburn was smart, and Szurko unquestionably, eccentrically brilliant, but Gordon-Palmer, as Crocker had learned from personal experience, operated from a cunning all her own. It wasn't simply her understanding of the Firm, of how SIS worked, that had made her C; she understood the political game as well, in a way that Crocker had never been able to master. It was a game she had played so deftly, it had cost the previous C his crown.

"Very well," C said finally. "If that's everything, Paul?"

"Yes, ma'am," Crocker said, and he left her office to return to his own, knowing full well it wasn't Tara Chace his C believed had stayed on too long.

CHAPTER SIX

SOUTHEND-ON-SEA—77 AVE ROAD, RESIDENCE OF DOROTHY AND KILLIAN NEWSOM
7 DECEMBER 0947 HOURS (GMT)

The woman who answered the door was stocky, pleasant, wearing a bright floral print apron and a just as pleasant and bright smile.

"My name's Tara," Chace said. "I called ahead about seeing your father-in-law?"

"Oh, that's right, come in, please do." She stepped back, allowing Chace through the doorway and into the narrow hall of the narrow house, shutting the door after her, and then literally having to squeeze past her again to lead the way into the front room. The whole house was filled with the smell of bacon, a late fry-up breakfast, and Chace could see boxes of Christmas decorations set out, waiting to be disinterred and mounted.

The woman offered her hand. "Dorothy Newsom, a pleasure. Da's upstairs. I should check on him first, if you don't mind?"

"No, I'm happy to wait," Chace replied.

Dorothy Newsom smiled, unfastening her apron as she stepped back into the hallway. Chace heard her climbing the stairs, treading heavily, and from above the sound of a television, audible but incomprehensible, through the floor. She moved further into the room, taking in the decorations, the various photographs on the mantel and walls. Dorothy and her husband had three children, it seemed, the eldest somewhere in mid-teens, if the pictures were recent. Chace didn't see any pictures she thought might be Jeremy Newsom.

The footsteps descended, as noisily as they had climbed, and Dorothy returned. The smile, this time, seemed more forced.

"You said you would want to speak with him alone, Miss Chace?"

"Yes, if that's possible."

"He's . . . he's having a harder time this morning, I'm not sure how with us he'll be today. Some of his days are better than others, you understand. Some days . . . his mind wanders."

"Is it Alzheimer's?"

"The doctor says senile dementia, but I suppose that's the same thing, isn't it?"

"Just you and your husband taking care of him?"

"The children help, of course, but yes. We couldn't bear to put him in a care home. I suppose we'll have to, soon, but not yet. Not until after the holidays."

"I shan't be long," Chace said. "It's just a couple of quick questions."

"This is about when he was with the Foreign Office, you said on the phone."

"That's right."

"May I ask you, miss, was he a spy?"

Chace looked at her curiously. "I'm sorry?"

"It's just that Killian says he thinks his father was a spy, only he never talked about it to him when he was growing up, you see, and now he can't really talk about anything at all. But Da says things, very odd things, places he's been that Killian never knew about. We'd started to wonder if there wasn't some truth to it, that perhaps it weren't all his mind going. So a spy perhaps, something like that."

Chace laughed softly, shaking her head. "No, my understanding is that your father-in-law was a special courier for the FCO, Mrs. Newsom. There was certainly a lot of travel involved, but nothing terribly glamorous or exciting."

"And that's what you need to ask him about?"

"We have some questions about a job he did, yes. Nothing that need worry you or your husband, I assure you."

Dorothy Newsom nodded, clearly not satisfied. "Well, you can go on up, I suppose. I was making myself breakfast. I'll be in the kitchen when you're finished, if you'd like a cuppa."

"Thank you, that's very kind," Chace said, and she headed upstairs to meet what was left of Jeremy Newsom, former Tehran Station Number Two, 1977–79.

It had been just past noon the previous day when the Ops Room had received responses to their separate queries. The first to come in had been from Thomas Bay, in Jakarta. It was a brief signal reporting that Falcon was present in theatre, and asking if there was a reason for the inquiry. The second had come from Barnett.

"The message was received via dead drop, all signals proper and confirmed," Lex had relayed to Chace. "The Number Two, Caleb Lewis, cleared it Saturday morning, found the message. The drop is currently assigned to an agent they're running, code name Mini. But it's not his code, and as Mini is hands-off right now, they can't confirm if he's been blown or not."

"Currently?" Chace asked.

"Direct quote," Lex answered, checking her copy of the signal.

Chace chewed on her lower lip, staring at the map on the wall. The callout for Operation: Bagboy was still positioned over Mosul, now with a notation reading, "Pending." Once Lankford was on the ground in Iraq, the label would change, declaring the op as "Running."

"Where'd we stash Ricks after he got back from Iran?" Chace asked, and when Lex shrugged, turned to Ron at the Duty Ops Desk. "Anybody know?"

"Think he's on leave." Ron picked up one of his many telephones. "I'll check with Personnel."

"Please." Chace made her way across the room, to Mission Planning and its companion Research Desk, taking a seat at one of the three terminals stationed there. Access from the Desk was limited, only to files graded Restricted or lower, but that was adequate for her current task. The system was painfully slow, the computers already several years out-of-date and creeping towards obsolescence despite the Systems Group's best efforts, and before she could actually begin her search, Ron called out to her.

"Confirmed. Terry Ricks is on leave, due for return to duty first January. I've got a leave address and contact number."

"Where'd he go?"

"Someplace up north, in the Ribble Valley. Clitheroe—"

"Right, Lancashire, I know the place," Chace said. Tom Wallace's mother, Valerie, lived some fifteen kilometers east from Clitheroe, in Barnoldswick. "Could you set me a call with him, please, Ron? Soonest?"

"As it is either that or resume struggling with my crosswords, I shall do the former."

Chace went back to the computer, started working through the message. She ignored the substitution code, working instead with the keywords from the book code as she came across them. She received two results for "grapes," the most recent from 1989, when the word had been used as code for automatic rifles during an operation in Cairo. "Water" kicked back nearly two thousand instances in the last ten years alone, and Chace realized it was useless, as whoever had inputted the information into the database had felt compelled to identify the use of "water" to mean any reference to any body of water in any operational theatre, ranging from the seven seas all the way down to a small lake in northern Cameroon. "Falcon" garnered five results, the oldest twenty years ago, in each instance used as a code name for a contact or agent, none of them in Iran.

"I've got Terry Ricks for you," Ron called from his desk, and Chace swiveled around to pick up the phone as the call was transferred over to her.

"Terry? Tara Chace."

"Hello, lovely. Calling to see if I'm lonely in Lancashire?"

"Everyone's lonely in Lancashire, Terry. Got two queries for you."

"Anything for Minder One."

"First one, does the name 'Falcon' mean anything to you?"

"Not at all. Should it, love?"

"That'll depend on the answer to the second question. It's about one of the cars you were using in Iran."

The levity vanished from Ricks' voice. *"Which one?"*

"Mini," Chace said. "He had his own parking space, yes?"

"All the cars did."

"Mini's space, was it yours, or was it inherited?"

"Ah, I see what you're asking. Inherited. The, ah, garage, as it were, has been using it since before Mossadegh's ouster."

"That pretty, is it?"

"It's like they say about real estate. Location, location, location."

"I understand."

"My little Mini having engine trouble?"

"Trying to determine that right now. Thanks for the help."

Chace hung up, logged out of the terminal, and sat, collecting her thoughts. Then she rose and headed out of the Ops Room, asking Ron to inform D-Ops that she'd be down in Archives should war be declared. She rode the elevator down to the first subbasement, stuck her head into the Pit, the cramped office that all three Minders shared. Lankford's desk was empty, but Nicky Poole was seated at his, elbows propped on the desk, head in his hands, apparently concentrating on the file open before him.

"You SAS types," Chace said, "can fall asleep anywhere."

Poole's head jerked up. "It's all those long nights I've been spending alone. Hardly getting a wink of sleep."

"C'mon, I've got something tedious and boring for you to do."

Poole closed the file, locking it away in his desk, before moving to join her. They started down the maze of identically decorated hallways, passing door after unmarked door, designed to preserve security between departments.

"You say boring," Poole said, "but I'll have you know, I am a discerning judge of tedium."

"We're going down to Archives."

Poole promptly pivoted on his toe, reversing direction one hundred and eighty degrees, heading back to the Pit, and Chace laughed and caught hold of him by his shirt.

"But I've been good!" Poole complained.

"That's probably why you're having so many lonely nights."

"Why are we being punished with Archives?"

"Need to go through the old records for Tehran."

"Aren't they in the computer?"

"The computer doesn't have anything older than twenty years or so. The rest are still on paper."

"We'll need written permission for the files."

"Only if they're graded above Restricted," Chace said, then added, "I turned in my resignation this morning."

"Very funny."

"Dead serious."

Poole stopped. "Tara."

"Hmm?"

"Dead serious?"

"Soon as the Boss finds a new Minder Three, I'm off to Mission Planning. He's going to make you Minder One. Don't look so bloody happy, Nicky."

"Do I?"

"No, you look like I just uprooted your herb garden, actually."

Poole made a clicking sound with his tongue. "You tell Chris?"

"Figured it could wait until he was back from Mosul."

"Probably best. If I tell you how much you'll be missed, it's not going to make a bit of difference, will it?"

"Not a whit of it," Chace said. "But the effort is appreciated."

It took two hours of searching through Archives before Poole found references to an agent named Falcon in the reports of Jeremy Newsom. For security reasons, the documents couldn't be removed from the room, so Chace and Poole spent another ninety minutes working at a set of facing desks, in surprisingly poor light, reading through the reams of paperwork Newsom had produced. All Stations delivered daily reports, normally no more than a page or two in length, but as the Revolution had approached, Newsom—along with his Number One, a man named Andrew Thurman—had seen the writing on the wall, and their signals had consequently increased in both frequency and length. SIS had, in turn, responded, accepting their analysis, and at several points Chace ran across "US–UK EYES ONLY" stamps, indicating that the information had, in fact, been shared with the CIA, only to be disputed and even disregarded, in turn, by the U.S. State Department.

There were only a handful of references to Falcon, but from what Chace and Poole could gather, he was a young man, a soldier, and had passed on some minor, but useful, information about support for Khomeini within the armed forces. His associated expenses totaled up to just under twenty-two thousand pounds, which led Chace to conclude Falcon had been a paid source, rather than an ideological one.

Nowhere within the files did either of them find anything that explained the phrase "the grapes are in the water."

As Poole was replacing the reports, Chace used the internal circuit to call up to D-Ops. Personnel files were kept by the Security Division, technically part of the Operations Directorate, and classified anywhere from Secret, in the case of general staff, to Top Secret, in the case of senior staff, for a minimum of fifty years from the date of recruitment to SIS. Access required written permission from D-Ops, or, in the case of senior staff, from the Deputy Chief or C.

Crocker came on the line with a characteristic growl.

"I need written permission to draw the personnel files of Thurman, Andrew, and Newsom, Jeremy," Chace told him.

"Who the bloody hell are they?"

"They *were* the Station One and Two for Tehran just prior to the Revolution."

"This is about Barnett's signal?"

"Yes, sir."

"I'll clear it."

The runner was waiting for them when Chace and Poole returned to the Pit, two massive files in his hands. Chace signed for the documents, handed over the one for Jeremy Newsom to Poole, and was about to settle in at her desk to read up on Andrew Thurman when she saw that the file had a "DECEASED" stamp across its face. She tossed it aside, and she and Poole each took half of the substantial Newsom file, trading papers back and forth as they read.

Jeremy Newsom was an old warhorse. He'd started in the Army in 1953, in the Prince of Wales' Division, the Sherwood Foresters, promoted to Sergeant while fighting against the communists in Malaysia. Recruited by the Firm at the height of the Cold War, he'd been sent to Oxford, where he'd studied Oriental Language and Culture, as it had then been called. His initial Station famil had been Cairo, followed by turns up and down the Persian Gulf, from Kuwait to Bahrain to Oman, with years spent in London in between, working a variety of Desks both in-house and in Whitehall. Security reports, evaluations, and commendations filled the rest of the folder.

From what Chace read, Newsom had been a good officer, if not an admirable family man. He had married while in the Army, and Chace found five separate Security notices regarding Newsom's liaisons with different women. Two had occurred while he was stationed in London, each with women working in the Firm itself, but it seemed that Newsom had developed the habit of taking up with some female member of the embassy staff while on Station. From what Chace could gather, none of the relationships had been compromising to SIS, but they exhibited a lack of judgment, and she suspected this was why Newsom had never been posted as a Head of Station.

His final field job had been Tehran. Following the Revolution, he'd been binned back to London and put onto the retirement track, which he'd accepted early. There was a note as to the effect that he and his wife, Mary, divorced just prior. Security audits continued intermittently over the next ten years, at which point it had been determined that any information Newsom had was so out-of-date as to be of no value to the opposition. The last entry was five years old, stating that Newsom was now living with his eldest son in Southend.

"Southend in December," Poole said, reading her mind. "Better dress warm."

Jeremy Newsom sat deep in an old lounge chair, wearing baggy black slacks and a bulky, hand-knitted sweater, watching *Grandpa in My Pocket* on BBC2. Chace held in the doorway at first, not wanting to disturb the old man, and for several seconds she did nothing but take in the room, the occupant in his chair, the voices on the television, the space in general. Pale winter sunlight slanted through a window to her right, and from some unseen duct, forced, hot air was feeding steadily into the room, raising the temperature to a few degrees above comfortable. There were no books anywhere that Chace could see, and no photographs, just a couple of framed, banal paintings, flowers and trees, and two hand-drawn pictures that she assumed had been done by one of the Newsom children, tacked to the wall beside the narrow bed.

"Mr. Newsom?" Chace said. "My name's Tara Chace."

The old man didn't move, didn't appear to hear her, and Chace took a step inside, closing the door gently behind her.

"I'm with the Firm, sir."

"You're not Dot." Newsom brought his head around slowly, and Chace saw that his face was lined and long and sad, his blue eyes remarkably pale.

"No, sir, my name's Tara."

Suspicion, then, but just for a moment, almost immediately eclipsed by a delighted smile, fed by false recognition. *"Jaanum,"* he whispered. "Oh, pet, I thought you'd gone."

The word, perhaps Arabic, perhaps Farsi, had no meaning to Chace, but she saw that Newsom was now struggling to get out of the chair, using both hands on the armrests and still unable to manage it, and she moved to him quickly, dropping to her haunches. Newsom responded, stopped trying to rise, instead now leaning forward and gazing at her with such relief and adoration it made Chace's heart ache. He reached out with one hand, touching her hair.

"Spun of gold." Newsom spoke softly, almost whispering, stroking her face with his fingertips. "Always so dolly, not like Mary. You were always so, *jaanum.* I thought you'd gone."

"No, I'm here." Chace took hold of his hand, pressed his palm against her cheek. "Falcon has come alive, Jeremy. Do you understand me?"

"No, we don't talk about that, eyes only and all that nonsense, you don't ask, I don't ask. Your business is yours. Mine is mine." His hand remained against her cheek, his palm soft and dry. The smile faded. "I had to leave, I'm sorry, *jaanum.*"

"It's all right, I understand. But now you're back. I need to know about Falcon."

"I don't know who that is."

"In Tehran," Chace said, and when Newsom grimaced, she added, "It's all right, Jeremy. You can tell me."

"They killed Robin, you know. Shot him dead as soon as that old bastard came home from Paris. Eagle, Swallow, too, anybody they could lay their hands on. I knew it, nobody listened. They said, they said, how bad can it be? But we told them, he won't give it up, he'll take over. It'll be a backlash, we'll never get our foot in again." Newsom's hand moved along her face, and he smiled once more, drawing his thumb lightly over Chace's lips. "God, I could kiss you for days, love."

Chace moved his hand gently, taking it in both of hers, returning his smile and feeling guilty. He so obviously was beyond competence, so clearly imagined her as someone else, and yet he had the answers she needed, was, perhaps, the only person yet living who did.

"Tell me about Falcon. Please, Jeremy."

"Falcon? Low-value, military, not worth your time, really. Fled after the Revolution, lost him, then. Probably to Paris, they always run to Paris."

"Who was he?"

"No, you can't ask that."

"But it's been cleared, all the way from the top. You can tell me."

He pulled his hand from hers, suddenly, looking at her with alarm. "I don't know you. Go away."

"My name's Tara. I'm with the Firm."

"Fucking Russians." He shoved her back with his foot, forcing Chace to drop to her knees to keep from falling over, then kicked at her again. "Go away!"

"Mr. Newsom—"

"Go away, you fucking whore! Fucking Russian whore!"

On the television, the show had ended, and in the pocket of silence she could make out footsteps rushing up the stairs. Newsom had twisted himself about in his seat, now resolutely staring out the tiny window, at the view of the rooftops across the lane. Rain had begun falling, and a sheet swept past, driven by the wind off the North Sea.

Chace got to her feet, reaching the door just as Dorothy Newsom opened it, catching it before it could come wide. The woman started into the room, but Chace shifted herself enough to block the entrance.

"It's all right," Chace told her.

"I heard shouting."

"He got agitated. It's all right."

Dorothy Newsom peered past her, sucking on her upper lip, to see her father-in-law. She looked up at Chace. "I think you had better go, miss."

"A few more minutes, Mrs. Newsom, please."

"You're upsetting him!"

"I don't mean to. But I need a few more minutes, please."

"Da?" Dorothy called past Chace. "Da, are you all right?"

"Dotty? Where's my tea, love?"

"You're all right?"

"I'd love a cuppa, Dotty. Can I have a cup of tea?"

"I'll go fix it for you, Da," Dorothy answered, then, reluctantly, and with a look rife with suspicion, backed away from the door, turning away only when she had reached the top of the stairs.

Chace closed the door again and went back to Jeremy Newsom's side. He was still seated as she had left him, still staring out the window, but his posture had relaxed. From her pocket, Chace removed her Security card, the pass that allowed her access to Vauxhall Cross.

"Mr. Newsom?"

"What did you say your name was? I'm sorry, I didn't catch it."

"Tara Chace, sir. From the Firm." She held out the card for him to examine, and he took it in his hand, turning it in the light before staring up at her again. For the moment, he seemed entirely present, and she pressed on. "We've received a message from Falcon, but we don't understand it. We need your help."

"You're very pretty," Newsom said. He examined the card. "What happened to the red pass?"

"They stopped using it. This is a new one, computer chip inside it, all the fancy security measures." She took her pass back, stuffed it again in her pocket. " 'The grapes are in the water.' Do you know what that means?"

"You say you're from the Firm. What Directorate?"

Chace was about to say "Special Section" when she realized that he'd never believe her. He would certainly never believe that a woman had been named Head of Section.

"Ops Room staff," she said. "Research Desk."

"Bet the Minders like seeing you there. Helps them remember what they're fighting for."

"Yes, sir."

"It's the lift code," Newsom said, abruptly. "Hossein's in trouble, he's asking to be lifted."

"Falcon is Hossein? Hossein who?" The old man stared at her, blinking, and Chace realized he was slipping away again. "What was the lift plan?"

"Something . . . something about a boat, in the north. Boats and goats in the north. What did you say your name was?"

"You called me *jaanum*."

He brightened. "I'll divorce her, I promise. Just you and me, my love. I could kiss you for days."

"Why would Hossein—Falcon—want to be lifted now, Jeremy? Why after thirty years?"

Newsom laughed. "Finally pissed the old fucker off, that's why. Limp-wristed bastard, Falcon was. Uncle's not going to protect him anymore, I'd imagine."

"Who's the uncle? Military? Government?"

"I hate the rain." He was looking out the window again. "The Ayatollah."

"The Ayatollah's dead."

"Is he? Evil bastard, good."

"Hossein Khomeini?"

"No."

"Jeremy, listen to me, this is important. Falcon is Hossein Khomeini?"

"No. You're saying it wrong."

Chace stared at him. "Khamenei?"

"That's right, *jaanum.*"

A gust of wind smashed drops against the little window. On the television, a high-pitched boy's voice started singing some nonsense.

"What was the lift plan, Jeremy?"

He didn't answer, still watching the rain. Chace put a hand on the old man's shoulder, and when that didn't work, moved it to his face, gently turning him by his chin to look at her. She tried to keep the urgency from her voice, but knew she was failing.

"You've got to remember," she insisted. "What was the timetable? The details? From drop-cleared until activation, what was the delay?"

He opened his mouth, then clamped it shut, suddenly frightened.

"Where was he to go to ground? What was the pickup? You've got to remember!"

"Tehran."

"He was to go to ground in Tehran? He was to stay in the city? What was the pickup, Jeremy? Falcon's in the open, do you understand? He's running, he's reached out to the Firm for a lift. You've got to tell me! How long from drop-cleared until the lift? Dammit, the clock's running, how much time do we have?"

She saw tears rising in his eyes, realized that what she'd feared, that she was losing him, wasn't what was happening at all.

"I can't remember," Jeremy Newsom sobbed. "God help me, I can't remember."

CHAPTER SEVEN

TEHRAN—198 FERDOWSI AVENUE, BRITISH EMBASSY

7 DECEMBER 1550 HOURS (GMT +3.30)

It was the first time that Caleb Lewis had ever received flash traffic from London, the communications cabinet suddenly bleating, loud and insistent, and it took him by such surprise that he actually jumped in his chair. For a moment he didn't know what the sound was, where it was coming from, and his mind flashed that perhaps it was an embassy alarm, that something was happening in the chancery, that perhaps he and Barnett and God only knew who else were about to be arrested and charged with espionage.

Then Barnett was up and out from behind his desk, unlocking the cabinet, and Caleb understood. By the time Barnett had the doors open and his key in the console, Caleb was standing over his shoulder, and together the two men watched the monitor and printer come alive together. They read the message as it decoded, character by character, on the screen, neither of them speaking, and when it had completed Barnett reached for the printout, tore it free from the feeder and handed it back to Lewis, then quickly typed the one-word response London had demanded.

Confirmed.

Barnett removed his key, closed and locked the cabinet, and only then did he look at Lewis.

"We're in the shit now, son," he said.

Caleb looked up from the signal in his hand, the one he'd already read through three times with mounting apprehension and comparable confusion.

"What does it mean?" he asked.

"It means, Caleb, that there's a Minder in our future."

The signal was unequivocal. Tehran Station was directed to, with all dispatch, effect the following:

First, they were to establish surveillance of the block of apartment buildings on the southern side of Nilufar Street, between Bustas and Aras Avenues, in Karaj, some twenty kilometers west of Tehran. Once established, they were to locate and identify Falcon, and, if possible, initiate contact. All caution and care were to be taken to avoid detection.

Second, the Station was directed to, with all haste, secure a safehouse in the north of country, in Chalus or Noshahr. The safehouse was to be stocked for three-to-five occupants for a duration of seventy-two hours, including sleeping arrangements, food, beverages, toiletries, and clothing. Additionally, a vehicle was to be provided for the location, in good condition and with current tags and registration. Upon acquisition, the Station Number One was to assign one of the embassy's Security detail to the location to standby.

The necessary equipment to provide proof of identity to London was to be furnished at said location.

The signal concluded by saying that Tehran Station had twenty-four hours to accomplish these goals.

"It's a lift?" Caleb asked. "They're lifting Falcon?"

"How it looks," Barnett said, spinning the combination on the office safe.

"But we don't know who Falcon is!"

"Presumably London does."

"Then why don't they bloody tell us that, instead of ordering us to make the identification? How are we supposed to identify him if we don't know who he bloody is?"

"That's the trick. Presumably, Falcon knows we'll come looking and hang a flag of some sort. You'll want to take a camera with you."

"Me?"

"Unless you'd rather be the one to drive up to Chalus and secure the house and car, Caleb, yes."

"Brilliant, so I'll just hop over to Karaj and drive around this block until I see someone who I think is Falcon?"

"Don't be daft."

"Thank you."

Barnett was into the safe now, pulling out stacks of cash, most of them Iranian rials, a few of Euros, and setting them on his desk. From the top shelf, he removed a Nikon digital camera and companion lens. He set the camera beside the money, grinned at Caleb around the cigarette in his mouth.

"No, you find a static position, someplace with a view of the whole block, if possible. Should be a café, something, someplace you can park your arse and take in the scenery. It can be in the open so long as you don't make a nuisance of yourself, I'd think. If I'm reading the signal right, Falcon is going to want you to spot him."

Caleb massaged his brow, feeling for an instant off balance and still horribly, horribly confused. He understood what the signal was telling them, understood that when Barnett had said a Minder was coming for a visit, there was a lift in the offing, and from the instructions for the safehouse, that it would be a defection rather than an abduction. He even understood that this was a direct result of the message from Mini's drop in the Park-e Shahr, that London had identified Falcon as a high-value asset, one that London was willing to pull out all the stops to secure.

So Falcon was important. Important enough that London was willing to risk a lift out of Iran, something that, to his knowledge, hadn't been attempted for years, even decades, now. But if London knew who Falcon was, why were they ordering Barnett and him to provide proof of identity at the safehouse, something that wouldn't be possible until after Falcon was in hand? It was arse-backwards, it didn't make sense.

Barnett shut the safe door, spun the combination, then stabbed out his Silk Cut in the crowded ashtray on his desk. He replaced the cigarette with a new one, leaving it to wait, unlit, while he held out one of the stacks of rials for Caleb.

"Five thousand," he said. "Try not to spend it all in one place."

The traffic, always bad, was fuck-awful out of Tehran, with almost constant gridlock, horns, and a new smattering of chilling rain that had the benefit of holding back the heavy smog that so often blanketed the valley south of the mountains. Once, Karaj had been a refuge from the bustle of the capital, where the well-heeled had retreated to get away from the city. Some such signs remained, including the spiral-roofed palace built in 1966 by the Frank Lloyd Wright Foundation for Shams Pahlavi, the Shah's sister, and the ancient Zoroastrian temple, Takht-e-Rostam.

That was then. Now Karaj was more a commuter extension of greater Tehran than a city all its own, though as a city it could boast a place as Iran's fourth or fifth largest, depending on which census Caleb wanted to believe. Current population was estimated between 1.5 and 2.5 million, and from the traffic alone, he was inclined to believe the larger number. The forty-odd-kilometer drive from the embassy just east of central Tehran to Karaj to the west took him nearly two hours, fighting rush-hour traffic all the way. The only benefit to the frustration and duration of the drive that Caleb could see was that by the time he wedged his Citroën into a space near the corner of Nastaran and Bustan, he was as positive as he could be that he hadn't been followed.

It wasn't until he was at the corner of Sonbol, perhaps two blocks from where he had been directed to establish his surveillance, that Caleb saw the police patrol, a group of four officers with their two parked cars. His first thought was that they were waiting for him, and the fear reared in his chest, growling, and for a half-second that seemed to stretch infinitely longer, he didn't know what to do. The immediate urge was to turn off, to turn away and head in a different direction. The pedestrian traffic was enough that he thought perhaps he might go unnoticed, but just as quickly he thought that would be a bad idea, the act of a man trying to hide himself, trying not to be seen, certain to draw more attention.

He continued forward, trying to master himself, and ten meters from the patrol one of the officers called out to him, waving him over.

"Papers," the officer said.

Caleb produced his wallet, his passport and visa card, handing them over. The officer used a small flashlight to look at them, peering at each document intently before shining the light into Caleb's face, checking him against his photograph.

"Why are you in Karaj?"

"Just sightseeing," Caleb said. "Went to see the palace."

The officer grunted, shining his light once again at the open passport in his hand. "British."

"Yes."

"You live on Mellat."

"Yes. Thought I'd wait until the traffic cleared up before heading home."

The light snapped off, the documents were returned. "You'll be waiting for a while. It never clears up."

"Lightens, then," Caleb said. "Do you know, is there anyplace nearby I could get dinner?"

"On Ladan, that way." The officer used the flashlight, still in his hand, to indicate the direction, then pointed the opposite way, to the east. "Or there, on Nilufar."

Caleb nodded, thanked the officer, and headed onto Nilufar, tucking his papers back into his jacket. It was marginally less busy than Bustan, still with a steady flow of Tehran commuters returning to their homes, their small apartments packed into the concrete, ugly buildings on both sides of the street. The ground floors of several were occupied by shops of one sort or another, and Caleb noted two restaurants and one coffeehouse. He stayed on the north side of the street, making his way to the coffeehouse, and inside ordered a cup of *ghahveh,* the traditional Iranian coffee, and a piece of date-filled biscuit, called *colompe.* With both in hand, he wedged himself into a table near the front, by the window, but the glare from within and the rain from without made visibility through the glass near-impossible. He looked around the crowded coffeehouse instead, watched as the postwork crowd of men and women pushed past, as urgent and aggressive as anything he'd ever seen in London, thinking about what he should do next.

Static surveillance from the street would be difficult, if not impossible, especially with the police patrol so close to hand. Never mind that there were at least a dozen apartment buildings crowded together on the south side of the street, opposite where Caleb now sat, and within those buildings God only knew how many apartments. One of them, according to London, held Falcon, but which one Caleb had no way to know. He considered trying to get a room on the north side of the street, but doing so would create a whole new set of problems, and it would limit his visibility of the buildings opposite him, to boot.

He sipped at his coffee, tasting the thick grounds as he reached the bottom of the cup. Barnett had suggested static surveillance, but now that he was here, Caleb simply couldn't see a way that was going to work, certainly not at night, certainly not with the police and the rain. Mobile surveillance wouldn't do, either; there was no way he could envision to both stay in motion and keep eyes on the whole block. It just wasn't possible. The only thing that Caleb could think to do, in fact, was to start working through the apartments one by one, knocking on each door in turn, and asking if, perhaps, anyone knew where he might find someone code-named Falcon.

The absurdity of the idea made him smile.

There was no way he could find Falcon, he concluded, certainly not without exposing the both of them.

Which meant that Falcon was going to have to find him.

There was no message from Barnett the next morning, but when Caleb stopped by the embassy before heading back to Karaj, he noted that at least two of the Security detail he was used to seeing on-site were nowhere to be found, and he concluded that Barnett must have already secured the safehouse. As part of the SIS position within the FCO, the Firm trained and provided guards for each embassy, with additional security provided by subcontracting through local agencies. The irony of hiring Iranians to guard the British Embassy in Tehran wasn't lost on anyone on either side, and it was accepted as a given that any local thus employed was delivering daily reports to someone in the Republican Guards or VEVAK or both about all they had seen during their shift. High-security areas were, of course, restricted to U.K. personnel only, and all operations were overseen by SIS Security.

It was three minutes to nine when he reached Karaj, the Nikon slung over his shoulder and a guidebook in his hand. This time Caleb approached Nilufar from the south, starting at Sepah Square. The square really wasn't, instead a large, finely tended grass roundabout where Aras Avenue converged with the multilane east-west highway that ran all the way back to Tehran. At the center of the roundabout stood a monument to the Sepah, four fine-featured soldiers facing in every cardinal direction, holding flags or rifles, all of them leaping skyward, as if ascending to heaven.

Caleb stopped and took several pictures of the monument, mostly to get the feel for the camera. He was careful to only shoot facing north; southeast of where he stood, fenced, patrolled, and guarded, was the Basij-e Sepah base. It took four and a half minutes before the traffic cleared enough that he could sprint across the road, north, to the next median, and from there it was only a short walk and a relatively shorter delay before he was able to cross west onto Nilufar.

There was a slight rise here to the road, another grass-covered slope dotted with trees, with a small gazebo set upon it. Caleb took a seat on one of the benches inside, checked the camera, and now looking down Nilufar to the west, took several shots in succession of the street. Shops were opening, first customers beginning to trickle into the coffeehouse he had visited the night before, as well as to the bank just south of where he was now sitting.

He watched the street for the next several minutes, pretending to alternately check his guidebook and his camera. The night before, he had arrived believing he would have to watch the apartment buildings, but today he gave them only a cursory glance. If Falcon was flying a flag from one of the windows, Caleb couldn't see it, and he was now increasingly certain that was because it wasn't there. Each apartment had an identity, a corresponding tenant or owner, and anything that drew attention to the location would logically draw attention to its occupant. Better to set the flag someplace more anonymous, somewhere Falcon could be just one of many, in one of the restaurants or shops along the street.

So Caleb watched the street—the bank and the restaurants and the coffeehouse—and while he did that he tried to keep an eye out for the police, and he tried to determine if he, himself, was under surveillance, and when it all became too much he rose and walked down Nilufar to buy himself another cup of *ghahveh*. He drank it at a table, was rising to leave when he looked back and saw, seated alone near the back of the room, a man in his late middle-age, graying hair and a neatly trimmed beard, sitting by himself, a book closed on the table in front of him. Caleb couldn't make out the Farsi from the distance, but he could see the illustration, the different birds taking flight on the cover, and the aftertaste of the too-sweet coffee turned sour in his mouth.

If there was a falcon in the flock on the cover, he couldn't see it.

He took his empty cup back to the counter, using the opportunity to take another survey of the room. The man had been seated when Caleb had entered, he was sure of it, and he was just as sure that the book hadn't been out at that time.

"Agha," Caleb said. *"Salam aleykum."*

The man smiled up at him. "*Salam aleykum.* Your Farsi is very good for a tourist."

"Thank you. You're interested in birds?"

"Yes, all sorts." The man picked up the book, turning it in his hand. "Though we don't see many here during the winter."

"I'd think you'd see some around here."

"A few. I don't get out often to look. You like birds?"

"Some more than others. I'm partial to birds of prey. Falcons, hawks, birds like that."

"Those are all good birds. There are, of course, many others."

The man seemed to consider, looking at the book in his hand, then offered it to Caleb. "I've read it several times. Perhaps you'll have more use for it than I."

"That's very generous of you," Caleb said, taking the book in hand. He freed the camera from his shoulder, turning to a nearby waiter. "Excuse me, could you take a picture for me? Of me and my friend here?"

"My pleasure."

"Just point and shoot. It's okay if you take a couple of them." Caleb moved beside the man, still seated at the table, held up the book with a grin. The waiter pointed the camera, and he heard the shutter click repeatedly before it was handed back. "Thank you."

The waiter moved off, smiling, perhaps amused, and Caleb turned again to the man at the table, who was now looking at him much more soberly.

"I hope you enjoy the book," the man said. "You should read it soon."

CHAPTER EIGHT

LONDON—VAUXHALL CROSS, OFFICE OF D-OPS
8 DECEMBER 2037 HOURS (GMT)

Paul Crocker sat on the edge of his desk, eating his dinner of takeaway salad from the commissary, and contemplated who he would most like to stab first with his plastic fork. On any given day, he would readily admit, the list would be a long one, populated by anyone from the file runner who didn't seem to understand that now meant now-god-dammit and not now-but-after-you've-had-a-nice-chat-with-my-PA, to the Head of Station in, say, Sucre, who couldn't mount an operation on his own without a coloring book and large-type instructions relayed in triplicate and signed by everyone from the PUS at the FCO to C to the Head of the Janitorial Staff.

And that was the list without the addition of politicians.

"I know that look," Julian Seale said. "Just tell me it's not me you're planning to murder."

Crocker shook his head, forcing down a particularly limp piece of cucumber. "You can relax. You're so low on the list they'll have caught and killed me long before I reach you."

Seale leaned forward in his seat, swiping a broad palm across his thigh to clear it of crumbs from his sandwich, before taking hold of the edge of the map laid out on Crocker's desk. He was a tall man, like Crocker, but broader, the body of an American footballer, as opposed to a British one. One of the few African Americans holding senior posts with the CIA, he'd held the Chief of Station office at the embassy in Grosvenor Square for just under five years now, an exceptionally long time for such a tour, and one that was due to end at the turning of the year. If Operation: Coldwitch resolved as everyone from Downing Street to the White House hoped it would, Seale would be leaving London on a high note, indeed.

"I like the placement of the safehouse," Seale said, after a moment. "That's, what, five klicks from the airport in Noshahr?"

"Just over four, yes."

Seale gulped the rest of his coffee, then got to his feet, craning his head for a better look at the map. "It's a sweet-looking operation, Paul. Your boys and girls really outdid themselves on this one."

"They damn well better have. Coast Guard is aboard?"

"Langley cleared it with the White House earlier today. Orders forthcoming."

Crocker made a last, halfhearted attempt to stab at an asparagus spear, just as limp as the cucumber, then gave up and dumped the remains of his dinner into the trashcan beside his desk. "I'll want confirmation."

"Obviously." Seale checked his watch. "When's Chace due to brief?"

"She's not." Crocker slid off the desk and began folding up the map. "The job belongs to Poole. He briefed this evening, will be on his way to Tehran at dawn."

Seale put a hand down on the desk, trapping the map, and Crocker was forced to look at him. "You can't do that. Paul, you can't do that, the terms of our involvement are that you send Chace. That's direct from Langley, this has to be handled by your most senior operations officer."

"You're moving up my list, Julian."

"This isn't a joke. The job has to go to Chace."

"Poole can do it just as well as she can."

"That may be, but those aren't the goddamn terms, Paul! Jesus, are you trying to kill the operation? It's *Hossein Khamenei,* it's not some fucking clerk in the post office, it's a high-value target of incredible intelligence value. You have to send your senior operations officer, you have to send Minder One."

"She's put in her resignation from the Section. I've accepted it.

She is not, therefore, the senior Minder. And get your fucking hand off my fucking desk, Julian."

Seale stepped back, glaring at him, and Crocker fought the map closed, fuming. The demand that Chace be the agent of record for Coldwitch was yet another of the many things he didn't like about the Tehran job.

"Why the hell weren't we told about this?" Seale asked.

"Because no one fucking asked me!" Crocker roared. "Because no one has listened to a word I've said for the last twenty-four hours! Ever since Chace made her report I've been fighting against this operation, and at every turn I've been either ignored or overruled."

"If I have to go back to Langley and tell them that she's not doing the job, that it's going to Poole, it'll scuttle the whole damn operation."

"Good."

Seale stared at him. "Is this about Chace or you?"

"What the hell does that mean?"

"Are you trying to end your career? Or protect hers?"

"I'm trying to protect my agents."

"So you're saying that even if Langley does approve Poole, you'll find a way to scuttle that, as well? And again if they agree on Lankford?"

"Too right I will."

"Have you lost your mind?" Seale asked after a moment, and Crocker thought he was genuinely curious. "They'll fire you, you realize that? They'll fire you and they'll fill that Desk with someone who, I don't know, believes in the radical notion of following their fucking orders!"

Crocker took his seat, looked up at Seale, now glowering down at him. "Hossein Khamenei is bait. That's all he is. You've got to see that."

Seale rubbed his eyes, and seeing that Crocker was still at his desk, that this wasn't a bad dream, turned his attention to the bust of Winston Churchill in the corner. It was a small bronze, capturing the former Prime Minister during the height of World War Two, one of only two decorations that Crocker kept in his office. The other was a black-and-white silkscreen print of a Chinese dragon, which hung on the wall opposite the door.

"Of course he's bait," Seale said, finally. "But he's a hell of a piece of bait, Paul. He's an irresistible piece of bait. And if we can pull him, it'll be worth the price."

"Not to me."

For several seconds the two men stared at each other. They'd never managed to become friends, but for the past several years had managed the pretense of professional courtesy, if not camaraderie. Crocker found himself again wishing for Seale's predecessor, Angela Cheng. It wasn't that Cheng had been more capable than Seale, but with her, Crocker had shared a fundamental understanding, that politicians were not to be trusted, that it was their duty to protect their respective services, the CIA and SIS, and their agents. Even when they argued—and they had argued often—they had stood on the same side.

From Seale's expression now, Crocker knew that wasn't the case.

"Get me an escort out," Seale said.

Crocker stabbed his intercom, Kate answering immediately. "Mr. Seale needs an escort out of the building."

"Yes, sir."

"They'll make you send Chace." Seale reached the door to the outer office. "And if you don't do it, they'll fire you and then they'll replace you with someone who will."

He stepped out, and Crocker waited until he heard the escort arrive and then depart again with Seale before getting to his feet. Kate was still at her desk, a paperback novel open in one hand, chewing on the end of a pen.

"She is technically still Minder One," Kate said, not looking up.

"Did you press a drinking glass against the door?"

"Didn't need one. You two were loud enough, the whole floor heard it."

"Go home, Kate. It's almost nine."

"You're done for the day?"

"Not yet."

"I'll stay."

Crocker glared at her, trying to determine if it was loyalty or pity that was keeping Kate at her desk. Then he went back to his chair, to await the inevitable call from C.

The problem was that Crocker had seen this all before.

Chace had no sooner finished telling him that Falcon was, potentially, Hossein Khamenei, than Crocker had known there would be an order to lift, an operation mounted, and he was just as certain Chace knew it, too. It was as inevitable as a car crash, and, worse, as potentially fatal for all those involved. As soon as their political masters in Whitehall and Downing Street heard that SIS might, just conceivably, be able to bring a member of the Supreme Leader of Iran's family to the West as a defector, they would go blind. They would see the result, not what was required to achieve it. What they wouldn't see, Crocker was certain, was the risk. And once those same men and women in Whitehall and Downing Street set their eyes on this new prize, there would be nothing Paul Crocker could do to stop them.

But he would damn well try anyway.

His first act after Chace finished her report was to demand that Kate get him D-Int, either on phone or in person; he had no preference as long as it was done with all due haste. All due haste, it turned out, had been via phone.

"Paul?"

"Daniel, do we have anything on Khamenei's extended family?"

"We have quite a lot, actually," Szurko said. *"As he has quite a lot of family. But what we have I'm not in love with, if you understand; I don't trust most of it."*

"He has a nephew named Hossein?"

"Yes." Szurko said it slowly, dragging out each sound in the word. *"Should be in his late fifties, maybe early sixties. Was Sepah in his youth, went to Paris after the Revolution, I think, but came*

home and went back into harness. Republican Guards, served a bit in the Iran-Iraq War. Not much more than that, I'm afraid. Married, at last report, with children, several of them, but no details. I can dig if you need digging. Do you need digging?"

"Everything you can, and anything that might indicate if he's in trouble. And if you can scrounge up a photograph or, better yet, a set of fingerprints, so much the better?"

"We're targeting the nephew of the Ayatollah?" Szurko sounded gleeful. *"I'll have the Iran Desk get all over it."*

Crocker hung up, hoping that Szurko wasn't as good at his job as he appeared.

His next act had been to inform the Deputy Chief. He'd made the report in person, heading down the long fifth-floor corridor to Rayburn's office.

"We have no confirmation that Falcon is Hossein Khamenei," Crocker told him. "Newsom is suffering Alzheimer's, and Chace said he has both difficulty focusing and staying in the present. There's no way to verify that what he told her is true."

"All the other participants are dead?" the Deputy Chief asked.

"Newsom's the only one still living, yes, sir. Minder One and Minder Two are going through Archives again for anything they might've missed the first time. But given the state of things when Newsom left post, what was happening on Station around the Revolution, I doubt there's more to find. I've already asked D-Int to dig up anything he can on Hossein Khamenei."

"Most of the Station records have been purged, if I remember." Rayburn used his chin to indicate to Crocker that he should take a seat, waited until he had, before adding, "There might be copies surviving in Whitehall. But Khamenei does have a nephew named Hossein, Paul—I remember that from my own days as D-Int. It's plausible he's asking to be lifted."

"But we've no verification he was even one of ours."

"He knew the Park-e Shahr drop. He used an established, albeit old, book code. I'd say he was definitely one of ours, at least for a short while."

Crocker shook his head, knowing the argument had been feeble, and already feeling that the coming battle was lost. Of all his peers in SIS, it was with Rayburn that he felt he had the best relationship. Not strictly a friendship, perhaps, but certainly they shared a mutual respect that had come from shared time in the trenches, Rayburn working his way through the Intelligence Directorate even as Crocker had climbed the rungs of Operations. When Alison Gordon-Palmer had been named C, she had needed to choose between her D-Int and her D-Ops to fill the position. Ultimately, she had gone with Rayburn, despite unspoken promises to Crocker that the job would be his. It wasn't a decision that Crocker could find fault with, even as he managed to resent it.

"Thirty years he runs silent, then he suddenly asks to be lifted?" Crocker said. "That doesn't sound plausible to me. That sounds like he's been flipped. We're being set up."

"Did you ask Daniel if there was any reason to believe Hossein might be about to have the skids put under him?"

"He's checking. According to Chace, Newsom indicated that he might be homosexual, but she advises that may be Newsom's own machismo speaking, rather than known fact about Hossein. When I checked with D-Int, he didn't mention it."

"Would his homosexuality be enough to have him executed?"

"I honestly don't know. Shi'a Iran isn't Sunni Al-Qaeda; they're not running a fundamentalist agenda despite what their mouthpieces are crowing. The Revolution ended in '81, when Khomeini realized he couldn't control the country with religion alone. Since then it's been less about religion per se than about expanding their power base."

"There's the Basij."

"More for propaganda than anything else. But at the same time, they might be willing to make an example of him. I think that's a stretch, Simon. As I said, I think we're being set up."

Rayburn tented his long fingers, rested them against his chin. It was a mannerism Crocker knew well, had seen him do hundreds of times as D-Int when he was sifting facts, trying to reach a conclusion. "To what end?"

"How much time do you have?"

"Moving on Basra?"

"Or something with the Kurds. Or something in Afghanistan. They're remarkably good at occupying our attention in one place while they bury another hundred Silkworm missiles along the Gulf."

"Might even be internal," Rayburn mused.

"Or it could be that they want to hurt us," Crocker pressed. "For the first time in decades we've actually got the start of a viable network in-country, Simon."

"And if we move to lift him, we risk exposing the network."

"Without question."

"To lift him would require Special Section support. You'd send a Minder."

"But the Station would have to prep for the operation."

Rayburn exhaled, brought his fingers down. "I have to present it to C, Paul. I've no choice."

"You know exactly what will happen if you do. We both do."

"I will stress to her your reservations."

"For all the good it'll do."

That earned him a look of reproach. "You've been in this job for too long to be making sullen asides. We both have."

"She's a political C, Simon, she's going to want to make the Prime Minister happy. And this will make the PM happy, with the added bonus that he'll be able to make the Americans happy."

"With good reason. We have an authenticated message from Falcon using an established lift code."

"I want more than that. I want fingerprints, some physical proof that Falcon is who he claims he is."

"Paul," Rayburn said, slowly. "You're not telling me you'd refuse to undertake the operation if the order should be given, are you? I know you, I know you're perfectly capable of sabotaging this before it gets off the ground."

"Iran is the single greatest threat to stability in the Middle East, I've felt that for years," Crocker said. "We handed them Iraq following the invasion, and we've all but handed them Afghanistan. They're deep in Lebanon, they're deep in Gaza. If someone—anyone—can prove to me that Falcon is for real, that this cry for help is legitimate, I will go to Tehran and get him out myself."

"Remember you said that, Paul." Rayburn got to his feet, watched as Crocker did the same. "Because I'll be sharing that with C, as well."

He'd been back in his office for all of eleven minutes following the briefing to Rayburn when Kate buzzed him on the intercom, saying that C wanted to see him. He'd gone directly up to the sixth floor, entered her office, and before he could even open his mouth, Alison Gordon-Palmer cut him off.

"Simon has explained your concerns, Paul, and I have to say I share them," C said, much to Crocker's surprise.

"I'm very glad to hear it."

"But as Simon has also no doubt made clear, I must bring this to the PM's attention. He's not an unreasonable man. Our reservations may carry some weight."

"But you doubt it?"

"I do, yes. The one thing you seem to have not taken into account is the American interest, and that is something the PM most definitely will do."

"There's no reason for the Americans to be involved at this point. They shouldn't even know about Falcon."

"But they will, no doubt in short order. And if it comes down to a choice between allowing CIA to lift Falcon or SIS, then I'm sure we're all agreed it should be SIS who takes the prize."

"It would have to be SIS anyway," Crocker said. "CIA doesn't have the backing in-country to mount a lift. They'd have to go for a military extraction."

"Yet another reason why I think we'd all prefer this stay with the Firm."

"If it's going to happen."

"If. Indeed." C shook her head slightly. "Get on to Tehran Station and have them begin prepping the ground for a possible lift."

"I'd rather wait, ma'am."

"I'm sure you would. Unfortunately we don't have the luxury. Now, if you'll excuse me, I don't wish to keep the PM waiting."

"You're going to have a hell of a time getting him out of the country," Chace told him later that afternoon as she and Poole discussed the operation in Crocker's office. "West you're in Iraq, east you're in Afghanistan, south you're all wet, north, you're not only wet but very cold."

"Gone swimming in the Caspian in December, have you?" Poole asked.

"Skinny-dipping, if you must know." She brushed hair back from her face, pondering the map on the wall. "None of the regional neighbors are going to be particularly helpful."

"Even if they were so inclined, they wouldn't," Poole agreed. "They're all scared to death of Tehran shutting off the tap."

"Caspian route would be your best bet. Get Falcon out in the middle of the water for a pickup."

"Provided we can get him that far," Crocker said.

Chace put her index finger on the center of the Caspian, marking an imaginary point. "The Americans involved yet?"

"Imminently, I'm sure."

"They going to try to steal it or support it?"

"C already marked the territory. It'll be ours if it goes through."

"What're you thinking?" Poole asked Chace.

"I'm thinking that there was a circular a couple months back about the United States Coast Guard's involvement in CTAP." Chase dragged her index finger across the water, until she reached the Republic of Georgia. "Training the Georgians, I believe."

Crocker heard Poole make a noise of pleasure that sounded distressingly close to sexual. "Oh, that's very good."

"Like that, do you?"

"Getting the American Coast Guard to pick us up under the cover of the Counter Terrorism Assistance Program? I think that's bloody brilliant."

"And I think you both are getting ahead of yourselves," Crocker interposed. "The Americans aren't involved yet. We have no reason to believe Falcon is who he says he is. And Tehran hasn't even begun to prep the terrain."

"Well, we can give them a place to start with Falcon, at least." Chace flashed him a smile, pulled a folded piece of paper from her jeans pocket, handing it over. "Not quite an address, but it narrows down the location on where Falcon's hiding. Nicky cracked it."

Crocker unfolded the sheet, saw that it was a copy of Barnett's initial signal from Tehran. The substitution code had been worked over in pencil, the string of letters converted into two sequences of eight-digit numbers.

"GPS coordinates?" Crocker asked.

Poole put a finger to the tip of his nose. "He used his name for the key. Hossein Khamenei, with 'H' as zero. Reasonably clever. You can't crack it if you don't know who sent it."

"And these coordinates are where, exactly?"

"West of Tehran, a city called Karaj," Chace said. "Fairly crowded area, too, from what the Iran Desk says, a good place to hide in plain sight. Presumably, that's where Falcon's gone to ground. It does make sense, Boss. He had to know that whatever lift plan he and Newsom established back in the day was dead and buried by now, that we'd have to work up a new one. He leaves us his location so we know where to find him."

"And stays there, one hopes, until the new lift plan is prepared," Poole said. "I like the Caspian exfil, too, Boss. If the Station can fix it so there's a RHIB somewhere near the shore, we can just shuffle Falcon aboard in a life jacket and zip north to the pickup."

"Seaplane," Chace said.

"Helo," Poole countered. "USGS, it'll be a helo."

"Have to do it at night."

"Absolutely, that's a given."

Crocker watched the two Minders at the map, listened to them discussing the relative merits of a pickup via airplane versus helicopter. Although neither of them had said as much, he knew that, as far as they were concerned, the job had already been confirmed, and Chace assigned to it. It was the logical expectation. The target was of exceptional importance to the Government, and the operation, if it should come to pass with a successful outcome, would reflect well on SIS. By necessity, then, HMG would demand SIS task the best agent for the job. By definition, that would be Minder One.

Crocker had to wonder what it meant that, not a day earlier, he'd accepted her resignation from the Section, and yet here she was, tête-à-tête with Poole, deep in mission planning. Nothing in what she had said to him the day before had indicated regret or even hesitation about her decision to leave. Yet all her actions now were to the contrary, and whether that was simply Chace doing her job, or being caught up in the moment, or in the excitement of an operation in the offing, he couldn't tell.

He was still pondering the question when Kate tapped on his door, then opened it without a word.

"What?" Crocker asked.

She ignored him, leaning past the edge of the door to find Chace. "Tara?"

"Me?"

"There's a Ms. Palmer calling for you from the Emmanuel School. It's about Tamsin."

"Oh, God," Chace said.

She had already slipped past Kate to the outer office before Crocker could say that it was all right, she could take the call at his desk. From outside, he heard Chace picking up the phone, identifying herself, and he looked sharply at Kate for further explanation.

"No idea," Kate whispered.

All three of them waited in silence for the better part of a minute before they heard Chace set the phone back down.

"She's taken ill," Chace explained, returning. "Been throwing up all afternoon."

"Go," Crocker said.

"I am sorry."

"It's understood."

She turned to leave, but Crocker caught her throwing one last glance back at the map before she was out of the room.

"Caspian route," Chace said to them. "It's the only viable exfil."

At twenty-two past eleven the next morning, Poole walked into Crocker's office carrying the latest signal from Tehran Station. The signal included a photograph of a middle-aged, gray-haired Iranian of Persian extraction, sporting a trimmed beard and looking absurdly stoic while a somewhat goofily smiling Caleb Lewis stood beside him.

"The book that Lewis is holding," Poole said. "Falcon gave it to him."

"Message?"

"Same book code, yes. 'Three west and three and third again.' "

"What do they make of it?" Crocker asked, examining the photograph closely and finding nothing in it that would allow him to call the operation off.

"Lewis thinks it's the direction to Falcon's apartment on Nilufar. The signal states that the book used for the code is quite ancient, and wouldn't allow for anything comprehensive with regards to direction. Therefore Falcon is working with what he has."

"Which puts the apartment where?"

"On Nilufar Street, number twenty-two. The apartment in question would be on the third floor, either number 3 or the third apartment on the floor, though if it's the latter, it's so vague as to be useless."

"Then it's the former." Crocker tossed the photograph onto the desk, annoyed by its unwillingness to help him. "Nothing so far has been vague, only inconclusive."

"That was my thinking. You want me to get onto Mission Planning about the initial exfil route?"

"They've worked up a cover?"

"They're holding off until you tell them who it'll be for." If Poole was feeling any expectation or anticipation about the job, or even any desire to take it, he was being as restrained about it as Chace had been the day before. “Tara’s at home?”

“She called in this morning to say Tam had been up all night with a fever. She was taking her to the doctor this morning.”

Poole nodded.

“Right,” Crocker said. “Go bother Mission Planning, Nicky.”

“We’re going to lift him, with the Prime Minister’s blessing,” C told Crocker after she returned from lunch. “Operation to be initiated at the earliest possible moment. The Americans are aboard, and willing to offer any and all support we might need. You can expect to hear from Mr. Seale before noon.”

“Very well,” Crocker said.

“Earliest possible moment, Paul. Where are you with the planning?”

“Still waiting to hear from Tehran. Once we have the details, Mission Planning will work on creating a cover for Poole.”

“Poole? Not Chace?”

“Chace is home with her daughter today. My intention is to send Poole.”

C studied him. “This is a high-value target in a high-threat theatre, Paul. As I understand it, the job should go to the Head of Section.”

“And as I informed you Monday morning, ma’am, Chace has tendered her resignation from the Special Section.”

“Pending the arrival of a replacement, Paul. And I’ll thank you to keep that condescension out of your voice when speaking to me in the future.”

Crocker hesitated, then offered the barest nod.

“Poole?” C asked again.

“Yes, ma’am.”

“Very well,” she said.

Crocker had wondered, at the time, why C had seemed so willing to let him send Poole rather than Chace.

Now, sitting at his desk, feeling both old and tired, the echo of Julian Seale still ringing in his mind, if not in his office, he knew why. The decision had already been made, most likely as part of the terms of the CIA's involvement in Coldwitch. C hadn't fought him because she hadn't needed to.

He raised his eyes to the clock on the wall, saw the second hand sweep time into the next hour, now eleven o'clock. If Seale had gone directly back to Grosvenor Square to report to Langley, then it was long past when Langley would have raised holy hell with the FCO. That Kate still sat at her desk with her paperback, that no phone had rung, puzzled him, and gave him hope that, perhaps, Coldwitch would die stillborn.

Then he heard the door to the outer office open, and from where he sat behind his desk he saw Kate straighten and then quickly get to her feet behind hers, and Crocker knew it was not to be.

"Ma'am," Kate said.

"Go home, Ms. Cooke," Crocker heard C say. "And if you find this office vacant in the morning, try not to be too surprised."

Kate glanced his way, her expression pained, then began gathering her things in preparation of heading home. She was still doing so when C walked into Crocker's office and shut the door softly behind her. Crocker got to his feet, thinking several things at once. The first was that wherever Alison Gordon-Palmer had been prior to returning to Vauxhall Cross, it hadn't been at home, unless she normally spent her evenings at home wearing a ball gown and her best pearls. The overcoat she'd donned to protect her from the cold made her seem all the more surreal, the fairy godmother of SIS come to wreak vengeance.

The second thing he realized was that her dress explained the delay. She hadn't been at home when the word had come down that Crocker wasn't playing ball. That led to the third, the fact that wherever Alison Gordon-Palmer had been that evening, it was clear from her expression that she would much rather still be there than here, and that she was as close to furious as Crocker had ever seen.

When she spoke, her voice was soft, and dangerously controlled. "I've just returned from being summoned to Downing Street, where the Prime Minister asked me why the President of the United States had felt it necessary to telephone him and inquire as to whether or not SIS was planning on lifting Falcon. When I told the Prime Minister that Coldwitch was to commence shortly, he said to me that he had been led to believe otherwise. He said to me that one of my Senior Directors had told COS London that there would be no Operation: Coldwitch, because he was refusing to brief or clear to run the agreed-upon agent for the mission."

"Poole—"

"Shut up, Paul," C said with such venom that Crocker was certain he could feel it pushing through his own veins. "Do you understand what I'm telling you? Do you understand that I was dressed-down by my Prime Minister less than an hour ago, made to look a fool, made to appear incompetent? Do you understand that you managed to do the same to the PM himself? Do you understand that you not only humiliated us, you humiliated the service?"

"I'm trying to protect the service," Crocker said.

"I am eager to hear how that can possibly be the case."

"If we send a Minder into Iran, if it's a trap—"

"And you have proof of that?"

"I have too many convenient explanations! I have an asset who's risen from the dead, an asset who, it turns out, is such a prize we're willing to shoot first and ask questions later! I have everything that makes this look irresistible, but the one thing I don't have is the time to check the facts!"

C stood motionless, and Crocker heard his own voice fading, the embarrassing desperation in it.

"Seale said CIA support was contingent on Chace being allocated," Crocker said, trying again. "Didn't it occur to you that's because they're suspicious, as well, that they don't want to risk any of their own people being caught and paraded on Iranian national television?"

"Of course it did," C said. "But that is neither here nor there. I told you that all consideration was given to your reservations, and that despite them, the operation was to go forward. From that point, your duty was to facilitate the operation, not to stonewall it, not to sabotage it. But since you couldn't have your way, you decided it would be best to try to undermine Coldwitch. In so doing, you caused embarrassment to myself, HMG, and the Service."

"That was not my intention."

"Paul, I know what your intention was. And now I'm going to tell you what you will do."

C stepped forward to the desk, lifted the handset for the red circuit and, with acute deliberation, pressed the button for the Ops Room. She put the phone to her ear, but not before Crocker heard the Duty Operations Officer identify himself.

"This is C. Hold for D-Ops." She lowered the handset, covering the mouthpiece with her free hand. "You will direct the Duty Ops Officer to bring Minder One in for immediate briefing. Then you will call COS London and tell him that Coldwitch is go, and you will do him the courtesy of inviting him to attend Minder One's briefing, as we have nothing to hide from our partners, and desire the CIA to be involved in every stage of the operation. Upon completion of briefing, you will contact Tehran and inform them they are now hands-off until rendezvous at the Noshahr safehouse.

"If you do all of these things, then you will find yourself still with access to this office come the dawn. If you do not, I will have Security remove you from the premises this instant, and tomorrow you'll be wandering up and down Whitehall in search of an open vacancy."

She held out the handset to Crocker.

"Make your decision now."

He took the handset, raised it to his ear.

"Minder One to the Ops Room," Crocker said.

CHAPTER NINE

IRAN—KARAJ, 22 NILUFAR STREET

10 DECEMBER 1821 HOURS (GMT +3.30)

If there was anything useful to be found in a roundabout, it was that it made flushing a tail easy; if a car followed you around it once, that was just some bloke heading the same way you were; if that car followed you around it twice, that was some bloke following you.

By the time Chace had made her second turn around Sepah Square, she was as sure as she could be that she wasn't being followed. She continued west another fifty meters before turning right, onto Bustan, then turned right again, onto Nilufar, looking for a place to park. The neighborhood wasn't what she'd expected, the dull utilitarianism of the buildings offset by the multitude of trees growing on each side of the street, denuded by the cold and the recent rain. It had turned dark, and a wind had come up, and as she guided her rental down the block her headlamps revealed quick glimpses of leaves as they flipped through the air like wounded birds.

At the east end of the street she turned right once more, and then immediately again, into a wide alley that ran parallel to Nilufar. Several cars were parked along here, and she found a space perhaps midway down and stopped, dropping the manual shift into neutral and letting the vehicle idle. The car was a Samand, essentially the Iranian version of a Peugeot 405, produced under license from the French, and while it was neither fast nor particularly reliable, it had the clear merit of being ubiquitous, something Chace had been able to verify during her long fight with the traffic out of Tehran.

With one hand, she adjusted the rearview mirror, as if inspecting herself in the reflection, and adjusted the black silk scarf she was wearing to hide her hair. A set of headlights flashed towards her, another car turning down the alley, and she watched from her periphery as it rolled slowly past, seeing two occupants, both men, neither of whom gave even the slightest glance in her direction. The car continued, made a left at the end of the alley, disappeared back onto Bustan.

Chace closed her eyes, trying to conjure the man from the photograph Crocker had shown her during the briefing, the man who was supposed to be Hossein Khamenei.

Instead she saw Tamsin, her cheeks flushed pink with heat, and she wondered if her daughter's fever had broken yet.

They had been sleeping when the call came, curled together in Chace's bed, each exhausted, but for different reasons. The previous night had been a marathon of sickness, with Tamsin ultimately reduced to spastic dry heaves that had made her sob.

"Why, Mommy?" she'd asked more than once. "Why am I sick like this?"

"It's your body trying to make you better, baby," Chace had told her, stroking her daughter's matted hair back from where it was clinging to her brow. "Just let it happen, don't fight it. You'll feel better soon."

It had been a half-truth. The vomiting had ceased, but the fever had increased, and after a second round of Calpol at four in the morning, Chace had begun to worry that perhaps this wasn't a cold but something else. She'd spent the rest of the darkness on her laptop, working up a fear that contained both the words "swine" and "flu," and by morning had already made an appointment to take Tamsin to the doctor.

No, not the flu, the doctor had said. Just a nasty bug. Home, rest, fluids. If the fever doesn't go down by tomorrow morning, I'll want to see her again.

Only marginally reassured, Chace brought Tamsin back to their home in Camden, tucked her into bed, and tried to do all the things a good mother should do. That Tamsin was willing to let her do such things was a sign of how sick she was; normally, getting her to stay still for more than four or five seconds at a time was a chore, and that included while her daughter was sleeping.

When the phone called out at just past midnight, it needed several rings before it could penetrate either of their sleeps, and Chace felt uncharacteristically groggy as she fumbled for the handset.

"Chace."

"Duty Ops Officer. Minder One to the Ops Room."

For an instant, the incandescent rage that consumed Chace threatened to make her say things, many things, she would regret. She was exhausted, her daughter was *ill,* for the love of God, and at—what was it, half midnight?—half midnight she was expected to summon a nanny for Tamsin and just rush off to the office? There were three Minders, dammit, why the hell weren't they calling Nicky?

But she didn't say any of those things. She said, "An hour."

"Confirmed."

Dial tone, and Chace blinked at the phone in her hand for several seconds, then pressed the speed dial for Missi Hegland. While it rang, Chace extricated herself from the bed and slipped out of the room, into the hall.

"Hello?"

"Missi, it's Tara," Chace said. "I'm sorry to be calling so late."

On the other end of the line, the nanny groaned. "Again?"

"I know, it's awful of me. Can you be here in half an hour?"

Chace heard a yawn. "How long will you be gone this time?"

"Only a couple of days, I shouldn't think. It's Australia, Hong Kong, and back."

"They do have other flight attendants, don't they?"

"You'd think," Chace said. "Can you be here in half an hour?"

When Chace returned to the bedroom, Tamsin was sitting up, bleary-eyed and disoriented. Chace climbed back onto the bed and wrapped Tamsin in her arms. They stayed that way until the knock came at the door. Missi was knocking a second time before Chace could let her inside.

"Tam's asleep?" Missi asked, removing her coat. She'd brought a small duffel bag with her, and Chace found it bitterly ironic that her daughter's nanny had, in essence, a go-bag. Chace's own was stocked and waiting in the Pit.

"She's down now, yes. She's been ill, running a fever all day. I took her to the doctor, he said rest, fluids, like that. If the fever hasn't broken by tomorrow, she'll need to see him again, and if it spikes, you should take her in right away."

"Tara," Missi said, her tone just shy of a reproach. She was a young woman, mid-twenties, a pretty blonde with an almost perpetual smile. "Why didn't you tell them no?"

"I can't, I just . . . I can't. This'll be the last time. On my word, this is the very last time."

"And you've got to go now, have you?"

"I do, I'm already late."

"Going?" said a small voice from the end of the hall, and both women turned to see Tamsin wobbling in the doorway of the master bedroom, matted hair and dazed understanding on her face.

"I'm sorry, baby, I've got to go to work—"

"Don't go!"

Chace moved to her daughter, scooped her up, held her close. "I'm sorry, baby."

The tears started, hot and fat. "Don't go! Don't go! *Don't go!*"

"I've got to go. This'll be the last time. I promise, Tam, this is the very last time."

The sobbing accelerated, becoming thicker and louder, and Chace carried Tamsin back to where Missi was standing. Tamsin refused to release her grip, wrapping Chace's hair in her tiny fists, pulling and screaming, until finally she worked herself into such outrage she was choking on her own tears. Chace managed to free herself from her daughter, and placed Tamsin into Missi's arms.

"You better leave," Missi told her, and though Chace knew better, she was certain it was a condemnation.

Hating herself, Chace headed to the Ops Room.

The wind cut into her as soon as she stepped out of the Samand, grabbed the tail of her manteau, and crushed it against the backs of her thighs. Chace tugged at the hem reflexively, making certain it stayed below midthigh. Iran wasn't as forbidding to women as Saudi Arabia or Kuwait, at least not this close to the capital, but there was still a standard of modesty that even Chace, as a foreigner, was expected to observe. Here, the *maqna'e* for her hair and the manteau, a shapeless trench-dress, sufficed enough that she could get away with blue jeans and boots.

It was quiet in the alley, quieter than Chace had expected considering the volume of traffic running on the road just to the south, the buildings on either side of her serving as a sound buffer. She locked the door of the car, tucked her chin against her chest, and began walking towards Bustan, eyeing the apartments on her right. As she passed the third from the end, she noted a rear door up a short flight of stairs, a single bulb in a fixture above it.

At the corner, she turned north, towards Nilufar, and immediately spotted four policemen standing beside two parked cars. There was nothing urgent in their manner, and as she approached she saw that three of the four were participating in some discussion with a group of locals, voices rising and falling with enthusiasm and laughter. Chace kept her eyes down. Almost everywhere else she could think of, avoiding an authority's eyes was a sign of guilt, guaranteed to raise suspicion; here, meeting a man's eyes could be perceived as a come-on.

"Khanom."

Now she raised her eyes, saw one of the officers beckoning to her.

"Khanom," he said. *"Shab bekheyr."*

"Pardonnez-moi," Chace replied. *"Mais je ne parle pas Farsi."*

The officer jerked his head back in surprise, realizing, perhaps, that she was a foreigner. He tapped one of his colleagues, which brought the attention of the remaining two, as well, and Chace heard the first officer speak, caught a word that she assumed was Farsi for "French."

"Non," said the smallest of the policemen to Chace. *"Non français. Anglais?"*

"Oui," Chace said. "I speak English."

"Are you alone?" he asked. "Are you lost?"

"Traveling alone, *oui.* But I have a . . . a colleague? He lives on Nilufar, I am visiting him."

"You are married?"

"*Non.* A widow."

The policeman's face fell in sympathetic grief. "May I see your papers, please?"

"Of course." Chace turned slightly, reaching beneath her manteau, then offered her passport and visa card to the policeman, watched as he and another of his colleagues examined them with a flashlight.

"You are a Swiss?"

"Oui."

"You are a doctor?"

"*Comment vous-parlez . . .* scientist?" Chace clamped her lips together and blew, inflating her cheeks. *"Poisson?"*

"Fish?"

"*Oui!* Sturgeon!"

There was a general sound of understanding from the group of officers. "Caviar," one of them said, and Chace nodded.

"Our caviar is the best in the world."

"Oh, yes," Chace agreed, taking her papers back as they were offered to her.

The policeman who had done most of the talking with her, the smallest of the group, indicated the street off to his left. "Nilufar is that way. Have a good visit to our country, Dr. Gadient."

"Merci. Salam aleykum."

"Salam aleykum."

"Tehran went sterile this afternoon at roughly fifteen hundred zone," William Teagle told Chace. "Your flight will touch down early evening tomorrow—well, today, really—so by the time you get your legs under you for the rendezvous, Falcon should have had seventy-two hours clear, no contact with anyone from the Station."

"They understand they need to keep the hell away from him?" Chace asked.

"Barnett knows the rules," Crocker said. "They won't go anywhere near Falcon prior to the lift."

"Cover identity is that of Dr. Pia Gadient, with the University of Fribourg. You're a marine biologist, in particular concerned with the declining sturgeon population in the Caspian Sea."

"I'm a marine biologist?"

Teagle slid a folder across the briefing table towards her. "You can read up on it. You've published a couple of very well-received papers on the subject, in point of fact. It's a very good cover for the job, Tara. Of all the countries on the Caspian, Iran is the only one to make any effort at sustaining the sturgeon population, and they're quite proud of the fact."

"I never did like caviar," Chace said, leafing through the folder.

"The cover also justifies why you'll be in the north, why you'll have access to a boat, why you'll be carrying a GPS, a sat phone. You can even get away with carrying a knife, if you like. After all, you've got to open those fish somehow."

"GPS will have the RZ coordinates?"

Julian Seale, sitting silently by Crocker and nursing a cup of coffee, spoke up. "Coast Guard will begin overflight of the rendezvous on the eleventh at twenty-three hundred hours. They'll continue flybys once an hour until oh-three-hundred morning of the twelfth. You'll have four shots at pickup before they have to break off and refuel."

"How do I signal them?"

"You don't. They'll be flying dark, using NVG. If you're there, they'll spot you."

Chace looked at the man, considered pressing the point, then decided against it. There was tension running between Seale and Crocker, even if both men were doing their best to conceal it, and she didn't want to inadvertently poke a nerve in the middle of a briefing.

"Exfil plan?"

"Tehran Number Two will be present in the safehouse on your arrival. He has acquired a RHIB, small Zodiac, already secured in Dr. Gadient's name, and will have the boat in position and moored by the time you arrive at the safehouse with Falcon. Once Falcon's bona fides are confirmed, you'll be free to proceed to departure. Sat phone to check in with London once you're on the water, then again after pickup by USGS."

Chace studied the maps on the table for the better part of another minute, then went through the documents again. The passport was Swiss, and according to the stamps, she'd made several visits to the countries that bordered the Caspian, including Azerbaijan, Turkmenistan, and Russia. This was her second visit to Iran in the last three years.

"Good," she said finally. "Now the big question: what's the fallback if it all goes to hell in a handbasket?"

"Instead of exfil to the north, you track west, to Tabriz," Teagle said. "From there you have your choice of borders, either into Iraq or, better, into Turkey."

"Is there a bolt-hole in Tabriz?"

"No."

Chace turned to Crocker. "Can we fix that, please?"

"I don't see how," Crocker said. "Not with the time we have left."

"So if it goes wrong I'm out in the open and on my own, that's what you're saying?"

"That's correct."

"Lovely. And I'm going unarmed?"

"Again correct. You get stopped carrying a knife, your cover supports it. You get stopped with a gun, they're liable to use it on you."

"Agreed," Chace said, immensely relieved that no one from on-high had insisted on her going armed. "All right, I'll need time to study all this, so if you want to sod off now, that'd be grand."

Teagle laughed, but neither Seale nor Crocker shared it.

"You make the approach to the apartment," Crocker said. "You make sure of the ground, Tara. You see anything—*anything*—that makes you unhappy, you abort back to your hotel in Tehran, take the next flight home, you understand?"

"Hold on—" Seale began.

"When it's your fucking agent, you can give the fucking briefing," Crocker snapped. "She's happy, or she doesn't do the job. It's that simple."

"Boys, don't let's fight," Chace said. "I'm a big girl, and I've played outside before. I know what makes me happy and what doesn't."

There was no security that she could see at the entrance of Number 22 Nilufar, just a set of three wide steps that followed the slope up to the front door of the apartment building. Chace took them with purpose, doing her best to appear like she knew exactly where she was heading. The door was unlocked, and she pushed into the narrow lobby of the building, smelling broiling meat and a mélange of spices that would have made her mouth water if it hadn't been filled with cotton.

To her right, running straight down, was a hallway that ended with another, smaller door, apartments alongside. The stairs to the first floor were at the end of the hall, so that one ascended facing towards Nilufar. She headed past them, to the door opposite the entrance, and it opened without difficulty, and she found herself looking out into the alley where she'd parked the Samand. She checked both directions, then looked up and, seeing no one, took the folding knife from her jeans pocket and, shielding her face with her free hand, whacked the closed blade against the lightbulb hanging over the door. The glass shattered, the light went out, and she slipped back into the building.

According to the briefing on Coldwitch, Falcon was on the third floor, either in apartment three, or in the third apartment there, but when she came off the stairs, her first thought was that their intelligence had been wrong. There were six separate apartments and none of them, at first glance, was marked with a three. The lighting in the hallway was weak, as well, and it made determining details even more difficult.

For a moment, Chace held on the landing, waiting and listening. From one of the apartments she could hear conversation, animated and happy, and from another broadcast voices, either the State-run television or the State-run radio, she had no way of knowing. Somewhere below she heard a door slam closed.

She moved forward along the hallway, checking each door in turn, and had reversed, was heading back towards the stairs, when she stopped, her eye catching on a chalk mark high on the wall. Three short lines, running parallel to the ground on the right side of one of the doors, and three more, barely visible, on the left.

Three and three again.

She knocked gently and waited, and after a moment, she heard a lock turn. The door pulled back, and the man who stood revealed matched the photograph, and Chace stepped immediately forward. She covered his mouth with her left hand, pushing him inside, then shoved him backwards against the wall, pinning him in place. With a foot, she shut the door. She put the index finger of her right hand up to her lips, and the man looked at her with eyes wide.

For nearly a minute she held him in place, neither of them moving, feeling his breath hitting the back of her hand as it left his nose, hearing her own heart pounding. Noise from the rest of the building filtered into them, a cough, the broadcast voices. A strain of music from somewhere above them. A laugh from the street.

Finally, Chace moved her hand from the man's mouth.

"Falcon?"

He nodded.

"It's time to go," Chace told him.

CHAPTER TEN

IRAN—KARAJ, 22 NILUFAR STREET

10 DECEMBER 1839 HOURS (GMT +3.30)

Shirazi stared at the flickering image on the video monitor, the live feed of the hallway outside the apartment, watched as the woman made her way carefully along the hall, her pace measured as she passed each door in turn. If he didn't know what he was looking at, he could believe she was simply lost and trying to find her way.

Then she saw the chalk marks, turning away from the camera, to look at the door to the apartment opposite where Shirazi and Zahabzeh now sat, and she knocked, and Hossein answered. She had him muzzled and inside so quickly, Shirazi was certain that if he had dared to blink, he would have missed it.

He motioned to the technician to his right, showed him two fingers, and there was the softest click of a button, and the image on the screen flickered and changed, now showing the interior of Hossein's apartment. On his left, he heard Zahabzeh inhale slowly through his nose, struggling against his desire to speak. Shirazi turned his head from the monitor, saw that Zahabzeh was looking at him, the question clear in his expression.

Shirazi shook his head, and Zahabzeh's mouth twitched, fighting off a frown.

Both men turned their attention back to the monitor.

The woman hadn't moved at all, still holding Hossein silent against the wall, so still that Shirazi could imagine the video was malfunctioning, that the image was no longer live but frozen, a moment trapped in time. The angle for this camera was such that he couldn't see her face, and the lack of appropriate illumination washed all color into shadow. Even if it hadn't, the *maqna'e* she wore concealed her hair.

It didn't matter. Shirazi knew who she was, and it took all of his self-control to keep from displaying the relief he felt at seeing Tara Chace, at knowing she was less than ten meters away from him. SIS had cut it close, had cut it very close. Another day and Hossein's absence would have been noted. A day more, it would have been inexplicable. Even now, Shirazi knew there wasn't much time left to him.

On the screen, the woman moved her hand from Hossein's mouth, speaking. Zahabzeh reached for the headphones running from the monitor, but Shirazi put his hand out, stopping him. There was no need, and despite knowing better, he feared that listening in might somehow, someway, reveal an unintended noise of their own.

Now the woman stepped back, and Hossein moved quickly down the hall, into the little room that served as the apartment's main living space. Shirazi showed the technician three fingers, but it was unnecessary, and even before he had done so the camera changed to the one placed on the far wall of Hossein's apartment, the one that granted the best view of the room. The woman had followed Hossein at a distance, staying in the mouth of the hallway, and Shirazi thought that was smart of her, that she was blocking the only exit, in case her defector suddenly tried to run.

But Hossein wouldn't run, not after waiting a week to prove his innocence to Shirazi, and by extension, to his uncle. He had already gathered up his meager belongings, one small satchel, and now the woman came forward and took him by the elbow. For a moment light and lens united, and Shirazi could see her face clearly, the look of concentration and focus, the restless eyes sweeping past the hidden camera. Despite himself, he smiled.

Then she was guiding Hossein back down the hallway, to the door, still holding him by the elbow, and the camera flickered, changed back once more to the very first position, and there she was, emerging with Hossein. They moved briskly to the stairs, then out of shot, and Shirazi wondered at how quickly she had taken control of Hossein. Even if Hossein hadn't been told to go with her, to do what she said, Shirazi doubted he would've been able to resist. Her presence had commanded him from the moment she had entered his apartment and taken his voice, and Shirazi had to wonder how long it would last.

Zahabzeh started to open his mouth, but Shirazi shook his head again, then carefully got out of his seat and moved to the window that overlooked the alley. With two fingers, he pulled the curtain back enough to look down, just in time to see the woman load Hossein into the Samand parked there. She moved to the driver's door, took one last, quick look around to all sides, and Shirazi let the curtains close before she could look up, as she had done when she'd first arrived. The glare from the light below had spared him there, and the move on her part had surprised him. In his experience, most people forgot to look up.

He listened for the sound of the car starting, waited until it pulled away, and only then was he willing to speak.

"Very well done," Shirazi said, aware that the others in the room, Zahabzeh and the technician and another one of the guards, would think he was praising them. "Farzan, get Javed."

Zahabzeh nodded and all but ran from the room.

"Break it down," Shirazi told the others. "We're done here. Leave no signs in either apartment."

Murmurs of assent, and Shirazi watched to make certain the two men were absorbed in their task, quickly disassembling the surveillance equipment, before he allowed his body to relax. Just for a moment, just for an instant, while nobody was watching; a moment of peace, a breath of relief.

Still far to go before this would be over, Shirazi knew. But now, at least, all the pieces were on the board, on his board, and that meant they were under his control, even if some of them did not yet know it.

Zahabzeh returned, Javed following close behind.

"It's placed?" Shirazi asked.

"Yes, sir," Javed said. "After she rounded the corner, I fixed one device to the rear bumper, as directed, and placed a second inside the car, beneath the driver's seat, just to be sure."

"Check them," Shirazi said, only to see that Zahabzeh was already doing so, the small GPS tracker in his hand.

"Good signal on one," Zahabzeh told him. He twisted the dial on the side, pressed the black button at the center of the unit. "And good signal on two."

"And Hossein's?"

"Still reading strong. If she takes him anywhere from here to Delhi, we'll know about it and be able to find them."

"I doubt she'll take him that far. Which direction is she heading?"

"North." Zahabzeh paused. "Not very quickly."

"Traffic. She's using the traffic to make certain they're not being followed, and that is why we use this method instead, Farzan, you see?"

"Yes, sir."

Shirazi rolled his shoulders, attempting to work some of the stiffness and tension that had settled in them free. "We have some time now. Come, let's get a cup of tea while the others clean up."

In the coffeehouse, the same coffeehouse where Hossein had met the thin British tourist who hadn't been a tourist at all, Shirazi and Zahabzeh sipped their cups of *chay*. Caleb Lewis had surprised him, Shirazi had to admit. Of all the new members of the British mission in Iran who had come in replacement of the old, he had been ready to dismiss Lewis as a possible replacement for Ricks. If it hadn't been for the constant surveillance on Hossein, it was likely Lewis would have remained unidentified as SIS for months to come.

"I do not understand why we didn't take her in the apartment," Zahabzeh said.

"You don't close the snare when the rabbit has only put his nose in, Farzan." Shirazi allowed himself a smile. "You wait until his whole head is in the noose."

"But we have identified at least one other, Lewis, from the embassy. Surely if we were to arrest either of them, we would get everything we could want to know from their interrogation."

"Perhaps, yes. But if this new agent can lead us to the larger network, if she can reveal all of their spies to us without ever meaning to, is that not better? There must be a plan to get Hossein out of the country, Farzan. We do not know how many people are involved, how much help she has."

"I just worry that we'll miss our opportunity."

"A concern I share, believe me. But we must balance what we have with what we may gain. The more we uncover of their network, the better."

"Yes. Yes, I agree." Zahabzeh looked into his empty cup, then up at Shirazi. "So now we follow them?"

"Until they have revealed all of their secrets," Shirazi confirmed.

CHAPTER ELEVEN

IRAN—NOSHAHR, 2 SHIR AQAI (SIS SAFEHOUSE)
11 DECEMBER 0017 HOURS (GMT +3.30)

"Vehicle incoming," MacIntyre told Caleb Lewis. "A Samand."

Caleb moved to the window, beside the larger man, peeked out between the curtains and the frame. How MacIntyre could tell the little car rattling down the unpaved road towards them was a Samand, he couldn't guess; the glare from the headlamps told Caleb that there was a car approaching, nothing more. But if MacIntyre was correct, if it was the Samand, then it would be the Minder and Falcon.

He thought that might grant his fear a reprieve. He was disappointed to discover that, instead, it only heightened what he was feeling, what he had been feeling ever since Barnett had sent him north and told him to wait at the safehouse. It wasn't that the house was bad, because it truly wasn't, though it was rather small. A well-chosen little cottage near the end of a tiny dirt track, in the foothills of the northern slope of the Alborz, just outside the town of Noshahr. From where he stood now, the Noshahr airport was just under a mile to the north, the boat for Dr. Gadient moored just under two to the northeast.

MacIntyre was moving to the front door, and Caleb followed him. The man was SIS Security, and Caleb supposed he was ex-military, possibly Royal Commando, though he wasn't sure, and even though the last two days had provided ample opportunity, he hadn't dared to ask. Over six feet tall and over two hundred pounds, MacIntyre had been quiet much of the time they waited, making walkabout of the cottage several times a day, to assure himself that there was no one watching them from the trees. The only manifestation Caleb had seen of anything like personality had been at mealtimes, when MacIntyre had used the small kitchen to cook up their food, always Iranian dishes, and always surprisingly good.

"Keep back," MacIntyre told Caleb, reaching out to switch off the interior lights before unlocking and opening the door.

Caleb did as instructed, trying to stay out of the way while still maintaining a view of the outside. A breeze entered the cottage, fresh and cold and sweet from the evergreens growing all around them. The Samand had stopped no more than fifteen feet away, the headlamps winking out as the engine rattled and died. For a moment there was nothing, no motion from the vehicle, just the sound of the wind and the pinging of the engine as it began to cool. Then the car creaked, and first the driver's, then the passenger's doors opened, and Caleb was surprised that he recognized the driver from the coffeehouse, the man he'd understood to be Falcon.

The passenger was a woman, or he assumed it was, because she was wearing a chador, her whole body, face, and hair all hidden beneath the tent of black fabric. Even as Falcon eased himself from behind the wheel and stood awkwardly beside the car, arching his back to stretch, she had closed her door and was coming around the side, and Caleb noticed that she'd looked their way only once, was now glancing all around her as she moved to the man's side. She grabbed his elbow, pulling Falcon with her to the entrance of the cottage, and before she had even stepped inside, she was tossing the keys to the Samand to MacIntyre.

"Ditch it," she said, her English, her accent, and her authority all coming as a surprise from beneath the chador.

MacIntyre caught the keys out of the air, stepped past them as they entered, making for the car. "Give me an hour."

"Close it," the woman said to Caleb, entering the cottage and shoving Falcon towards the couch. "Sit."

Caleb moved to the door, shutting it, and when he turned back, Falcon was seated and the woman was already shrugging off the chador, revealing blond hair to her shoulders, blue jeans, and a burgundy-and-gold manteau beneath it. The manteau was open, unbuttoned, and even in the poor ambient light, Caleb could see her pale and bare skin, the dark shadow of her bra across her chest.

"Bloody burning up in that thing," the woman said, tossing the chador onto an empty chair. "Chace."

It took him seeing her extended hand before he realized she was giving him her name, and Caleb shook it, saying, "Lewis."

"And this is Falcon," Chace said, indicating the man on the couch. "But he says we should call him Hossein."

"We've met," Caleb said. "I enjoyed the book, sir."

Falcon looked confused for an instant, then nodded, managing a weak smile. "I am most glad to hear it."

The lights snapped back on in the small living room, and Caleb saw Chace move away from the switch on the wall, briskly making a circuit around the space, opening the few doors she found and leaning half into each room, one after another. He knew who she was, of course, now that he had her name. Minder One, Tara Chace, Head of the Special Section, and he tried not to stare at her, just as he tried not to notice that she still hadn't buttoned up her manteau, and that the bra was in fact black and perhaps silk. When he glanced back to Falcon, he noted that the man was looking resolutely away from her; whether that was the result of cultural modesty or something else, Caleb didn't know.

Chace finished her survey, turned back to Caleb. "No trouble?"

"It's been very quiet."

"Good. We need to ID him now."

Caleb nodded, grateful for something to do other than stand there. The inkpad and cards were already on the small table by the couch, and he moved to lay them out while Chace and Falcon watched him.

"If you'll come over here, please, sir."

Falcon rose slowly, still stiff from the long drive. He glanced back to Chace, then just as quickly away again, and as Caleb took hold of his right hand by the palm, he asked, "Why do you take my fingerprints?"

"Just procedure. Thumb first, thank you, sir. Then your index finger, very good."

"You don't believe I am who I say I am?"

"Of course we do, sir. We would hardly be here otherwise, would we? Left hand now, sir."

One by one, Caleb copied Falcon's prints off his fingertips and onto the card. While he worked, Chace made another circuit of the cottage, and this time, when she emerged from the bathroom, she was buttoning up the manteau once more. Caleb caught her eye, and the grin she gave him was surprisingly sheepish. He wondered if she truly had forgotten her top had been open, or if it had been a deliberate move, a way to keep Falcon off balance by playing on his cultural and religious standards.

"All done?"

"Just finishing," Caleb told her.

"We'll rest here for a while, Hossein," Chace said. "It's safe and we should have everything you might need. There's fresh clothes for you in the room over there, and the bathroom has a shower, if you'd like to get cleaned up. Certainly, you'll want to wash your hands. Are you hungry? Thirsty?"

Falcon considered for what seemed a very long time, staring at his ink-stained fingertips. When he spoke, he sounded unsure. "I think I would like to shower. And perhaps if I might have a cup of tea before lying down? I am afraid I do not feel very hungry."

Chace gave him a smile that was nothing less than radiant, full of reassurance and understanding.

"No, I don't imagine that you do, sir." She took him gently by the elbow once more, guided him to the bathroom, and once Falcon was hidden behind the closed door, she turned back to Caleb. "How are you for coms?"

"For audio, not terrific. We have a sat connection to London, but I don't trust it for more than ninety seconds at a time. The Iranian monitoring apparatus is very good, as I'm sure you know. Better to use the letter drop on the Internet."

"Then let's get to it."

Caleb hesitated, looking towards the bathroom. There was no noise coming from behind the door, no sound of water running, nothing.

"He's not going anywhere," Tara Chace assured him. "Even if he wanted to rabbit, the window's too small."

"So what's he doing in there?"

"I suspect trying not to be sick. The drive over the mountains was murder. Ice in the pass, traffic didn't let up until we reached Chalus, and I made him do most of it himself to avoid suspicion."

"You weren't stopped?"

"Once, coming into Marzanabad. I was in the chador by then, and he did all the talking. Didn't last more than two minutes once they saw his ID card, and then they practically offered to give him an escort through town."

"So who is he, then?"

Chace grinned at him. "They didn't tell you?"

"I've only known him as Falcon. We figured he was someone important, but no idea who."

"Let's just say he comes from the right family," Tara Chace told him.

The shower came on as Caleb finished uploading the scan of Falcon's fingerprints to the webmail program he was using. The e-mail would never be sent, in fact, but rather would remain in the drafts folder on the server until deleted. Once he logged off, a program running at the Main Communications Desk back in the Ops Room in London would inform the Coms officer that the server had been updated, and the officer would then read the draft and thus receive the message. It was a beautifully anonymous and safe system, and one that SIS could take no credit for discovering; it had been in use by various militant terrorist cells to communicate and coordinate their plans for years before the Firm had adopted it to their own purposes.

"Anything else you want me to add?" Caleb asked, and when Chace didn't immediately answer him, he turned in his chair to look at her. She had taken Falcon's place on the couch, was sitting with her head tilted back against the cushions, eyes closed.

"No," she said finally. "No, nothing more."

Falcon emerged from the bathroom minutes later, wearing his fresh clothes, his hair wet, and while he looked moderately refreshed, there was no mistaking his fatigue. Caleb made tea in the kitchen for all three of them, and they drank their cups of *chay* in silence, for the most part.

"When do we leave?" Falcon asked, finally.

"Soon," Chace told him. "When the time is right."

"But how long will that be?"

She shook her head, gave him the same reassuring smile as before. "It's all well in hand, sir, I promise you."

Falcon looked doubtful, seemed ready to press the point, when the front door rattled and he froze as if suddenly sheeted with ice. It wasn't until MacIntyre was through the door and out of his coat that the man seemed to relax, and Caleb saw that Chace had noted the change, too.

"Car's taken care of," MacIntyre told them. "You lot want to get some sleep, I'll take watch."

"Yes," Chace said. "That's probably a very good idea."

She rose and waited for Falcon, then escorted him to the room that would be his for the rest of the night. Caleb gathered up the empty teacups, returned them to their place in the kitchen, and when he came back, Chace was speaking to MacIntyre, her voice so low he couldn't make out a sound, let alone a word. MacIntyre nodded, and Chace turned to Caleb.

"If London sends a response, wake me," she told him, and then headed off to the only other bedroom.

After she had gone, Caleb asked, "What was that about?"

"What was what?" MacIntyre said.

"What did she say to you?"

"His clothes are still in the bathroom?"

"I think so, yes."

"That's what it's about. She wants us to search them. Then she wants us to burn them."

The fear, the same, cold, sickening fear came flooding back into Caleb's chest.

"I'll get a fire started," he said.

CHAPTER TWELVE

LONDON—VAUXHALL CROSS, OPS ROOM
10 DECEMBER 2134 HOURS (GMT)

Crocker stared up at the plasma wall in the Ops Room, watched as the top left quadrant redrew itself, northeastern Russia vanishing as the display filled with Falcon's fingerprints, freshly downloaded.

"Can we confirm?" he demanded.

"Technical division is looking at it now," Ron Hodgson assured him.

"How long will it take them?"

"No idea. The only fingerprints of Hossein Khamenei available for match are courtesy of the CIA, and there's been a hiccup."

Crocker spun on the toe of his patent leather and made straight for the Duty Ops Desk. "Hiccup how?"

"CIA has asked we send the prints to them for verification, not the other way around."

"Get Seale."

Hodgson nodded, reaching for one of his many phones as Crocker stepped up to join him on the raised platform, then turned back to survey the room. No less than four people were gathered at the Mission Planning Desk, including Nicky Poole, who, despite having been told to go home and take the night had decided to spend his Friday in the Ops Room, keeping one eye on Coldwitch, another on Bagboy.

"Julian Seale, sir," Hodgson said, handing over the phone.

"What the hell are your people playing at?" Crocker demanded.

"She has him?"

Crocker eyed the clocks above the plasma screens. "They reached the safehouse in Noshahr without incident forty-two minutes ago. Why are you withholding the fingerprints?"

"Must be some mistake," Seale said. *"I'll have Langley release them now."*

"Did you really think I was going to box you out, Julian?"

"I don't know what you're going to do, Paul. Taking out a little insurance seemed wise."

"I see. And will you withhold sending the Coast Guard to the rendezvous as insurance, as well?"

"No," Seale said. *"I think you got the message."*

"Yes, I did. Now I'd like the fucking fingerprints."

"Should be there within the next five minutes."

Crocker slammed the phone down, hard enough to bring the Ops Room to a sudden, if brief, silence.

"Bastard," Crocker said to no one in particular.

"Yes, sir," Ronald Hodgson agreed, cheerfully.

Crocker stepped down from the platform, started to cross to Alexis at MCO, when Poole intercepted him.

"Boss, we may have a problem."

"Are you going to tell me or do I have to buy you dinner first?"

"You can't afford me." Poole offered him a printout, the ink still tacky on its face. "Weather in zone for tomorrow night is taking a turn for the nasty. There's a storm brewing, looks to sweep down from the northwest across the Caspian, heavy rains and wind. If Tara takes Falcon out onto the water in the Zodiac in that weather, they could end up swamped."

Crocker looked at the satellite image, the blanket of clouds that seemed to be folding over itself. "Probability?"

"They're saying ninety percent chance. It'll bring the temp down, and it's already going to be damn cold out on the water. Winds could reach fifty KPH, possibly higher."

"It just gets better and better, doesn't it?"

"Not really, no, sir."

Crocker stared up at the plasma wall again, this time not seeing it, trying to sort his thoughts.

"Daylight in zone is when?" he asked abruptly.

Poole called out to Ron, relaying the question. There was a pause, then Ron called back, "Morning twilight in zone tomorrow, oh-six-twenty-five, sunrise oh-six-fifty-three."

"And it's oh-one-twenty there now," Poole added.

"How long from the Zodiac to the rendezvous?"

"It's not close. David? Can you put the RZ for Coldwitch on the map and give distance from Noshahr?"

On the plasma wall, a red dot appeared on the Caspian.

"Two hundred and eighty-seven klicks," Poole said. "Top speed of the RHIB is going to be maybe—*maybe*—seventy knots."

Crocker did the conversion in his head. "A hundred and thirty kilometers an hour. There's no chance in hell she'll be able to go that fast."

"She'd be lucky to push forty knots."

"Which would still mean four hours exposed on the water. If she leaves *right now* she'll have the cover of darkness for the trip. Otherwise, she'll be out there at dawn, when everyone and their goat can see her."

"That's not the major worry," Poole said. "Will the Coast Guard even attempt the pickup during daylight?"

Crocker snorted. "Absolutely, even if they scream bloody murder about being forced to do it. If she has Falcon with her, they'll be there."

Poole stared up at the map. "No chance we can have them move the RZ further south?" Exasperation had crept into his voice.

"None. They want to stay as far from Iranian airspace as possible. They move further south, they'll risk their own cover. It's why the site's so far north in the first place."

"Not good."

"No," Crocker agreed. "Not good at all."

"Maybe the fingerprints won't match," Poole offered, hopefully.

"With our luck?" Crocker said. "Of course they will."

They did, Daniel Szurko bringing the report directly down to the Ops Room in person, cheerful and excited to be entering a domain normally forbidden to him.

"Positive eighteen-point match, Paul," he said. "It's confirmed, Falcon is Hossein Khamenei."

"You informed C?"

"I thought I'd leave the pleasure to you, though you don't look terribly pleased, I must say."

"That's because I'm not," Crocker said. "Nicky, inform the DC, C, and the FCO that Falcon's identity has been confirmed. Ron, I need Seale again."

"Ahead of you already, sir," Ron said, trying to hand him the phone. Crocker had to reach for it twice, because Szurko had climbed onto the platform to get a better look at the room and, realizing he was now in the way, kept moving in the absolutely wrong direction to get out of it.

"You've confirmed Falcon's identity?" Seale asked.

"It's a positive match with the prints you provided," Crocker said. "But we've got another problem."

"Which is?"

"Weather in zone for tomorrow has gone ugly. I want Chace to take Falcon out tonight. Can you move up the RZ?"

"How soon can she move?"

"If we push and everything goes the way it should, she could be on the water by oh-three-hundred in zone, oh-three-thirty at the latest."

"That'd put her at the RZ well after sunup."

"Between oh-seven-hundred and oh-eight-hundred, I'd think. If there's no trouble on the water."

"Hold on," Seale said, and Crocker heard the line go mute. Szurko hopped down from the platform with both feet, began talking excitedly with Poole about the Ops Room and how they really must get some better equipment in here, certainly have the ICT lads upgrade the computer system. The line clicked, and Seale's voice returned. *"Jesus, you weren't kidding. She tries to take him out in*

that, they won't need the Coast Guard for a RZ, they'll need them for a rescue."

"Can you get them to move up the timetable?" Crocker insisted.

"I'll get on it. You going to clear her to run now?"

"Not until I know if she's got a flight home."

"I'll call you back."

"Quickly, Julian. If they don't start before dawn, there'll be no point in going. I'll have to order them to stay put another day."

"Yeah, I get you. I'll call you back."

The line went dead.

Seven minutes and twenty-six seconds later, according to the Ops Room clock, Seale called back.

"Go," he told Crocker.

CHAPTER THIRTEEN

IRAN—NOSHAHR, AZADI SQUARE, SHALIZAR HOTEL
11 DECEMBER 0252 HOURS (GMT +3.30)

He had just descended far enough into sleep for the dream to begin, the long, blond British spy staring at him past the hidden camera, knowing he was there and watching her. She reached for the silk scarf covering the back of her head, pulled it free, and she opened her mouth, started speaking to him, but the words weren't hers; they were Zahabzeh's.

"They're moving. Sir, they're moving again, Hossein just left the house, they're heading north, our direction!"

Shirazi stared dumbly up at his deputy, winced as the lights came on in the hotel room.

"They're moving!" Zahabzeh said. "They're not waiting, they're going now!"

"I'm awake," Shirazi said, twisting himself out of bed, reaching for his glasses on the nightstand. "How long ago?"

"Two minutes, perhaps three. If they're heading for the airport, they'll be there any moment!"

Shirazi began pulling on his shoes, grateful he'd slept in his clothes. "Get Javed and Parviz over there, immediately, tell them to stay in radio contact. They're to make no move, no effort to apprehend, without my direct order."

Zahabzeh was already heading to the door. "Do you want me to go with them?"

"No, get the others down to the cars. I'll join you there in a moment."

He finished pulling on his remaining shoe, got to his feet. Zahabzeh had left the door open, and he could hear him shouting orders to the men, intense and excited. Shirazi waited until the voices faded, the men rushing to do as ordered, then crossed to his go-bag and quickly unfastened the top flap. He dug in deep, beneath the change of clothes and past the papers and money, finding his pistol and the silencer that went with it. He racked the slide, tucked the gun beneath his shirt at his belly, then thrust the silencer into his pocket. He hoisted the bag onto his shoulder and headed out.

Javed and Parviz had already gone in one of the cars when Shirazi stepped out the front of the hotel, Zahabzeh pulling up immediately and leaning across to open the door for him. The remaining two cars, each driven by Shirazi's handpicked men, idled behind. Shirazi climbed inside the car, keeping his bag slung, and Zahabzeh had them rolling before the door was shut once more. Taking one hand from the wheel, Zahabzeh handed him the receiver for the tracking device they had planted inside Hossein.

"They're headed to the airport," Zahabzeh said.

Shirazi doubted that, had doubted it the moment they'd determined the location of the safehouse. It was too obvious an exfil, and too difficult to accomplish; according to all of his information, Tara Chace was many things, but she wasn't a pilot, and neither was Hossein. Checking the receiver in his hand confirmed the fact.

"No, they're not," Shirazi said. "Now heading northeast. Past us, two hundred meters."

Zahabzeh spun the wheel, whipping the car in a turn around Azadi Square, heading north. Shirazi had chosen the Shalizar Hotel upon their arrival in Noshahr some three hours earlier not because of its cozy décor or its beautiful daylight views of the mountains to the south and the port to the north, but for the simple reason that it had been built almost dead-center in the heart of the town. That decision was saving them right now, and as they headed up Allameh, Shirazi could see Hossein was staying a steady two hundred meters ahead of them.

"They're heading for the water," Zahabzeh told him. "You were right."

"Yes."

"We checked all the piers, we didn't find a boat."

"Then we clearly missed it." Shirazi reached for the radio on the dashboard, brought it to his mouth. "All units converge at Farabi."

Confirmations came crackling back, including Javed. *"Confirm, sir? We are to join on your position?"*

"Correct."

"Understood."

The blip on the receiver was slowing, now turning east. "Right ahead," Shirazi told Zahabzeh. "Slow down."

"If we lose them—"

"We're not going to lose them. Slow down. This is a trap, Farzan, not a chase. Take the left."

Zahabzeh took the turn as instructed, and they crossed a narrow bridge, spanning one of the many canals that ran throughout Noshahr and dumped into the Caspian. They were less than two kilometers from the shore. Shirazi stared out the windows, searching for any signs of their quarry. On the receiver, he saw that Hossein's progress had come to an almost complete stop.

"They're out of their vehicle," Shirazi said, and added, to the radio, "Stop at Danesh, south side of the park, no lights on approach."

Confirmations over the radio, and Zahabzeh slapped the knob to his left, killing their own headlights. They slowed, turning onto the grass at the southern edge of the little park that ran along both sides of the canal here, and as soon as they had stopped, Shirazi got out of the car, the receiver still in one hand, the radio in the other. He heard the engine die, and Zahabzeh was out now, too, coming around the back of the vehicle and opening the trunk.

The other two cars stopped on either side of them, but Shirazi kept his attention on the receiver for another moment. Hossein was still moving, but much more slowly, and he was sure that meant they were now going on foot. Wherever they had stashed the boat, it had to be close, along the canal, certainly no more than two hundred meters away.

When he raised his head again, the other two men had joined them at the rear of the car, now checking the weapons Zahabzeh had handed them, a compact submachine gun for each, to accompany the pistols they carried. Zahabzeh, Shirazi saw, was offering him one, as well. He took it in his free hand with a nod, raising his radio once more.

"Javed, where are you?" Shirazi asked.

"Coming from the southwest of the park. Should be there in another minute."

"Stop before the bridge and wait for me there."

"Yes, sir."

He lowered the radio again, looked at the group of men, each of them attentive and focused and flushed with anticipation for what was to come. It was cold, cold enough that each breath sent clouds of condensation curling around their faces. Shirazi turned back to the north, searching the bank on either side of the canal. Somewhere in the darkness, hidden by the shadows and the night and the denuded trees, their quarry was preparing to escape.

"Now?" Zahabzeh whispered to him.

"Yes," Shirazi said. "Now. Take Sina and Rostam along this side of the canal. Javed, Parviz, and I will take the other side. And remember, Farzan, we want her alive. No one shoots unless it is to return fire."

"Understood."

"I want her alive," Shirazi repeated.

They spread out, Zahabzeh leading the two others into the park, all of them moving quietly and quickly. Shirazi headed for the edge of the canal, jogging back down towards the bridge, and across, to where Javed and Parviz were just now pulling to a stop. He slowed long enough to give the men time to join him, turning north again, this time along the canal's western edge. Behind him, he heard the clack of metal sliding over metal as bolts slid into place, weapons being made ready.

He moved fast, almost faster than he dared, hearing the steady, soft crunch of his boots on dead leaves and frosted grass. Now and then he caught glimpses of Zahabzeh and the others through the trees on the opposite bank. His heart was beginning to pound, and when he checked the receiver once more, Shirazi saw that his own pulse was making it jump ever so slightly in his hand. Hossein's progress had slowed yet further, and he thought they most certainly must have reached the boat by now.

Clearly, SIS had set their rendezvous for the Caspian itself, somewhere out on the water. He was cutting this very close, Shirazi knew; if Chace got Hossein onto the water, his only option would be to intercept her before the canal reached the sea, either that or be forced to call out boats, and if he did that, the entire operation would fail, as far as he was concerned. But nowhere ahead could he see them, and it was agonizing; to come this far, to be this close, and to lose it all at the last minute, would be unbearable.

Then he saw them, two figures moving through shadows, low to the canal, and he saw the boat, covered by a tarpaulin, moored against the opposite bank, Zahabzeh's side. Chace was leading towards it, still wearing the manteau and head scarf he'd seen on her back in Karaj, Hossein lingering at the base of the wooden steps, perhaps two meters behind. Shirazi held up a hand, coming to a stop in shadows of his own. Javed and Parviz pulled up immediately behind him. Shirazi tucked the receiver into his pocket, pointed.

"I want her alive," Shirazi whispered, then motioned them forward, watched each of them drop into a crouch, their pistols held in both hands, low and ready before them. Shirazi looked to the opposite bank, Zahabzeh visible for an instant as he motioned his own men to spread out.

He slung the submachine gun from its strap over his shoulder, letting it rest against where he wore his bag, and from his pants Shirazi pulled the silencer to his pistol, then quickly screwed it onto the barrel of the gun. Going low himself, he moved quietly forward, Javed just visible to his left, Parviz a little further ahead on the right. He checked the water again, saw that Chace had removed the tarp covering the boat, revealing a slim and low rigid-hulled craft, perhaps only eight meters long, two large outboard motors at its stern. Small and fast and perfectly appropriate for what she was trying to do.

They were nearly opposite her now. Shirazi scanned the far bank again, trying to find Zahabzeh, saw him for a moment between trees, and then he saw Hossein, backing up the stairs from where the boat was moored. He reached the top, Chace now ascending after him, and Shirazi couldn't read her body language, but Hossein took a half-step back in response. She started to lunge for him.

That was when Zahabzeh and his men opened fire.

CHAPTER FOURTEEN

IRAN—NOSHAHR, JAME CANAL

11 DECEMBER 0258 HOURS (GMT +3.30)

Something was wrong.

Chace had seen hints of it at the safehouse, before Falcon had gone to take his lie-down. It wasn't so much that the man was nervous or even afraid; those were to be expected, those were basic human emotions, and if a man fleeing for his life from the country of his birth didn't exhibit them, *that* would have been beyond suspicion, that would have been confirmation, and Chace would have known just what to do; she'd have broken his neck and dumped him on the side of the Chalus-Tehran Road, and damn to his family name and his potential value to SIS and the CIA and the Parks and Rec Commission and all the rest.

But it wasn't just that he was scared.

It was that he was the *wrong* kind of scared.

Caleb Lewis woke her with a gentle touch on the shoulder, bringing her instantly and fully awake. She'd been asleep for less than forty minutes.

"London," the young man said. "Timetable's moved up, they're saying you have to go now."

She sat up, began pulling on her boots, asking, "Did they say why?"

"They're worried about the weather tomorrow night."

"Get Falcon."

He left the room without another word. Chace got to her feet, tying her hair back beneath her silk scarf. She smoothed her manteau, checked her pockets, making sure she knew where everything was. Papers, cash—rials and Euros—the GPS unit, sat phone, and her little folding knife. From the next room, she heard Caleb's voice, speaking Farsi, and Falcon answering. The older man's words were coming fast, and she could hear the anxiety threading each of them, didn't need to understand the language to guess at his meaning.

MacIntyre was standing in the main room when she emerged.

"Get the car ready," Chace told him.

She took half a moment to find her smile, then brought it with her into Falcon's bedroom. As much as the GPS unit and the knife in her pocket, the smile was another tool, to be used with the same precision. Whether he liked it or not, Falcon had already defected, had done so the moment he left Karaj with Chace. He had left his own country and moved into hers, and so she smiled to let him know that he was welcome, that he was safe, that she would care for him.

Falcon was still speaking in Farsi, but he switched to English when he saw her. "You said we would be able to rest here. You said we would have time here."

"Yes, I did say that. But it's better this way. The sooner you're out of the country, the less chance of discovery. You'll have to trust me, Hossein."

"I need my clothes, my things."

"Everything's in your bag," Chace told him. "Come along, sir, we've got to get moving."

She took his elbow the way she had several times already, and guided the man out of the bedroom. Caleb went ahead, picked up Falcon's small duffel, and the front door opened, MacIntyre returning. Along with the breath of cold air, she could smell the exhaust from the car idling out front.

"Do we have a coat?" Chace asked. "It'll be cold."

MacIntyre pulled a parka from the peg by the door, helped Falcon on with it. Chace motioned to Caleb to follow her, then stepped outside, to the car. She waited while he shoved the duffel into the backseat.

"His clothes," she said. "Did you find anything?"

"Nothing. Nothing in the bag."

Chace chewed on her lip. Through the open door, she could see MacIntyre zipping the parka closed, as if dressing a child. Falcon wasn't looking at him, nor was he looking out, at her, and that struck her as odd, as well. She was his lifeline now, she was the one who would keep him safe. In her experience, defectors subconsciously fixated on the first ally they encountered during their escape, rarely letting them out of their sight. She wondered if the business with the manteau had been too much, if she had offended him so deeply by showing skin that she'd destroyed his trust in her.

"You know what to do now?" she asked Caleb.

"We'll sterilize the house as soon as you're gone," he told her. "Our initial plan was to head back to Tehran as soon as you two cleared out, but given the hour I'm having second thoughts. We may push out departure until morning. Less suspicion, I'd think, if we're driving in daylight."

Chace considered, remembering the checkpoints she and Falcon had passed on their way north. "Probably wise."

The young man looked relieved. "I'll be glad to be out of here, if you don't mind me saying."

"I don't mind you saying it at all." She offered him her hand, and he seemed surprised by that, needed a half-second before shaking it. "You're ever in London, let me know, I'll take you round the pub."

"That'd be wonderful."

Caleb smiled awkwardly, and Chace again thought how very young he looked. She opened the passenger's door, motioned for Falcon to come and join them. MacIntyre followed him out. She got him into the car, closed the door, then climbed behind the wheel herself, rolling down the window.

"Straight up Shir Aqai," Caleb told her. "Then right on Farabi. The road will curve northeast along the park. Mooring point is in your GPS."

Chace nodded, put the car in gear.

"Pleasure doing business with you," she said.

"Godspeed," MacIntyre told her.

The road signs were marked in both Farsi and English, and Chace found the park without difficulty, stopping on the northeast corner. There had been almost no traffic on the roads, only distant headlights that had turned away before she could even see the cars that made them. She checked her mirrors again, and again didn't see anything that alarmed her. Beside her, in his seat, Falcon was doing the same thing, but more obviously, twisting around, trying to look in every direction at once.

She killed the engine, leaving the keys in the ignition, then reached around to the backseat for Falcon's bag and set it in his lap. "We're on foot now."

"Is it a boat? We're taking a boat?"

"This way, sir."

She climbed out of the car, pulling the GPS from beneath her manteau and switching it on without looking, instead watching as Falcon came around to join her. There was a street lamp some two meters away, and in its illumination she could see the shine of sweat on the man's face, despite the cold. She checked the GPS, got her bearings, and, putting one hand on Falcon's shoulder, began leading him through the park.

They moved in silence, just the sound of their steps and Falcon's heavy breathing as they threaded their way through the trees. They passed a picnic area, then a small gazebo, and when the GPS told her that she was only eight meters from where she wanted to be, Chace saw the canal and stopped them both in the shadows. She switched the device off, stowed it away once more, checking the terrain, straining to hear anything other than the slight rustle of the wind and the water. Still nothing.

A wooden platform had been constructed on the side of the canal, ahead, and as she led Falcon forward she saw the steps running down, perhaps no more than eight feet, to a small landing. The RHIB, covered, was tied up against it, rising and falling ever so slightly on the swell. She led him down carefully, scanning the opposite bank before looking back to check their own. No one and nothing. The wooden stairs were slick with frost, and Falcon moved painfully slowly, as if afraid he might fall.

She had to let go of him at the base to uncover the boat. She freed the tarp, bundling it up and stuffing it beneath the wheel, at the bow, and when she turned back to Falcon, she saw that the man had retreated, now backing up the stairs. Chace hissed at him to get down, starting up after him, and suddenly the thing that had been wrong all along, the thing she had missed, struck her, as clear and cold as the night itself.

She was supposed to be Falcon's savior. She was supposed to be his protector. He had abandoned everything to fly with her to safety. By all rights, he should have been sticking to her like a shadow. Yet whenever he could, he would put as much distance between them as possible. It wasn't because she was a woman.

It was because he had no intention of leaving with her at all.

"You son of a bitch," Chace said.

She pushed hard off the last step, nearly slipping, reaching for him. He tried to turn away, to run, but she caught him at the collar, and to her right Chace saw a muzzle flash, heard the air rip. Falcon screamed, went dead-weight in her grip, and she stumbled forward as another chatter of shots rang out, nearly falling, and this time the flash was almost directly ahead of her, perhaps ten meters away. The air shivered and sung around her head. Movement, now to her left, and shouting from behind, a man's voice screaming in Farsi from the opposite bank. All in an instant Chace realized Falcon was dead, that she had been boxed, that if she went for the Zodiac their crossfire would chew her apart. As ambushes went, it had been perfect, leaving her with only two choices: she could surrender or she could die.

Even as she understood all of this, she realized she was moving, heard herself screaming filth and obscenities, and there was a man directly in front of her, a strobe-light impression of a narrow, clean-shaven face and eyes open too wide, whites bright in the darkness. She grabbed the barrel of his gun with her left hand, twisting and pulling, as she ran into him, through him, punching straight into his trachea with her right, feeling her fingertips crush and shatter cartilage. He went down choking on his own blood, backwards, and Chace did, forward, tumbling over him, saw the grass and soil bursting around her as she regained her feet. She had his submachine gun in her hand, pointed it left, heavy on the trigger and firing blind, running for her life. Shots followed her.

The car was where she had left it, her lungs aching, burning, by the time she reached the door. More voices were shouting in Farsi. She yanked the door open, and bullets crashed into the metal to her right, where she had stood half an instant before, as she dove into the car. She dropped the submachine gun, twisted the key so hard in the ignition it broke in her hand, but the engine gave life, and she stomped the accelerator, ducking her head as the windows on her side exploded in sequence, showering her with glass. The car shot forward, bumped, and Chace brought her head up, heaving the wheel to point herself back towards the road. More bullets crashed into the car, the rear window disintegrating, the front windscreen suddenly a spider's web.

Then she heard only the sound of the car, the cold winter air rushing in from every direction, the sound of herself sobbing for breath. She turned right, then left, then right again, driving too quickly, all the turns at random, until she saw the sign for Chalus to the west, and the symbol of an airplane on a post, an arrow directing her towards the airport, and she followed it. She tried to get her breathing back under control, and in the glare of the airport lights, she saw blood all over the steering wheel, her hands, the seat, the dashboard.

There was a car park on the left, ahead, and she turned into it, came to a jerking halt. She pushed open the door, and a shower of broken glass fell from the still-running car onto the pavement. She followed it out, taking the gun with her, hearing more glass fall from her clothes, where it had caught in the folds of the manteau. That explained the blood, she thought, all the glass, she'd been cut, it was a miracle she hadn't been cut to ribbons, in fact. She was still out of breath, still light-headed from adrenaline. There was another

Peugeot nearby, a knockoff made by Khodro, a Suzuki, a Benz, another Samand. She began trying doors, finding them locked, until finally she used the butt of the submachine gun to shatter the driver's window on a dark green Nasim, and then again, once inside, to break the housing over the ignition on the wheel.

Her fingers fumbled with the wires, and by the time she managed to get the engine started she was gasping for air, and she knew that the blood still spilling out of her wasn't from the glass. The pain came up suddenly, as she put the Nasim into gear, a kick in the back so furious and cruel it made her sob aloud, and her vision blurred with tears from the intensity of it. She managed to get the car out of the lot, back onto the road to Chalus, and every breath was a struggle between pain and pressure. Her vision fogged gray, cleared, then clouded again. She gulped uselessly for air, each attempt met with an ever-worsening agony. She was reduced to breathing through her nose, short, ineffective sips of oxygen that were only prolonging the inevitable.

Everything had gone wrong. The boat was gone. Falcon was dead. She would never make the RZ on the Caspian. The safehouse was compromised, MacIntyre and Lewis both either arrested, dead, or escaped and heading for Tehran. She was alone in a police state, her cover blown, and certainly would be the target of a massive manhunt, if she wasn't already.

But the worst of it was, she knew now that she'd been shot. She was suffocating, and from everything her body was telling her, it was getting worse. At the most, she had ten minutes of consciousness left to her. Chalus was six minutes away to the west.

If Chace could find a doctor's office, even a veterinarian's, she might survive.

If she couldn't, she was going to die of asphyxiation.

CHAPTER FIFTEEN

IRAN—NOSHAHR, 2 SHIR AQAI (SIS SAFEHOUSE)
11 DECEMBER 0317 HOURS (GMT +3.30)

Sterilization of the safehouse was completed within eight minutes of Chace's departure, a relatively minor affair concluded in short order. Caleb took the card with Falcon's fingerprints into the bathroom, setting fire to it over the toilet and letting the paper burn until the flames threatened his fingers, before dropping it into the bowl. The charred paper sizzled out, and he flushed what remained of it away before making a second sweep of the green-and-white-tiled room, checking the shower stall, the reservoir tank on the toilet itself, the sink, all the cabinets. He found nothing.

He took the bedroom that Chace had used next while MacIntyre went through the other, where Falcon had slept, albeit briefly. Minder One had lain above the covers rather than beneath them, and aside from the slight crush of sheets, the memory of her body, there was no sign other than the impression her head had made in the pillow and a single blond hair. Caleb puzzled over the hair for a second, taking it with two fingers and for a moment wondering what he was meant to do with the incriminating item before accepting that he was, perhaps, being overly paranoid. He opened his fingers, watched the hair fall and float back to the bed.

He was back in the main room, packing up the laptop, when MacIntyre emerged from the other bedroom, saying, "Clear."

"Then I think we're good," Caleb said.

"We'll be good when we're back in Tehran, sir," MacIntyre said, and then, as if fearing there'd been too much reproach in his voice, added, "I was thinking of putting on the kettle."

Caleb snapped the clasp on the laptop bag closed, set it beside the chair, was about to agree that, yes, a cup of tea would be nice about now, when he heard the echo from outside. He looked to MacIntyre, already halfway to the kitchen, saw that the other man had stopped, hearing it as well.

"Helo," MacIntyre said, his voice dropping. "Two of them, sounds like."

"What do you think?"

MacIntyre shook his head, still listening, and Caleb listened, too, then tugged at his left cuff, exposing his watch. Thirty-three minutes past three in the morning, and two helicopters flying overhead, already the Doppler echo fading, maybe heading north, to the water, though with the foothills bouncing the echo he couldn't be sure.

"They'd be on the water by now," Caleb said.

MacIntyre waited until the sound faded, then looked at him, not needing to say what both were thinking. They'd be on the water now if everything had gone right.

And two helos flying overhead at half-past three in the morning meant that things had certainly not gone right.

"I should inform London," Caleb said. "Barnett, at the very least."

"And say what? That we just had an overflight by two helicopters? That maybe it's gone tits up?"

"We should do something."

"There's nothing we can do, Mr. Lewis," MacIntyre said. "You want to go out there, do a recce? If they've brought in helicopters, they've damn well turned out the police and the local militia, as well. We stomp around in that, we're going to get done for ourselves. Nothing we can do."

"We can't just sit here. If she's in trouble, if she's running—"

"We let her run. Nothing we can do."

They stared at each other for several seconds. There was no flaw in MacIntyre's logic, Caleb knew that, but the frustration rose in an overwhelming crest all the same. The only benefit to it that Caleb could find was that it was such a strong sensation, it consumed the lead pill of fear in his stomach.

Then they heard the sound of cars racing down the road, coming their way.

"Fucking hell," MacIntyre muttered. "Motherfucking hell."

The cars stopped, engines dying, and from outside Caleb heard multiple doors slamming, but no voices, no orders. No question at all that they were about to have company, and very little question as to the nature of that company, as well. Militia or police about to knock on the door, and he wondered how they had found the safehouse so quickly, and his mind flashed on the idea that Chace had somehow been taken alive, that she had given them up, but as soon as he thought that he disregarded it; the timing was wrong, it didn't make sense, not unless Minder One was precisely the devout coward that Caleb feared he himself was, and maybe he was, but she certainly wasn't.

But they were here, they were knocking on the door of the safehouse, almost pounding, and how no longer mattered, only why. MacIntyre was beginning to move, to answer, and Caleb stepped forward quickly, ideas, realizations, plans all swimming, half-created, in his mind.

"Me," he told MacIntyre. "Let me talk. Follow my lead."

MacIntyre hesitated, and another battery of fist meeting door filled the brief pause. Caleb reached out, unlocked the door.

Two men stood there, with another one visible just at the edge of the light's reach, and Caleb counted three cars, and he understood that there had to be others, most likely circling around to the back of the house, to cover any possible exits. Three men he could see, and the one waiting by the car had a submachine gun in his hands, now aimed at the ground, but that could quite obviously change, and change quickly.

They don't have her, he realized. *They think she's here.*

The shorter of the two men was also the elder, perhaps in his late forties, neatly trimmed beard, balding, wearing glasses, and Caleb knew he was looking at Youness Shirazi. His companion, at his shoulder, was at least ten years younger, taller and broader, but with the same clean lines of facial hair, and if the one was Shirazi then this had to be Zahabzeh, his deputy, though Caleb couldn't be certain; of the two, Barnett had only ever shown him photographs of Shirazi.

"You were awake," Shirazi said in Farsi. He had been looking past Caleb from the moment the door opened, only now blinking slowly up at him. "There's been an incident, we have reason to believe an enemy of the State may be taking refuge inside this house. We require entry to make a search."

The man standing at Shirazi's shoulder, presumably Zahabzeh, took a step forward. There were grass stains on his trousers, damp spots on the knees, and a smear of dirt at his elbow, and now, in the illumination that spilled from the front door, Caleb could see a sheen of perspiration on the faces of each man, despite the cold.

"I'm sorry," Caleb said, and he surprised himself by the firmness in his voice. "I'm afraid I can't permit that."

Zahabzeh moved closer, the physical threat implicit. "We are State Security, we have reason to believe—"

"This building is attached to the British Mission to Iran. As such, it enjoys the same diplomatic protections as any consular or embassy structure." Caleb looked from Zahabzeh to Shirazi. "My apologies, gentlemen, but I cannot grant you access."

Behind him, Caleb felt more than heard MacIntyre shift, coming in closer behind him.

Shirazi blinked again, then offered a thin smile. His hands, at his sides, clenched into fists before relaxing again. "Mr. Lewis, isn't it?"

"Yes, sir."

"If the British Government is harboring an enemy of the State, you will be initiating a gross diplomatic incident, Mr. Lewis. Your refusal to grant us entry has the appearance of guilt. Is this something you wish? Or do you not think it would be wiser to permit us to come inside and perform our search?"

"I've no desire to antagonize your government, sir. But I simply don't have the authority to waive diplomatic protocol."

"Then may I suggest," Shirazi said drily, "that you contact someone who does?"

Zahabzeh, who had been glaring at Caleb, now looked sharply at Shirazi, then touched the man's shoulder and bent to whisper in his ear. Whatever it was he said, he said it too softly to be overheard, and Shirazi's expression didn't alter, remaining as placid and reasonable as from the start. The smaller man turned to his deputy, returning an answer just as softly, or almost, because this time Caleb caught two words distinctly. "Wounded" and "bleeding."

Shirazi turned his attention back to Caleb. "We will wait."

"Just a moment," Caleb said, and he shut the door, felt it latch beneath his hand, felt his hand begin trembling the instant after. His heart was racing, and he needed a moment to collect himself, a moment that MacIntyre didn't give him.

"What do they want?" MacIntyre whispered. "They want to search the house? That it?"

Caleb stepped away from the door, reaching for the phone in his coat. "You don't speak Farsi?"

"My Farsi's shit, Mr. Lewis. You're refusing the search?"

"Technically the house is an extension of the mission." Caleb looked at the phone in his hand, the glow of the screen, at a momentary loss as to who he should call. "They've got no evidence anyone is here aside from us, no reason to force a search, which means it's at our discretion."

"Then they don't have them."

Caleb looked up, to MacIntyre. "Doesn't seem like. Though Shirazi said someone was wounded."

MacIntyre turned his attention back to the front door, reacting. "That's Shirazi?"

"Yes." Caleb stared at his phone again, then stabbed in a number with his thumb. "I'm calling Barnett."

"Caleb?"

"Sir, we're still in Noshahr. Package went out under an hour ago, but something's fouled up in transit, and we've got company wants to come inside and take a look around. I've told them we're part of the mission, and that's holding them off for the moment, but they're still asking to come inside."

There was a moment's pause, and Caleb heard the click of a lighter as Barnett fired up one of his Silk Cut, then coughed. He'd probably been sitting up all night, chain-smoking, waiting for the phone to ring.

"Is it clean?"

"We'd just finished when they arrived, yes, sir."

Barnett swore. *"You're sure?"*

"Yes, sir."

Barnett swore again, more vehemently, and Caleb empathized. Waiving diplomatic immunity would set a bad precedent, one that Barnett certainly didn't want to take the responsibility for doing. At the same time, antagonizing the Iranians was never a good idea, and now all the worse of one, especially if Chace was still running, with or without Falcon. Ideally, Caleb knew, Barnett would want to check with London, get some direction from Crocker or, better, the FCO itself.

"All right," Barnett said bitterly. *"Grant them access. The FCO and the Ambassador will both have fits when they find out, but I can't see another way. I'll call London, give them the bullet. Call me back as soon as you're clear."*

"Yes, sir." Caleb closed the phone, tucking it away again as he told MacIntyre, "Let them in."

The front door opened once more, MacIntyre stepping out of the way, and Caleb turned to face Shirazi and Zahabzeh, only to discover that they were no longer waiting, but instead were heading back to the parked vehicles. MacIntyre shot him a puzzled look, and Caleb shook his head, stepping out into the now-frigid night air.

"Sir?" Caleb called out. "I've been told to grant you access to the house."

Two other men were emerging from the darkness at the side of the house, moving to one of the cars. The remaining men were climbing into their vehicles, including Shirazi, who now paused at the passenger door of his car as Zahabzeh slid behind the wheel.

"Perhaps later," Shirazi said.

Caleb felt his throat tighten. "You found what you're looking for?"

The question was clumsy, inelegant, unsubtle, and Caleb hated himself for asking it. The engines were starting up again, including Shirazi's car, but Shirazi himself hadn't moved. Light from the house reflected on his glasses, hiding his eyes, and Caleb was certain they were fixed on his own, that the Head of Counterintelligence for VEVAK was staring at him now, taking his measure, and finding him lacking.

"Some advice for you, Mr. Lewis," Youness Shirazi told him. "I would stay away from Chalus tonight. I would stay inside. Yes, that is what I would do, if I were you."

Shirazi disappeared into the car, the door slamming closed, and then all three vehicles were moving, one after the other in a tight turn, accelerating away from Caleb, down the road. Taillights faded, vanished, and there was a fraction of silence before that, too, was broken by the sound of rotors, of helicopters, flying west, towards Chalus.

Caleb thought of the single blond hair on the pillow in the bedroom.

"Run," he whispered.

CHAPTER SIXTEEN

IRAN, CHALUS, SHAHRIVAR STREET
11 DECEMBER 0320 HOURS (GMT +3.30)

There was no doctor's office, and there was no veterinarian's, and damned if she was going to roll up into a hospital with her last breath and surrender her liberty for her life. Her vision was swimming, graying at the edges, threatening to wash white, then clearing briefly as she sucked weakly, quickly, trying to bring air into her body from her nose and mouth. Lights along the street flashed past her at inconstant intervals, patches of darkness, headlights, then street lamps, white and bright, faint and ghostly, cycling, and Chace didn't know what she was looking for, the same way she was no longer aware that she was driving the Nasim, everything now reduced to instinct and a desperate, hungry need to survive.

There was only that, and the absurd, pathetic sound of her wheezing, as each breath became more painful even as it became more and more pointless.

She caught the sign out of the corner of her eye, to her left, just after she'd crossed the bridge into central Chalus, a flickering green glow that registered deep, and she spun the wheel hard about, and the pain it caused in her chest made her expel precious air in a weak scream, enough to shock herself back to her senses, if only for the moment. The Nasim squealed, tires breaking from pavement, and Chace ground gears, found the green light again, the glowing sign, and there were cars parked on the street here, in front of the pharmacy, but there was a gap, and she pointed the nose of the car towards it and floored the accelerator. The engine growled feebly, popped over the curb onto the pavement, and then shattered its way through the storefront. Shelves, boxes, bottles flew and crashed, and Chace was fumbling open the door before the car had stalled, toppling out of the vehicle, dragging the submachine gun behind her with a free hand, a sick toddler pulling along its favorite toy.

Her voice was gone now, she could hear herself squeaking like a rusted chain between gasps. The headlights on the Nasim were still on, enough light to see what lay ahead, and Chace heaved herself upright using the front of the car, swaying amidst the debris, looking about desperately, and there, top shelf, still standing, she saw the boxes, printed in Farsi, the line drawings of syringes in various shapes and sizes. She lurched forward, stumbled again, crashing into the display and bringing the whole thing down around her, boxes of gauze and cold remedies and herbal extracts and sanitary napkins. She abandoned the gun, both hands searching, hands and knees, saw blood dropping from her mouth in the glare of the headlights, spattering on white packaging, and she found the syringes again, the wrong size, and she shoved the box aside, blinking, shaking her head, knowing that she was wasting oxygen, that she didn't have any to spare. She saw the label, printed in Farsi, the numbers Roman, grabbed at the box, the right gauge, the right size to save her life.

Her fingers weren't working properly anymore. She dragged at the flap twice, before using her teeth on the package, ripping the box apart and scattering its contents. Plastic-wrapped syringes flew away from her, out of the light, out of sight, and she whimpered, reaching out, found one again, and, this time forcing herself to slow down, brought it to her teeth once more. She peeled the plastic wrapping back, took the fat tube in her right hand, and, again with her teeth, ripped at the cap covering the large-gauge needle. The cap dropped out of her mouth, and she turned the syringe, bit at the base of the plunger, wrenching it likewise free and letting it fall.

She worked herself upright, onto her knees, steadying herself with her left hand, then tore at the top of the manteau. Buttons popped free, spun away, clattered on linoleum out of sight. She ran her fingers down from her neck, over her left breast, pressing down, counting ribs, searching for the space between the second and third intercostals. Marking with her left hand, Chace brought the needle to her body with her right, and through the pain, the dizziness, felt the bite of the point against her skin. Her left hand moved, joined the right, and if she'd had the air to spare she'd have taken a breath then, steeled herself for what would come next, but she didn't, and so instead drove the needle into her chest as hard as she possibly could. The last of her breath exploded out of her, a pitiful sound of pain and misery, the lance of steel sinking into her body, slowing imperceptibly before finally popping through membrane into her chest.

Air hissed past her hands, spilling from the syringe, and Chace gasped, and then, discovering she could breathe once more, gasped again, falling back, needle still held in her body with both hands. Another breath, and another, and the pain was exquisite, but her vision was clearing, the roar fading in her ears, and she knew she had to move again, quickly, but for the moment all she wanted was to just lie there. Just to lie there, amidst the debris of the ruined pharmacy, on boxes of knockoff over-the-counter medications, of sticky plasters and cough syrups and disposable diapers and deodorants.

Lucidity returned, self-diagnosis, understanding of what she'd known but hadn't realized. She'd been clipped when Falcon had gone down, maybe on the way to the car, maybe at the car itself, but it couldn't have been from the submachine guns, because if it had been, she was certain she'd be dead. A handgun, then, a small-caliber round, but whatever it was, it had punctured the chest cavity in such a way that air had invaded with it, had torn her left lung from the pleural wall, collapsing it, but the wound must've sealed itself, sparing her the misery of a sucking chest wound in exchange for a . . . pneumothorax, that was the term. The air pressure in her chest cavity had collapsed her lung to the size of a golf ball, and that same trapped air had begun pressing on the right, making it harder and harder to inflate. The needle had allowed the trapped air to escape, the pressure to equalize, and the lung had reinflated. She could breathe once more.

Until it happened again.

She had to move.

With a tug, Chace pulled the syringe from her chest and tossed it aside, and the pain was no less awful, but now she had the air to fight it. She gave it a second, pressing a finger to the puncture site, assuring herself that the skin had closed, sealing her chest once more. She stumbled back to her feet, found the submachine gun again, then scanned the shelves and the floor, quickly pulling packages down, checking them in the light from the Nasim, discarding what she didn't need. Three of the prewrapped, large-gauge syringes were visible on the ground, and she took them, stuffing them into the pockets of the torn manteau, along with two crumpled boxes of gauze and a roll of tape, as well as a package of something she thought might be amoxicillin, and another that she hoped was a pain reliever of some sort.

Chace straightened, the act itself making her back ache, then turned her attention to the Nasim. There was no way in the world she would manage to get it running and out of the pharmacy. She picked her way out of the wreckage, stepping carefully over broken glass that shattered further beneath her boots, and the flashing lights cut into her periphery as she emerged onto the street, the police car slewing as it took the corner, its headlights falling full upon her as it skidded to a stop.

There were two policemen, their doors opening immediately, each shouting at her in Farsi as they began to emerge. Maybe they had seen the submachine gun in her hand, maybe they had been warned, knew who she was; maybe they were simply responding to the crash. It didn't matter, there was no choice for Chace to make.

She brought her weapon up to her shoulder, settling it into place with the same instinct and practice that had driven her flight thus far. She felt her cheek against the stock, lined up her shot, squeezed the trigger once. She shifted, repeated, squeezing the trigger again, and the submachine gun went dry during the second burst, but not before its work was done.

Chace ran awkwardly towards the police car, dropping the empty gun, a fresh bloom of pain wrapping around her torso as she moved. The driver was dead already, his partner dying, and she searched them quickly, taking their wallets, tossing them into the still-idling police car. Each carried a pistol, a Sig-Sauer knockoff, and spare magazines, and she took those, as well. The partner coughed blood up at her, eyes unfocused and vision fading, and for a moment, Chace thought about sparing him, thought that he was her only a few hundred seconds earlier, that his life could be saved.

But she was hunted and he was hunter and she had already left too much behind.

"Sorry, mate," she murmured.

She shot him with his own pistol, once, between the eyes.

Three and a half miles along the road, heading northwest, before curving to follow the shore of the Caspian westward, Chace pulled in to the lot of a large manufacturing facility. Sodium lights and steam wafted distantly in the air, mixing with light fog, but the lot itself was dark enough, and she killed the engine and exited the vehicle. Outside, she could hear the machinery churning, and beyond and above, the sound of a helicopter as it circled back towards the center of Chalus. There was a vague smell of fish in the air.

There were several cars to choose from, more of the same makes and models she had seen at the airport what seemed like a lifetime ago, and this time she went with another Samand, simply because its door was unlocked. She threw the pistols, wallets, and spare magazines onto the passenger seat. Back at the police car, she popped the trunk, where she found a first-aid kit and a large wool blanket. She took both, moved them to the Samand, then stopped and made another survey of the immediate area. There was no one to be seen, no voices to be heard, only the constant grind from the plant. Even the helicopter had faded.

Chace checked her pockets, found the folding knife and snapped it open. The car immediately beside the Samand was another Peugeot. She dropped to her knees behind it, experienced another sharp surge of pain from her back as she did so, a warning that seemed to both climb and fall at once. Her breathing was, at least for the moment, steady and sure, but each inhale, each exhale, came with a constant discomfort.

As quickly as she dared, she unscrewed the bolts holding the license plate to the Peugeot. Then she moved to the next car in the line, a Sarir, and removed its rear plate. She did the same to a Suzuki Vitara, and to a Miniator, and a Mercedes-Benz, and finally to a Citroën Xantia, all parked in a row. She closed the knife, took her collection of plates back to the Samand, and set them on the floor of the passenger's seat before cracking into the ignition and hot-wiring the car.

The original exfil plan had been to the west, via Tabriz, and it made good sense; good enough sense, in fact, that Chace was certain anyone searching for her would see it, as well. From Tabriz, one could run to Iraq, to Turkey, to Azerbaijan, to Armenia, and every single one of those borders would be monitored, watched, guarded. With the ruined pharmacy, the dead policemen, the abandoned cars, and now with the license plates, her trail would only confirm the suspicion: she was running to the west.

So not west. But a run east was out of the question, too far and too long and ultimately ending in western Afghanistan, where the Republican Guards had made strong inroads with the local populace. Given the state she was in, the pain still cruelly riding her, taking to the Caspian wasn't any more viable; the RHIB was gone, and even if she could secure another vessel, even if she could somehow avoid the airplanes and boats that would surely be patrolling the coast, there was still the threat of the weather. "Drowning" was just another word for asphyxiation.

Which left south, back to Tehran.

Chace put the Samand into gear, and feeling her chest twinge, pulled out of the lot, turning east, then south.

Back into the heart of enemy territory.

CHAPTER SEVENTEEN

LONDON—VAUXHALL CROSS, OPS ROOM

11 DECEMBER 2359 HOURS (GMT)

The silence had come upon Alexis Ferguson calling to Crocker, "Tehran Station, update on Coldwitch," all activity ceasing instantly, all movement, all motion, coming to a stop. Crocker felt the weight of every gaze in the room as he crossed the floor, took the offered headset, and pressed it to his ear.

"D-Ops," Crocker said, and then he listened, aware that the room was listening with him, to him, as Lee Barnett in Tehran told him that everything he had feared had been true, that he had been right all along. He took it all in, staring at a point beneath the toes of his shoes, and when Barnett concluded, he asked the one question that hadn't been answered already. "Minder One?"

"No idea, sir," Barnett said. *"Lewis thinks she's still at large, but believes she may be injured. He confirms it was Youness Shirazi who came to the safehouse, which has to mean that VEVAK is all over this, they'll be turning out the Sepah, the Basij, everyone and everything."*

"But it means they haven't caught her yet."

"I'd think it's only a matter of time."

Crocker considered, looking up at the map, the clock above it reading the current time in Iran. To his left, he heard Nicky Poole speak, asking for maps of northern Iran, times of the next available flights, and that broke the silence, the death-watch, and the room came alive again even as Crocker continued staring at the map on the wall.

"Sir?"

"Find out what the hell happened, Lee," Crocker said. "And see if we can't get confirmation on Minder One, if she is wounded, if they've taken her."

"Working on it, sir."

"Notify immediately with any new information, no matter how small. I'm handing you back to MCO. Keep the line open."

"Understood."

Crocker handed the headset back to Lex. "Open line."

"No matter how small, yes, sir."

Crocker strode across the room, heading for Duty Ops. "Ron, call C at her home and inform her that Coldwitch has gone bust. Tell her that we have reason to believe Minder One is running in the open, still at liberty, but no word on disposition of Falcon. Soon as she arrives in the building, I want to know. And someone get me a line to Grosvenor Square."

"Yes, sir. Here, sir."

"Julian?"

"What's our status?"

"We've been fucked," Crocker said. "Best guess right now is that Hossein was bait all along. No confirmations, but we've reason to believe Chace is still at liberty, though she may be wounded."

"Falcon?"

"Not a word, no idea. Is USGS still en route to the RZ?"

"Last I heard. You want me to tell them to abort?"

"Not if there's a chance in hell of Chace making it in time."

"Is there?"

"Again, no idea. Can you beat the bushes on the Iraqi side of the border, see if your lot has intercepted any traffic, anything that can put light on this? We're in the dark."

"I'll get on it now. You want me to come over?"

The question threw him, Crocker uncertain if Seale was simply offering professional courtesy or something more, something that might approach sympathy. The question was enough to make him think of Chace, of Tamsin, and of the visit he would have to make if Coldwitch had really become the nightmare it appeared to be. That Coldwitch had failed was already understood, but until Seale had offered company, Crocker hadn't allowed himself to believe Minder One was lost.

"Your choice," Crocker said.

"Fifteen minutes," Seale told him, hanging up.

"Just how bad is it?" C demanded.

The question was one that Crocker had spent much, if not all, of the last eight minutes pondering, while waiting for C's arrival, and although he'd begun to describe the edges of understanding, he'd yet to reach its center.

"You want the worst-case scenario?" he asked.

"No, Paul, what I want are facts." She shrugged the coat off her shoulders, let it fall onto her chair as she turned to face him from behind her desk. The haste and the hour, Crocker thought, both were telling on Alison Gordon-Palmer's face. "Speculation later, for now, what do we know?"

"Very little. According to the Station Number Two—lad named Caleb Lewis—he and one of our Security personnel, Adrian MacIntyre, dispatched Chace with Falcon to the exfil point directly as ordered."

"They were supposed to go out tomorrow night, weren't they?" She took her chair, indicated for Crocker to take one for himself.

"Initially, but weather in zone made that unviable."

"Continue."

Crocker sat, leaning forward, elbows on his knees. "Lewis reports that shortly after he and MacIntyre completed their sterilization of the safehouse, they heard helicopters making overflight, and within a minute of that a team of VEVAK security personnel presented themselves at the location and demanded entry. They claimed they were seeking a foreign agent and had reason to believe that agent was in the house."

C's eyes narrowed. "They knew the location of the safehouse."

"Gets better—or worse, depending on your point of view. Lewis reports that the team was led by Youness Shirazi."

"I don't know the name."

"Not surprising; we don't have much on him."

"Significance?"

"Shirazi is the director of VEVAK's counterintelligence group. Lewis reports that Shirazi addressed him by name, made the request to enter and search. Lewis refused, citing diplomatic grounds."

"Did he just?" C managed a bare smile. "A stance on principle?"

"Perhaps. It was only Lewis and MacIntyre in the house. Shirazi pressed the issue, Lewis said he could not make the decision to allow them entry, Shirazi in turn told him to speak to someone who could. Lewis rang up the Station Number One—"

" 'Budgie' Barnett, yes."

"Barnett told him to grant entry. Lewis made to allow Shirazi and his men to search the premises, but instead found them in the process of departing. The conclusion that Lewis reached, and with which I agree, is that between him contacting Barnett and relaying permission to enter, Shirazi got a lead on Chace in another location, and was able to discount the safehouse. It was around this time that Lewis overheard enough conversation between Shirazi and his deputy to ascertain that Chace may have been wounded."

"And no mention of Falcon at all?"

"None whatsoever."

"Yet every indication that a manhunt is under way for Chace as we speak."

"Yes, ma'am."

C gazed at him thoughtfully, then closed her eyes, pinched the bridge of her nose between forefinger and thumb. Her brow creased, and Crocker had to wonder if her head was hurting as much as his now was. For fully half a minute she remained silent before speaking again.

"So you were correct, Paul. We were set up."

"I'm not certain," Crocker said.

Her eyes opened in surprise. "Chace was ambushed at the exfil point with Falcon. She managed to escape, Falcon told . . . Shirazi, is it? . . . told Shirazi the location of the safehouse."

"But why wait?" Crocker asked. "If it was a setup, they were tracking Falcon. Why wait? Why not take him at the safehouse?"

"Mr. Lewis' excuse. Diplomatic privilege at the site."

Crocker grimaced, shook his head slightly. "But they could have taken everybody at the house, there were only four of them there. Arrest our three and what would we say? You can't do that, that's our safehouse? Lewis could only claim embassy involvement after the fact."

"Paul," C said slowly. "What are you getting at?"

"I don't know." Crocker shook his head again. "It's not . . . something's not right. Shirazi was *on the ground* in Noshahr. The Head of Counterintelligence doesn't go into the field, he has a deputy for that, he has men for that. Why was he there?"

"I think it's clear," C said. "Your initial assessment of the situation was the correct one. Falcon was never more than bait, the object of the exercise was to lure and then capture an SIS officer. The object of the exercise was to capture Chace."

"But there were other opportunities. When she made the pickup in Karaj, for instance. The safehouse. Anywhere along the Karaj-Chalus highway. If they were watching Falcon, they could've picked their moment. Why did they wait?"

"You're overcomplicating it, Paul." C rose, picking up her coat. "And now I have to go and brief the Prime Minister. They'll need to begin formulating a response."

Crocker stood, waited until C had donned her coat. "Which will be?"

"Denial," C said bluntly. "We'll deny all of it."

"Even Chace?"

C stopped, looked at him. "Will she let them take her alive, do you think?"

"If she's been wounded, she may not have a choice."

"Hmm." C turned away, opening the door. "Unfortunate. It would make things much easier for us if she died."

CHAPTER EIGHTEEN

IRAN—CHALUS, NAMAK-CHALUS MANUFACTURING
11 DECEMBER 0423 HOURS (GMT +3.30)

"More blood." Zahabzeh shone the beam from his flashlight slowly over the driver's seat of the abandoned police car, lingering at a point high on the upholstery, roughly shoulder level to where the driver would have been seated. "Hers?"

"Probably." Shirazi held up a palm, shielding his eyes, and the beam dropped. Zahabzeh slid back, out of the car, clicking the light and straightening up, his expression as pinched now as it had been half an hour earlier, outside of the pharmacy on Hasankeif.

"What now?" Zahabzeh asked.

Shirazi turned away, not bothering to answer, thrusting his cold hands deep into his pockets. It was always coldest before dawn, and tonight, for so many reasons, had been very, very cold. Around him, local militia scurried through the lot, checking cars, overseen by a middle-aged commander who was far too excited to have his men mobilized by VEVAK. Another police car sped past on the road, Route 22, heading north, and Shirazi watched its progress. The road ran northwest out of Chalus before curving to run along the Caspian shore, west for almost two hundred kilometers before it would begin curving southward, towards Rasht.

It wasn't the best place to have dumped the vehicle, Shirazi decided. Only two directions in which Chace could have gone, east or west, and heading east, back the way she came, would have been an act of madness. West, Rasht, her choices would be limited again, north to continue following the Caspian, to Arbadil, or south and over the Alborz once more, down into the plains. Both routes would take her towards Tabriz, and from there she could have her choice of any of three borders. Well-guarded, well-monitored borders, but there were always gaps.

She was in a car, Shirazi was certain of it, her third in the last ninety minutes as far as he knew, this one another Samand. Had that been intentional, too? Chace could hardly have done better in pursuit of anonymity; the Samand was as ubiquitous in Iran as a mosque. And the license plates, that she'd had the presence of mind to take several of them, made him admire the woman all the more. One car, one plate, that would be easy enough for a roadblock or a checkpoint or a patrol to remember. But ask the militia to remember five or seven different ones? Better to not even ask them at all.

Zahabzeh had moved off, speaking into his radio, and Shirazi heard Faradin's reply, that they were finished at the pharmacy, coming to join them now.

"No," Shirazi interrupted. "We will meet them at the airport."

The order was relayed without comment, and Shirazi motioned for the militia commander, speaking on a radio of his own now, to join him. "We have the roadblocks?"

"Yes, sir, at Mo'allem Square and again at the foot of the highway, before it climbs into the mountains. Another east of Noshahr, and two more along the Beltway."

"And the boats are still out, you're still patrolling the water?"

"They can stay out for another three or four hours, if you need. But the helicopters are low on fuel, they need to land."

"Soon as they can, put them up again. I want them to the west." Shirazi pointed, sweeping his hand to follow the curve of the roadway, up towards the water. "Careful attention along the sides of the road. She'll need to pull off someplace, somewhere. She needs to rest." Shirazi put a hand on the man's shoulder. "Your involvement in these efforts will be noted. As will your discretion."

"You may rely on me."

Shirazi nodded, turning away and moving back to his car, where Zahabzeh was waiting for him. They started out of the lot, turning back towards the heart of Chalus, and Shirazi sank back against his seat, removed his glasses, and closed his eyes. A wash of fatigue ran down his back, made him shudder involuntarily, though he doubted he could sleep, even if he wished to.

The pharmacy had been informative, he reflected. The desperation apparent at the scene, and the murder of the two policemen. Clearly, Chace had been wounded, badly enough that she had been willing to crash her Nasim through the front of the store. Yet her behavior at the plant had been anything but, which could only mean that, whatever the injury, she was now managing it. He wondered at the nature of the wound, if it would slow her down appreciably.

Too many variables.

Shirazi had worked so hard to limit variables, and all it had taken was one fool who had thought Hossein's life was in danger to destroy months, even years, of planning. That Chace hadn't been murdered as well was small consolation to him. She had been so close, she had almost been in his hand, and at the last moment, he had lost her. The taste was still bitter in his mouth, as bitter as it had been when they had reached the safehouse in Noshahr. Even before Caleb Lewis had answered the door, Shirazi had known she wasn't there.

A blond, Western woman, injured and fleeing in Iran. How hard could it be to find her?

And they *had* to find her, there was no question of that. Even if everything that had come before this night had been in pursuit of Shirazi's agenda alone, Hossein's death implicated them all.

The situation had, to say the least, changed.

Hossein Khamenei had lain dead on the ground, his upper torso on its side, his hips turned so that his lower body lay skyward, his mouth open, the wound that had killed him shining black in the side of his neck. Steam had still been rising from the blood leaking out of his body when Shirazi had reached him. More shots had rung out amongst the trees, and he'd heard the car, seen Zahabzeh with one of his men attempting to chase the vehicle down even as it fled. Zahabzeh's other man lay on the ground, only eight, perhaps ten meters from Hossein, his face swollen, eyes wide in death.

"Enough!" Shirazi shouted. "Enough! Regroup on me!"

"The spy—" Zahabzeh yelled back.

"On me!"

Javed and Parviz had caught up to Shirazi by then, breathless from their sprint, clouds of mist every time they exhaled, and Zahabzeh had returned with the other, Kamal, each still holding his weapon. Zahabzeh was reloading the small pistol in his hand, the little Russian PSM that he always had with him.

"I hit her." Zahabzeh's face shone with excitement, zeal, even in the poor light. "I hit her, at least once. She won't get far."

"You fucking fools!" Shirazi pointed to Hossein's body, glaring furiously at Zahabzeh, then Kamal. "You goatfucking fools, what have you done?"

"She was . . . ," Kamal said. "She was going for his neck—"

Shirazi slapped him hard, across the cheek, feeling himself vibrating with fury, and the silence that followed was awful. "He's dead. He's fucking dead. The Supreme Leader's nephew is dead, do you understand me? Do you understand what I am saying to you?"

"The spy." Zahabzeh looked up from Hossein's body, and Shirazi saw that he, at least, understood how their world had changed in the last thirty seconds. "We can . . . it was the spy, we all agree it was the spy. He was murdered by the British spy before we could rescue him. A . . . it was a kidnapping attempt, that's what we'll say. She was trying to abduct him, we moved in to make a rescue, and she killed him."

"It was me," Kamal whispered. He was a young man, only in his early twenties and baby-faced, and now his expression struggled to become that of a man's. "My shot. I take . . . I will take the responsibility."

Shirazi shook his head in disgust, moved his glare from Zahabzeh to Kamal while the others remained in stunned silence. "Fine, then you will be the longest to die. But if you think that will spare the rest of us, you're fucking wrong. None of you sees it yet, do you? It's *our* bullet in his neck! And when they find that—and they *will* find that—they will want to know why we murdered the Supreme Leader's nephew. And they will want to know why we are acting against the State. And they will want to know when we joined the counterrevolutionaries. And then—*then*—they will shoot us."

Javed started to speak. "But we aren't—"

"They won't care!" Shirazi shouted.

Zahabzeh looked to the body of his other man, Mahmoud, then back to Shirazi. "If we find the woman . . . if we find this spy . . ."

"Yes," Shirazi said. "Alive."

"Alive she could talk. Dead, she won't be able to argue."

"No one will hear her. No, she must be brought in alive. Questioned. Put on trial. And then she can take the bullets meant for us. That is the only way."

The other men were motionless still, the only signs of life the regular puffs of condensation that marked their breathing. Shirazi and Zahabzeh stared at each other, and Shirazi was certain he saw accusation, even the hints of suspicion, in his deputy's eyes. He knew what the younger man was thinking; that this had always been Shirazi's folly, that he had pushed too far, and taken unnecessary risks. And now, Shirazi was sure, Zahabzeh had to wonder if this next gamble would play like the ones before, if it would fail, if it would bring all their ends.

"All of us must agree," Shirazi said. "All of us together, or all of us will die."

Another moment, and then Zahabzeh gave the slightest nod, reached into his coat for his phone. "Local police?"

"And militia. Roadblocks, helicopters, boats on the water, all of it. Give them the description of the spy, and stress that she's to be taken alive." Shirazi indicated Hossein's body. "Inform them about this, but give no details, no identification of either body. Bring the cars around. She can't have gone far, not if she's wounded. We'll try their safehouse first."

Men scattered, Zahabzeh speaking quietly, authoritatively, on the phone, and for a blessed moment, Shirazi had no eyes on him, nothing he had to say, and he had time to think. After a moment, he knelt on one knee, took the small penknife he carried from his pocket. Murmuring an apology to the dead man, he lifted Hossein's shirt, feeling his way along the cooling skin until he found the bandage at the left side of the corpse's abdomen. Shirazi ripped it free, then, with the tip of his blade, dug into the half-healed flesh until he freed the tiny transmitter he and Zahabzeh had implanted in Hossein's side. He stuffed it into a pocket, closed the knife against his thigh, rose.

Zahabzeh had finished his calls, and already the sound of sirens could be heard in the distance. "I told them to check the airport first."

"Good."

"It won't take them long to identify him," Zahabzeh said. "As soon as they do, they'll notify Tehran. Tehran will have questions."

The cars were pulling up now, the sirens crying louder, coming closer. Shirazi could see the first flashes of red and blue through the trees of the park. Tehran would indeed have questions, many questions, and unless they could find Tara Chace, and find her quickly, Shirazi wasn't at all sure his answers would suffice. From the start, he had decided that she was the one he needed, the only one for him.

Until this moment, he hadn't known how right he was.

They were at the airport, the tiny terminal between Chalus and Noshahr, where Shirazi had unceremoniously taken over the administration offices, the dawn beginning to bleed in through the windows. Six men standing around a large map that had been pulled down from the wall and spread on the table, Parviz marking checkpoints with a pen. He handed it off to Kamal, who drew in the patrol routes of the boats, the helicopters, then gave it in turn to Javed, who marked each and every roadblock that had been set up along the major roads in the last two and a half hours.

Shirazi gazed at the map for a long time after the markup was completed, not moving, lost in his thoughts. Someone offered him a cup of tea, and he took it without thinking, drank it without tasting it, lost in the lines of terrain. His eyes kept going back to the water, back to the Caspian, what had to have been the initial exfil point. There had to have been a ship waiting for them, or a helicopter, something far from the shore. That had been clever, he thought, that would have worked.

But Tabriz, he realized, that wasn't clever at all. That was expected.

She wasn't going to Tabriz, he realized, and he turned his head, put his hands on the map, covering the routes east and west from Chalus. North and south—not north, either, because certainly the exfil was blown, and there was no way she could have cleared the shore unnoticed. South, it had to be south, and it was such an absurd thing for her to have done that he was all the more certain she had done it.

"Sir?"

Shirazi looked up, saw Zahabzeh standing only two feet away, holding out his phone, his expression grave. Shirazi hadn't even heard it ring.

"Sir," Zahabzeh said. "Your presence is requested in Tehran."

CHAPTER NINETEEN

IRAN—ALBORZ MOUNTAINS, 38 KM SSW CHALUS
11 DECEMBER 0746 HOURS (GMT +3.30)

Chace sat in the driver's seat of the stolen Samand with a new syringe in her hand, the car half-hidden in a copse of spring pines, snow on the ground, and a view that would have been spectacular if she'd had the time or inclination to pay it any heed. The pain in her chest had grown appreciably more acute in the last hour, her breathing shallowing with the increasing pressure from within, now becoming, once again, dangerously short.

She hadn't meant to put it off for this long, in fact, but circumstances had prevented her from acting prior. Twice on the drive south she'd narrowly avoided roadblocks, each time tipped off to their presence by the line of cars backed up along the roadway. The first time, she'd turned before becoming stuck in the traffic jam, had followed side roads through forest and fields, circling around back to the highway. The second time, as soon as she'd seen the congestion, she'd reversed, taken the first turn she could off the road, ending up on a dirt track that wound its way steeply higher and higher into the mountains until she'd crossed into snow. Every time she'd thought it safe to pull off and stop, another car had appeared, each of them heading the opposite direction, none of them official-looking, but they had been enough to make her keep going.

Checking her mirrors and the view out the windows, Chace thought she was as safe as she was likely to get for the time being.

She stepped slowly out of the car, moving cautiously, stiffly, the syringe still in her hand. The air bit at her, cold and yet surprisingly pleasant against her skin. She was still wearing the torn manteau, had driven with the wool blanket from the police car wrapped around her shoulders and covering her head. Somewhere along the line, she didn't know where or when, she had lost her *maqna'e*. She made another survey, listening to the world as much as trying to see it, all the while fighting the creeping panic caused by her slowly increasing breathlessness.

She heard nothing, saw nothing.

Carefully, she spread the blanket out over the hood of the car, then brought out the first-aid kit, as well as all of the supplies she'd managed to grab from the pharmacy. The owner of the car had left an unopened bottle of Zam Zam Cola rolling around on the floor, and she took that now, opened it, and then opened the box of amoxicillin. She swallowed two of the antibiotic pills, and used the soda to wash them down, the cola tepid and sticky sweet in her mouth. Last, she put one of the pistols she had taken from the police on the blanket, within easy reach, should she need it.

Stepping back from the side of the car, Chace raised her right leg and threw out a kick at the driver's side mirror. It broke away easily, snapping clear of the Samand with a crack that bounced off the snow and vanished amongst the trees. The kick had hurt, cost oxygen, and she needed a moment to steady herself against the car, for the bright spots of light to fade, before she was ready to bend and pick up the mirror.

Thus far, the only examination she'd been able to give herself had been cursory, as opportunity had allowed. The arrival of daylight had made things a little easier, and she'd confirmed what she already knew as she drove; she hadn't taken a hit to the front. While the chest pain had been significant and constant, an ache that moved through her like a tide, she'd begun to discern within it a purer note, high on her back, below the shoulder, where she couldn't reach and couldn't see.

Chace set down the mirror long enough to remove the manteau. Free from her arms and off her shoulders, the long shirt began to slide down, but then snagged, and she had to bite back on a cry as fresh misery sliced along her back. Gravity continued to pull, and the manteau suddenly fell the rest of the way, and instantly Chace could feel blood trickling down her back, and just as quickly, the pressure in her chest expanded, her ability to draw breath stealing away.

Fighting panic, Chace picked up the mirror in her left hand, turning her head to catch its reflection, and she saw the blood leaking down her back, followed its trail to the wound, a small, narrow, leaking hole above the back of her bra, just inside the shoulder, narrowly missing the scapula. The fabric of the manteau had sealed it, had acted as a bandage, allowing a clot to set, and she understood now what had happened to her, what was happening, what was going to happen. Removing the manteau had reopened the wound, allowing air to again invade her chest to crush her lungs. She was still standing, albeit with difficulty, still had enough air to know she had to work quickly.

There were multiple bandages in the first-aid kit, various sizes, squares of gauze, rolls of tape, even fabric for fashioning a sling, but not what she needed, no occlusion bandage. Putting gauze over the wound—even if she could somehow reach around to it, which she couldn't—would do nothing; the dressing would be too permeable. She needed something solid, something with which to make an airtight seal.

She abandoned the kit for the moment, tried to keep herself from moving too quickly as she climbed back into the car, searching the interior. The thought struck her that the bullet was still inside her, and a new surge of panic tried to take hold, clawing, this time more desperately. If the bullet was rattling around in her chest cavity it could be cutting up organs, arteries, her heart. She could be hemorrhaging internally, not a tension pneumothorax but a hemothorax, bleeding slowly, filling her like a bottle until she drowned in her own blood.

"One thing at a time."

It took her a moment to realize the whisper was her own.

She snapped open the glove box, pulling the contents free. Crammed in the corner, crumbs of some substance lining the bottom, she found a small, clear plastic bag, and she grabbed it, extracted herself slowly from the car. She was sipping for air now, hearing herself wheezing with each tiny breath. Her throat ached.

Using the roll of tape from the pharmacy, she laid four lengths around the plastic bag, working as quickly and carefully as she dared, making certain each segment overlapped. The seal would have to be perfect, nothing could come between the plastic and the wound, and with difficulty she reached back and unfastened her bra, letting it drop. She took one of the scavenged syringes, stuck it in her pocket, and then, taking the makeshift dressing carefully in one hand, moved to the boot of the car, where she set the bandage flat, adhesive side up.

Chace hiked herself into a sitting position on the boot, her back to where she had placed the plastic, and slowly leaned herself backwards, trying to position herself and the wound atop it. The posture took even more of her air, balance awkward, the shock of the colder metal against her already cold, bare skin. She saw blue sky, points of white light swimming in her vision. Then she was lying with her back against the car, cold stealing into her skin, legs over the side. She tried a breath, and its success was limited, and she didn't know if that was because the bandage was in place now, or simply because the boot itself was sealing the wound. In either case, the wound was, for the moment, closed.

But there was still too much air in the pleural space, still too much pressure for her lungs to work properly.

Without sitting up, Chace took the syringe from her pocket, carefully stripping its wrapping away. She pulled the cap, the plunger, brought the needle to the point she had punctured herself before, and, like before, with both hands, drove it into her chest. The release of pressure was instant, this time the hiss of air lost behind her involuntary scream. She sobbed fresh oxygen into her lungs, her hands falling to her sides, pounding on the car in furious pain. It had hurt before, but this time it was worse, this time it was almost unbearable.

But she was breathing again, she realized, breathing the way she should, and with careful hands she withdrew the needle from her chest, heard it roll against the boot, fall to the snow. With effort, she sat upright, and the pain that moved with her was manageable, and still she was breathing. When she turned her head, she could see a smear of her blood on the car, but the bandage was gone, where it needed to be, fixed to her back.

Chace slid back to her feet, moved to the front of the car. Her bra lay in the snow, and she picked it up, shaking it clean, then slipped herself back into it, closing it gingerly at her back. She heard the plastic crinkle, pressed further against her skin by the shoulder strap. Its aid to the bandage was questionable, she supposed, but anything would help, anything to keep the wound sealed.

The sun found her through the trees as she cleared the hood of the car. Using her knife, she cut a hole in the center of the blanket, large enough for her head, then drew it over her, wearing it like a poncho. She examined the manteau, bloodstained and torn, and again with the knife cut as large a clean strip as she could, then used that to cover her hair. She shivered beneath the blanket, exhausted, took another look around her, seeing the trees and the mountains and the snow shining.

It was going to be a beautiful day, she realized.

The Alborz were both an aid and a hindrance. Certainly, the terrain made the chance of running into anyone, let alone a checkpoint or a roadblock, that much more unlikely, but conversely, anyone she was liable to meet would be justifiably more suspicious of a strange foreigner in their midst. She had no map, either, only the GPS, and her desire to head south, back to Tehran, notwithstanding, she had to follow the road where it led.

That wasn't the worst, however. The higher the road went, the more the air pressure outside changed, the more the pressure in her chest would be exacerbated. She had two needles left, and no desire at all to have to use either of them.

Shortly after ten in the morning, Chace judged she had put enough distance between her last stop and her present position that she pulled to the side of the road. By some miracle, she'd managed to keep hold of both the small GPS unit and her sat phone, and now, for the first time, she felt it was safe to try using both. Her breathing, while still wildly uncomfortable, was steady and effective.

Exiting the car, Chace took one of the two pistols, tucking it into her jeans at her waist. She used the GPS first, taking a reading, and saw that she was further west than she had hoped, though without a map to aid her, she was unsure of her precise position. She noted the altitude, as well, almost seventeen hundred meters, and that was cause for worry. She would need to descend, and soon, or else risk further complications to her injury.

She left the GPS on, setting it atop the roof of the car, then opened her sat phone and switched it on. To her chagrin, the battery indicator was reading less than a quarter charge. The phone beeped, the screen clearing, ready and waiting.

Chace dialed from memory, waited, and when she recognized Lex's voice on the other end, said, "Minder One, black, repeat black, am on open line."

"Minder One, confirmed," Lex said. And Chace could swear the woman, for the first time in their acquaintance, had relief in her voice. *"Status?"*

"Coldwitch is bust, opposition was waiting at exfil. Falcon is dead. I am blown and wounded, repeat, blown and wounded, confirm."

"I confirm. Are you mobile?"

"Am mobile. Location, stand by." Chace reached for the GPS with her free hand, checking the coordinates once more. "Am at thirty-six point forty-three sixty-one seventeen by fifty-one point naught-six twenty-three eighty-seven, confirm."

"I confirm. Coms check?"

"Low battery. Fifteen minutes, probably less. Note, cannot exfil by air, repeat, will require medical treatment prior to airlift."

"I confirm, negative air. Next communication, seven minutes from mark."

Chace checked her watch, saw that blood had dried on its face. She scraped at it with a nail. "Mark."

"Out."

The line went dead, and Chace switched the satellite phone off, then the GPS, climbed back into the Samand. In six minutes she'd switch the phone on again, and thirty seconds or so after that it would trill, and Alexis Ferguson or, better, Paul Crocker would be on the other end. D-Ops' voice, sharp and sure, telling her what to do, where to go, how to proceed. Telling her how he was going to bring her home.

Chace shivered again, drew the wool poncho closer around her body, heard the plastic bag on her back crunch as she moved. Sunlight lanced through the windscreen, suddenly and deliciously warm on her face, turning her drowsy. She closed her eyes, mind wandering free, instantly finding Tamsin, so far away. The fever, had it broken yet? Was she all right? Then she was seeing Tom Wallace, perfect in memory, a flight of fancy as Tara held their daughter in her arms, showing her to him. Look what we made, look at this beautiful creature we created.

Her eyes snapped open, Chace starting in the seat, quickly checking her watch. For a second, she couldn't remember the mark, then saw it had been six minutes, six minutes already, and she hurriedly climbed out of the car, turning the sat phone on, and no sooner had it beeped, confirming its signal, than it was ringing.

"Minder One," Chace said. "Go."

"Here's what you're going to do, Tara," Paul Crocker said.

CHAPTER TWENTY

IRAN—TEHRAN, MINISTRY OF INTELLIGENCE AND SECURITY (MOIS)
11 DECEMBER 0927 HOURS (GMT +3.30)

The Minister was waiting for Shirazi in his office, seated at his desk. He was a slender man, in his fifties, his left shoulder sitting at an angle higher than his right, the remnants of a wound taken during the War of Iraqi Aggression. He had come alone, but Shirazi took no comfort in that. As a member of the National Security Council, all it would take was a word, and the whole of Shirazi's department would turn against him. That was real power, and both men knew who held it.

"I am meeting you here, Youness," the Minister said, "as a courtesy to you and your service, because you have never failed us in the past. And because we wish to hear your explanation for the madness that took place early this morning in Noshahr."

"I appreciate your consideration, sir."

The Minister settled his hands on Shirazi's desk, folding one atop the other, gazing at him evenly. "I am pleased to hear that, because your position at this moment is an exceedingly delicate one. The Supreme Leader has already been informed of the death of his nephew. He is anxious for an explanation. Extremely anxious. Extremely concerned, Youness."

"I am ready to explain."

"Do so, then."

Shirazi measured his words. "I regret to say that Hossein Khamenei was murdered this morning in Noshahr by a foreign agent, possibly British, during an aborted attempt to kidnap him. When we moved to apprehend this agent, she executed the Supreme

Leader's nephew, as well as murdered one of my men, before escaping."

The Minister blinked at him. "A woman?"

"Yes, sir."

"This woman is still at large?"

"We are searching for her even now."

"To no result, it would seem." The Minister blinked again. "You say British. Why would the British attempt to abduct Hossein Khamenei?"

"The most obvious reason, sir, is that he was a target of opportunity, someone they wished to bring to the West, perhaps to be used as pressure against the Supreme Leader himself. Of all his family, Hossein was possibly the easiest for them to identify and locate."

"The British?"

"That is our suspicion."

"You are lying to me, Youness," the Minister said.

Shirazi said nothing.

The chair behind the desk creaked, the Minister turning in it, and from one of the drawers he withdrew the thick file on Hossein, bulging with photographs and documentation, that Zahabzeh and Shirazi had prepared. He set it tenderly on the desk, flipped it open casually, and perused its contents.

Without looking up, the Minister said, "You think we didn't know?"

Shirazi hesitated, then shook his head. In truth, he *had* believed Hossein's involvement with the British had been long forgotten, that, perhaps, the Supreme Leader himself had ordered it covered up. But now, watching the Minister as he lifted one photograph, then another, holding them up to better see in the light from the window, the look of mild disgust on his face, Shirazi realized he had been foolish.

"I know you brought him here, to this office, at the end of November. Had he reached out to the British already?"

"We feared what the reaction would be if we informed the Council," Shirazi answered. "That the Supreme Leader would . . . overlook his nephew's actions."

The Minister lowered the photograph he was holding, one of the photographs of Hossein as a young man, indulging himself with another young man. "He had gone to the British, then."

"Yes," Shirazi lied. "He made his approach shortly after the replacements began arriving. When we realized who he was, we were obligated to investigate."

"But not obligated to take it further."

"We couldn't ignore it, sir." Shirazi allowed a hint of enthusiasm into his voice, trying to follow the story the Minister had clearly already constructed. "And the opportunity was too great, the chance to feed the British false information, or even to uncover their network, especially now, especially with the pressure the West has put us under."

The Minister dropped the photograph, clearly offended by its contents. "I think you should tell me all of it, Youness."

Shirazi did so, mixing truth with enough fiction to maintain the portrayal of Hossein as the villain of the piece, an enemy of the State who had, upon being confronted and turned by VEVAK, reached out again to the British. Once they realized that, Shirazi said, they saw a new opportunity: certainly the British would come for him, and when they did, VEVAK would move, capturing both the traitor and the spy. But it had gone wrong at the last moment—Shirazi was careful to avoid assigning blame to any one individual—and Hossein had been shot, the spy had escaped.

"Not how it was intended to go," the Minister said coldly. "At all."

"No, sir, never."

"This kind of operation cannot be permitted without oversight, Youness. You never should have undertaken it without clearance from the Council."

"I recognize that, sir."

"It is salvageable, however." The Minister glanced to his left, to the portrait of the Ayatollah on the wall, clearly considering the situation. "In fact, it may serve us very well, indeed. But only *if* you can capture this spy. If you can do that, Youness, your failure will become a success, one that will bring you much forgiveness."

"We're doing everything we can."

"I would expect nothing less. But now I want more. You will have the State media release news of Hossein's murder, but leave the identification of the perpetrator vague at this time. Unknown foreign enemies will suffice. Once we have this spy in hand, once we can put her on television, then we will implicate the British, and they will have to respond publically."

"Will you release her to them? Make an exchange?"

The Minister's smile was anemic, and as close to amused as Shirazi had ever seen. "It will depend how badly they want her back. But any exchange will only occur after a trial, after she has been sentenced. For that reason, we *must* have her alive, Youness. We must have her alive and healthy for the cameras."

"Yes, sir."

With his knuckles, the Minister rapped the folder of photographs. "Destroy these. All evidence that Hossein was ever in collusion with the British, destroy it all. Who else knows the details, the extent of his corruption, his betrayal?"

"Only Zahabzeh," Shirazi said. "And Farzan will never betray our secrets."

"No, he would not." The Minister pushed himself back from the desk, rising. "You are not safe yet, Youness, do not mistake me. You know what you must do."

"Perfectly."

"Then do it," the Minister said. "Someone must pay for this failure. And if not this British spy, then you yourself, Youness, will do nicely."

CHAPTER TWENTY-ONE

LONDON—WHITEHALL, OFFICE OF SIR WALTER SECCOMBE, PERMANENT UNDERSECRETARY AND HEAD OF THE DIPLOMATIC SERVICE (FCO)
11 DECEMBER 0804 HOURS (GMT)

"I heard it from the Foreign Secretary, who heard it from the Prime Minister, who heard it from C." Sir Walter Seccombe motioned Crocker to the large, leather-upholstered couch in his office. "And now I want to hear it from you, Paul. How likely is it that we'll be seeing Minder One's face on Al-Jazeera?"

Crocker rubbed at his temples, then sat down, heavier than he had intended to, on the couch. Seccombe's office was always dangerous ground, with its centuries of history, floor-to-ceiling bookshelves laden with leather-bound tomes, thick rugs that had been brought from the Orient during a time when "the Orient" still meant something very specific. It was a room that had housed men who had overseen the erection of the Empire, and its subsequent dissolution. It was a room that remembered.

"There's a chance, yes," Crocker said, taking the offered cup of coffee, certain it wasn't decaffeinated and sipping at it anyway. "But it's not as bad as it looked when C went to brief the PM."

"And that's why your PA called, insisting that I see you at the earliest possible moment?" Seccombe moved to one of the high-backed reading chairs, settled himself into place, running a palm over his silver hair. The PUS was well into his seventies now, Crocker knew, with over half a century in the Foreign and Commonwealth Office behind him, but, like the room itself, he might as well have been timeless. The PUS wielded enormous power; more power, in many ways, than C herself. While Crocker didn't work for Seccombe directly, SIS was a part of the FCO, and thus the PUS could bring remarkable pressure to bear on the Firm if and when it suited him. That if and when most normally followed after the desires of the Foreign Secretary, who in turn was beholden to the Prime Minister.

A conversation with Seccombe, therefore, was effectively whispering straight into HMG's ear, and Crocker's ability to do so was entirely at Seccombe's discretion, and never the other way around. They weren't friends, though there had been times when Crocker had suspected Seccombe held some sort of fondness for him, perhaps as his mentor, perhaps seeing him simply as an amusement. More than once, Seccombe had urged him to take a more active hand in the politics of SIS, to consider the job, the operation, yes, but also the effect of his actions within the Government, as well as without. It was a lesson that Crocker had refused, and he knew it had cost him dearly. Twice that he could think of, the PUS had saved his career, and those were only the times Crocker knew of; he was reasonably certain there had been many others, and, in fact, suspected that the only reason his job was still waiting for him when he had returned after his heart attack was due to Seccombe's direct intervention.

Crocker finished the coffee, set the cup in its saucer gently on the coffee table, then leaned forward, towards Seccombe in his chair. "Chace called into the Ops Room just after seven this morning. She's alive—wounded, but alive—and mobile."

"How badly is she wounded?"

"Badly enough that she'll need medical attention before we can fly her out of the country."

Seccombe sucked air through his teeth, clearly not pleased. "She goes into a hospital, she won't come out except in Sepah custody."

"I'm not sending her to the hospital," Crocker said. "I want your permission to bring her to the embassy."

The displeasure deepened, then dissipated, Seccombe's expression becoming curious. "Paul?"

"They've set up roadblocks, checkpoints, they are actively searching for her. Her last coordinates put her just under ninety kilometers from Tehran, but she's in the Alborz, and she's had to veer far to the west to avoid the major highways. There's a village, Nowjan, roughly at the midway point. I've ordered her to head there."

"To what end?"

"Ideally, to have the Station Number Two rendezvous with her there. He can put her in his car, drive her straight to the embassy. We can bring a doctor in to see her, to stabilize her enough for transport, and then get her the hell out of the country. With your word, she could be on a flight home by tonight."

The sucking noise again, air drawing through his teeth, as Seccombe considered, looking away from Crocker as he did so. "They'll be stopped. Once the Number Two heads back into Tehran, they're sure to be stopped."

"It's almost guaranteed," Crocker agreed. "But the Number Two has diplomatic credentials, and the vehicle will be from the embassy, as well."

"Meaning Chace will have diplomatic immunity."

"It's the only way I can think to bring her in, sir."

"The Foreign Secretary won't like it."

"I suspect he'll like seeing footage of her trial rebroadcast on the BBC even less."

"Indeed." Seccombe, still looking away, smiled, then returned his attention to Crocker. "She's on the way to Nowjan, you said?"

"Yes."

"Meaning you've already committed to the course of action. I daresay you've informed Tehran Station of what you wanted them to do, as well. Still seeking permissions after the fact, Paul."

"I'm not going to leave one of my agents to die in Iran."

Seccombe shook his head, dismissive. "Hardly the point. Even at this late stage of the game, you still insist on playing by your rules."

That made Crocker pause. "What do you mean?"

"Someone was going to end up on the chop for Coldwitch, Paul. Even if Chace gets out of Iran, someone might still. Could be you. The Americans were extremely eager at the thought of bringing

Khamenei's nephew in for a few questions, never mind what we could've wrung out of him. Chace makes it home, very good for her, but the operation is still a disaster."

"I was against the operation from the start," Crocker said.

"I'm sure you were. But C certainly won't take responsibility for its failure any more than she already has, nor will the Deputy Chief. Unless you're willing to lay the blame on Minder One, it will have to come to rest somewhere. My understanding is that she is retiring from the Special Section anyway, yes?"

Crocker started to respond, could feel the argument forming on his lips. He felt very, very tired suddenly, as old as the room, and nowhere as well preserved. Seccombe was watching him, an eyebrow gently arched, curious.

"It's not the first time," Crocker said finally.

"No." Seccombe considered him a moment longer. "But it may be the last."

"So you believe I've stayed too long, as well?"

"I didn't say that, Paul. You clearly still have a contribution to make. But you have also made it clear that, when the time comes, you've no intention of going gracefully."

"I could say the same about you, sir. Twenty years as PUS now?"

"It'll be thirty in January. I'm still in the process of grooming my replacement, you see."

"I haven't gotten that far yet."

"Something for you to consider, at any rate." Seccombe nodded, rose fluidly from his chair, scooping up Crocker's empty cup. "Go ahead and inform Tehran Station to proceed, if you haven't done so already, Paul. I'll expect the good news from you before close of play today."

Unlike C, Crocker had no Bentley at his beck and call, in fact no official vehicle of any sort, and while he could have justified a taxi fare that morning, he needed time to think, time to clear his head, and the walk back to Vauxhall Cross could provide him that. He set out, walking south, passing Downing Street and then the Treasury, hands stuffed deep in the pockets of his overcoat, eyes ever wandering over the faces making their way along the street. It was early yet, but not so early that the work of Government wasn't already in full swing, and he saw faces he recognized, this one from the Admiralty, that one from the JIC. Some nodded in recognition when they met his eyes, others looked quickly away.

Seccombe had been correct on almost every account. In the handful of minutes between the red phone ringing in his office, where he and Poole had been sitting in silent commiseration, pretending to go through the morning's paperwork, and Crocker's reaching the Ops Room to make contact with Chace, he had already constructed the frame of what would become the new exfil plan. He'd ordered Mission Planning to bring up the map of Iran, working from the coordinates Chace had already relayed, and God bless them one and all, they were ahead of him, had already picked out Nowjan as the best location for a pickup. It was Chace's wound that had made any further considerations moot; the embassy route was the only possible way to save her.

Crocker had no sooner cut the connection with Minder One than he'd picked up the still-open line to Barnett in Tehran and told him what he wanted, how they would make it happen. Barnett, in turn, had reported that Lewis and MacIntyre were on their way back from Noshahr, that they would make the pickup on the way into Tehran. He'd have a doctor waiting for Chace at the embassy, he promised. They'd get his girl back to him in one piece.

There had been one other option, of course, the one that C had almost, but not quite, been willing to put voice to as she was leaving her office to brief the Prime Minister. Crocker could have told Chace that there was no way home, that there was no help coming, that she was on her own. He could have told her how dire the situation looked. He could have concluded by saying, simply, that she could not let herself be taken alive. And if that hadn't made the point painfully clear, he could have asked, finally, if she had managed to arm herself. The instruction would have been implicit. She would have understood.

Whether or not Chace would have put the gun in her mouth and pulled the trigger, Crocker didn't know. He was profoundly grateful that he hadn't been forced to find out.

C hadn't been entirely callous when she'd said that things would've been infinitely easier if Chace had died. At that moment, with the little knowledge available to them, capture had seemed imminent. Objectively, then, the death of Minder One would have spared them the political shitstorm that would've come with her arrest.

As soon as Chace had made contact, however, everything had changed. She was mobile, and she was still at liberty, and that meant there was the possibility—the very strong possibility—that they could get her out of Iran before Shirazi managed to lay hands on her. If they could do that, the political fallout of Coldwitch's failure, at least in the public eye, would be minimized. The Iranians could scream and shout to their heart's content, could blame SIS and HMG and the CIA and the Mossad, too, for the death of Hossein Khamenei, but there would be no proof, and in the end, then, it would be only what it so often was out of Tehran: noise, loud and incomprehensible, designed to mask their true intentions.

He was passing the House of Commons now, Big Ben just beginning to strike the hour, walking along Millbank. Ahead of him, still on this side of the river, just past Lambeth Bridge, stood the headquarters of Box, the Security Services. He turned before reaching it, started across the Thames on the bridge.

Doubt was nagging him, and he tried to isolate it, identify it. He'd been correct about Coldwitch, but he knew, as well, that he was wrong, that he was missing something, but he was damned if he could see what it was. If Falcon had only ever been bait, why had Shirazi waited so long to close the trap? Even after missing Chace, why hadn't he taken Lewis and MacIntyre, diplomatic immunity notwithstanding? The rental in Noshahr wasn't the embassy; that far from Tehran, Shirazi could have easily brought both men in for questioning, made his apologies later.

He stepped off the bridge, turning south once more, now walking along the Albert Embankment. He could see the SIS Headquarters in the distance, the absurd cubic pyramid of tinted and mirrored glass, as distinctively unsubtle a work of modern architecture as ever beheld. From this angle, at this distance, its nickname of Legoland had never seemed more appropriate.

Seccombe had been trying to tell him something at the end, Crocker realized, had been trying to warn him, perhaps, that this was the last favor, the last back-channel chat they would be having. Another person ringing the death knell for Paul Crocker's career.

Crocker shook it off, producing his pass as he approached the gate. The watch logged him back in, and he crossed the enclosed courtyard to the entrance, showed his pass a second time, then, inside, swiped it through the reader as he passed through the metal detectors. He couldn't count the number of times his career had been threatened. Frances Barclay, Gordon-Palmer's immediate predecessor as C, had practically made a sport of it, in fact. Yet Barclay was gone and Crocker was riding the lift back up to his office as he had done hundreds, even thousands of times before.

There would be fallout from Coldwitch, Crocker had no doubt. But he couldn't worry about that now, wouldn't allow himself to be distracted. For C, for Seccombe, for Seale and the CIA, Coldwitch was over, was bust.

But not for Crocker.

Not until he could bring Tara Chace home.

CHAPTER TWENTY-TWO

IRAN—SHEMIRANAT COUNTY, TEHRAN PROVINCE, NOWJAN
11 DECEMBER 1639 HOURS (GMT +3.30)

The news came over the radio between the second and third roadblocks on the Karaj-Chalus highway, leading at the top of the hour. Caleb, riding in the passenger seat while MacIntyre held the wheel, reached out and turned up the volume, listening closely to the rapid-fire Farsi now coming from the speakers. The report concluded, Iran pop music returning, and Caleb rolled the knob until the radio clicked off.

"They're reporting the death of the Supreme Leader's nephew," he told MacIntyre. "Hossein Khamenei, shot dead by foreign agents in Noshahr during an abortive abduction attempt early this morning."

MacIntyre glanced to him, his expression flat, then put his attention back to the road.

"Falcon," Caleb said. "Jesus Christ. That's what she meant when she said he came from the right family."

MacIntyre shrugged, disinterested, slowing, and Caleb saw out the windshield yet another line of cars and vans all at a standstill, turning the two-lane road through the Alborz, yet again, into a single-file car park. They came to a stop, and Caleb rolled down his window, pulled himself half out, to get a better look. A switchback ahead of them reversed the road one hundred and eighty degrees, turning it north again, and perhaps thirty meters below them he could see the actual roadblock itself, the police cars and officers. He slid back into the car.

"At least an hour," Caleb said. MacIntyre shrugged again, then switched off the ignition. The drive from Noshahr down to Tehran would've normally taken no more than four, perhaps five hours with the winter weather in the high pass and the planned detour in Nowjan, but, by Caleb's watch, they were now into the seventh hour of their journey.

"Stop looking at your watch."

Caleb dropped his wrist. "We're going to be late."

MacIntyre chuckled.

"It's not like she's got somewhere else to be, Mr. Lewis," he said.

They cleared the third roadblock at seven minutes to six in the evening, with night falling. Just as with the prior two checkpoints, both MacIntyre and Caleb were required to produce their documents, and just as before, the officer who took them immediately summoned his supervisor as soon as he realized their nationality. Caleb did the talking all three times, the conversations in Farsi all remarkably similar.

"British?"

"With the embassy in Tehran, yes."

"Where were you in the north?"

"Chalus and Noshahr."

A frown or a scowl, and then, "Just a moment," and the supervising officer would step away, speaking into his radio, and for three or four minutes Caleb and MacIntyre would wait. Then the supervisor would return, peering past them, trying to see if anything was hidden in the car. Sometimes there would be more questions, had they seen anything unusual, had they been approached by anyone, were they carrying anything, and in all cases Caleb's answers were the same, no, no, no, until ultimately they would be waved through.

This third time, though, Caleb thought they had been detained longer than before, and he wondered if it had been deliberate, if they were being intentionally delayed. When Barnett had reached him late that morning, directing him to stop in Nowjan before returning to Tehran, the call had come over Caleb's cell phone. Barnett had used open code, never mentioning Minder One nor anything directly incriminating at all, and the whole of the conversation couldn't have lasted more than thirty, perhaps forty seconds at the most. But that could have been long enough for VEVAK to have overheard what was said, and it wouldn't take a genius to understand their meaning.

Seven kilometers past the roadblock, MacIntyre turned them off the highway, west, down a narrow unpaved road into a valley between the mountains. Full dark had descended, and within the car, the only view of the world was via the headlamps, and one of them, it turned out, was broken. The car was an older Benz, a four-door, and Caleb thought that once in its life it had quite possibly been grand, perhaps even used by the Ambassador himself, but that would have been twenty years ago now, at least, and every rock and dip in the uneven ground translated clearly through the chassis, into his spine.

By the map, it was only three and a half kilometers from the highway to Nowjan, but that implied a straight line. The truth was over three times the distance, the road—if it could be called that—twisting north, then south, then west, then east, then west again, repeated curves and turns through the valley. The Alborz rose on both sides of the car, steep, showing the pale glint of snow high along the slopes.

They hit pavement abruptly, the ride smoothing as the road straightened, descending further, and ahead of them, Caleb could now see Nowjan, a handful of lights burning in homes that clung to the hillside. They passed an orchard, trees bare from winter, another house, and then they were rolling into the tiny town square, the mosque on their left, a squat building ahead of them. MacIntyre turned the car about slowly, and their single headlight revealed a faded portrait of Khomeini painted on one nearby wall.

There was absolutely no one about, absolutely no movement that Caleb could see at all. He turned in his seat, looking to one of the houses, saw its lights wink out, go dark. The thought that they had just driven into a trap asserted itself, called his fear up to duty once again. They were too late, the delays had cost them. Minder

One had come and instead of Caleb and MacIntyre and their old Benz she had been met by Shirazi and the Sepah, they had already taken her away. Or they were holding her now, watching as the Benz made a second turn around the square, as it came to a stop, waiting to spring upon them when the moment was right.

MacIntyre reached out, touching his elbow, not speaking, and Caleb turned to see that he was indicating something ahead of them, to the right. A shadow moved, indistinct, began shambling towards them in the darkness. Caleb saw the pistol in its hand, felt the fear surge, trying to become panic, and then he saw the pale face, realized it was Minder One, and he was out of the car before he could think about it, moving towards her even as she brought the pistol up in both hands and pointed it at his head.

"It's all right," Caleb said. "It's all right."

She wobbled, the pistol remaining trained on him for an instant longer before she brought it down, as if the effort of leveling the gun had taken all the strength in her arms.

"Late," Chace mumbled. "Thought they'd got you."

Caleb moved in, taking the pistol from her hand, laying his other arm across her shoulders, trying to support her. She made a noise of pain as his arm came down, her elbow shooting out, catching his ribs, and he released her, more surprised than hurt. She was bent at the waist, hands on her thighs, stray hair dangling from beneath her makeshift *maqna'e*.

"Back," Chace managed. "Hit me in the back."

Feeling like a fool, Caleb reached out for her again, this time taking her arm. "Let's get you in the car. Get you out of here."

She nodded weakly, straightening with obvious pain as he took hold of her. MacIntyre had emerged from the Benz, had the rear door open, looking around at everything but the two of them. With care, Caleb led her to the back of the vehicle, helped her climb inside. He closed the door, moving around to join her in the backseat.

"Let's go," he told MacIntyre.

"Don't have to say that twice, mate."

Caleb climbed in beside Chace. MacIntyre started the Benz

again, swung them around and back onto the road the way they had come, accelerating, driving in darkness until they were off the pavement once more, and only then switching on the headlamp. The car rocked and jumped, Chace swaying with every motion, and Caleb understood she could barely keep herself upright. He reached out for her, and only then saw that she was still holding the pistol, and he stopped, not knowing what to do with it.

"The pistol," he told MacIntyre. "What do I do with it?"

"Fucking hell." MacIntyre reached back with one hand. "They stop us and see that thing, we're done. Give it here."

Caleb handed it over, and MacIntyre leaned to his side, stuffed the weapon into the glove compartment, snapped the door shut again.

"They search the car—" Caleb started to say.

"They search the car, Mr. Lewis, a hidden pistol will be the least of our worries."

Beside him, Chace made a croak that Caleb understood was meant to be a laugh. Her head pitched forward, as if she'd fallen suddenly asleep, then jerked back, and she mumbled something he couldn't make out. Caleb reached out for her once again, taking her face in his hands, trying to see her eyes in the darkness of the backseat, and she let him. Her skin was damp and cool, her eyes open, but he couldn't make out her pupils.

"She's in shock," Caleb told MacIntyre.

"Can you do anything about it?"

"Not unless we stop."

"We're not stopping, Mr. Lewis."

Chace mumbled something else, and Caleb caught the word "not" and the word "stop" and he nodded at her, saying, "We're going to get you to the embassy. We're going to get you somewhere safe."

She closed her eyes, leaning forward, putting her weight into his hands. The car turned, hopped back onto paved road, back on the highway. The Benz accelerated, and Caleb, not knowing what else to do, brought Chace's head against his shoulder, then, gingerly, wrapped his arms around her, supporting her against him. He listened for a sound of protest, of pain, but she made none, just relaxed into him further.

"Safe," Tara Chace murmured.

They hit their last roadblock just north of Karaj, east of Vasiyeh, and Caleb had his papers in hand when the officer came to collect them, shining his flashlight around the interior, settling it on Chace, half-asleep and half-unconscious, Caleb still with one arm around her. The moment the beam hit her, the officer turned away from the vehicle, shouting out, and quickly the car was surrounded by men. Caleb could see one of the officers already speaking on a radio, another with a cell phone in his hand, dialing.

"Get out of the car," the officer ordered.

"This woman is ill," Caleb said. "We're taking her to our embassy for medical care."

"You must get out of the vehicle now."

In the front seat, MacIntyre didn't move, his hands still at the wheel, staring fixedly ahead.

"We are British embassy personnel," Caleb said. "As such, we are accorded diplomatic privileges and rights. This vehicle belongs to the embassy, and as such is an extension of the chancery, and to be considered British soil."

The officer reached for the door.

"Don't do it," Caleb warned. "You open that door, you will initiate an international incident. You will violate British sovereignty, potentially committing an act of war, and you will certainly destroy the reciprocal protections enjoyed by your government in its embassies and missions around the world. *Your* actions. *You* will be responsible."

Head still against his shoulder, Chace moved, resting her cheek to his chest. Outside of the car, the lead officer stood, hand extended, uncertain, the others around him. Caleb glanced quickly out the front, saw that the one on the radio had lowered it, scowling, that the man on the cell phone was still speaking, now turning away from them. Caleb returned his look to the officer at the door, glaring at him.

The officer stepped back without a word, turned, moved to join the one speaking on the phone. The phone came down, a hushed exchange, another scowl in their direction. The phone came up again.

"We're there?" Chace murmured.

"Not yet," Caleb told her. "Soon. Just hold on."

The officer was motioning at them, and for a second, Caleb thought he was ordering them out of the car again. Then the others surrounding the car stepped back, and he saw that they were being waved through. MacIntyre shifted the Benz back into gear, the car moving forward, and Caleb looked back as they began driving away, saw the one with the phone still speaking on it, the other officer writing in a notebook in his hands. Then the roadblock and the police and all of it were out of sight, the Benz speeding south, next turning east onto the Karaj Highway, back towards Tehran, until, finally, they were deep in the city traffic, slowing again, stopping and starting at the lights on Jamhuri Avenue.

Caleb thought they were going to make it, he really did.

Right up to the moment the van rammed them in the intersection at Vali-ye Asr.

CHAPTER TWENTY-THREE

IRAN—TEHRAN, JAMHURI AVENUE/VALI-YE ASR

11 DECEMBER 2107 HOURS (GMT +3.30)

When the call came, Shirazi almost missed it.

He'd been working out of his office since the Minister's departure, was still coordinating Republican Guards and Basij search teams along the Alborz, when Zahabzeh returned from Chalus with Parviz, Kamal, and Javed in tow. They had nothing by way of good news. Several times already, false alarms had reached them, though this last had seemed more promising at its outset. An officer manning one of the roadblocks out of Chalus, at the mouth of the highway, had seen a salmon-colored Samand peel away from the traffic jam waiting to clear the checkpoint. He hadn't gotten a good look at the license, only a partial; but the partial had matched enough of one of the stolen plates that Zahabzeh had ordered another canvas of Chalus, believing that Chace had again reversed direction, was trying to run back to the north.

But if she had, there had been no sign of her.

"This woman is injured, exhausted, alone," Zahabzeh complained. "She has no friends, no support. How is it we can find no sign of her?"

"She's extremely good," Shirazi said.

"Or maybe she's dead," Javed suggested. "Pulled off somewhere, and her wounds finally caught up to her. She could be dead, and that's why we haven't found her."

None of them liked that suggestion, and the looks Javed received as a result turned him quiet for several minutes, before he offered to go out and bring in some food. Shirazi told him that it was a fine suggestion, and that Kamal and Parviz should go with him.

After they had left, Zahabzeh asked the question he'd been waiting on since returning. "What happened?"

"The Minister was here when I arrived. He informed me that the Supreme Leader knew about his nephew's collusion with the British, and had known for quite some time. He took my initial explanation of the situation as an attempt to protect Hossein's memory, on behalf of the Ayatollah."

Zahabzeh's grin was rife with relief. "Thanks be to God."

"It's not ideal, but it could have gone far worse. The belief now is that Hossein had sold himself again to the British, that we got wind of the plot, and attempted to capture the spy with Hossein. The Minister stated that our intention was admirable, if poorly considered."

"Meaning we should have obtained clearance first."

"Correct."

Zahabzeh thought, scratching at the stubble on his face. Shirazi expected he looked the same; none of them had been given a chance to shave, let alone bathe or change clothes, in over twenty-four hours now. "If so . . . then the Minister knows exactly what we were trying to do, just not *how* we tried to do it. Do we have official clearance now? Retroactively?"

"Provisionally, I think, on the successful capture of the spy. They already have plans for what they'll do with her, I think. He wants her brought in alive. He was very clear on that point."

"Of course."

"And he was clear on what would happen to us if we failed."

Zahabzeh grunted. Nothing more on that point needed to be said.

They moved to one of the conference rooms, and Shirazi ordered a radio set brought in, and more phones, as well as maps of the country, thus transforming the space into a makeshift command post. Javed returned with the others, bringing *kubide* for all of them, and they ate hungrily. The phones rang regularly, and twice within the first hour came calls reporting the missing Samand, and each time Shirazi took the handset from Zahabzeh, only to learn that, on closer inspection, there had been some sort of mistake, an overreaction, an error.

This continued into the night.

Shirazi was plotting all of the possible sightings thus far on the master map he'd hung on the wall, working the old-fashioned way with thumbtacks and a ruler, when one of the phones on the conference table began ringing again. He didn't bother to turn to it, letting Parviz answer it. The plots on the map were ridiculously irrational, many around Chalus, which was regional, but at least one as far east as Gorgan, which would have put Chace heading into the Balkans, and another as far south as Rafsanjan, over eight hundred kilometers from Chalus, an impossible distance for her to have covered already.

"Sir?" Parviz said, and then repeated it, the second time unable to keep the excitement from his voice. "Sir! We have her!"

Everyone in the room turned, fell silent, and Shirazi held out his hand for the phone.

"This is Director Shirazi. Whom am I speaking to?"

"Director, sir! Captain Bardsiri, sir, with the—"

"I don't care. You have her?"

Hesitation. Then, *"No, no we've had to let them go."*

Shirazi wasn't certain he'd heard correctly. "You've what? What did you say?"

"We couldn't arrest her, sir, we—"

"You had her, alive, and you let her go?" Shirazi heard his voice rising, was aware that the attention from his men in the room had become that much more intense. "Is that what you're telling me, Captain Bardsiri?"

"She had—she was traveling under diplomatic protection! We couldn't do anything, we had to let them go! I'm sorry, sir, I just didn't have the authority—"

Shirazi held out the phone to Parviz, hearing the captain continuing to excuse himself, his voice now small and agitated. "Get the location, a complete description of the vehicle, the license plate, everything."

Parviz took the handset, nodding, and Shirazi turned to Zahabzeh. "She's with her own people, they picked her up somewhere in an embassy vehicle."

"Diplomatic immunity does not extend to murderers," Zahabzeh said.

"Something Captain Bardsiri either doesn't know, or decided he didn't want to risk. But still, if she's traveling with embassy staff . . ."

"If they get her back to the British mission, we will lose her."

"Agreed." Shirazi considered for a moment, all the time he needed. Whatever possible political fallout would come of violating British sovereignty, he truly didn't care. He needed Chace, he absolutely had to have her, and Zahabzeh was correct; once she reached the embassy, she would become untouchable. Removing her from the mission grounds would be impossible.

But taking her from a mission car while it made its way to the embassy, that was another matter entirely.

Parviz was off the phone now, a paper in his hand. "They were heading south towards Karaj."

"They'll take the highway," Zahabzeh said. "Quickest route to the embassy."

"We need to be quicker," Shirazi said.

Shirazi got out of the van last, holding back, as he should, as his role required, despite his passionate desire to be first. But when the doors at the back of the van opened, he made sure it was Zahabzeh leading, and Shirazi let Kamal, and then Parviz, follow after him before exiting himself.

The Benz had stalled in the intersection, bent metal and a cloud of steam, shattered glass glimmering on the ground. The three men in the lead had drawn their weapons, Zahabzeh already covering the driver, the one called MacIntyre, who was only now beginning to regain his senses. Behind him, Shirazi heard the whine of the van as Javed put it in reverse, backing it closer.

Behind the cracked windshield, MacIntyre righted himself, started to move, then saw the guns and arrested, raising his hands before laying them flat on the dashboard. Shirazi had a moment's relief that the man was intelligent enough to have read the situation, to have seen the inevitable outcome. He sincerely hoped MacIntyre wouldn't change his mind, decide now was the time to become a hero; if he did that, Shirazi would have no recourse but to order him shot, and his desire was very much that no one die. Not yet, at least.

Without ceremony or hesitation, Shirazi walked to the rear of the Benz. There was young Caleb Lewis, blood running down the side of his face, looking appropriately dazed and frightened. And there, too, was Tara Chace, slumped against him, and behind the glare of streetlights off the window, Shirazi saw her turn her head, blinking at him blearily, sluggishly. Shirazi tried the door, found it locked.

"Parviz!" Shirazi called, and the young man instantly holstered his gun, running around to join him. The baton was in his hand before he came to a halt, extending out with a snap of the wrist, and Shirazi stepped back to give him room, saw Caleb Lewis flinch, hand moving to shield Chace's head. Then the end of the metal baton hit the window, the glass exploding into fragments. Parviz rammed the baton against the side of the car, collapsing it, stowing it, then brought his gun out again.

"If he moves," Shirazi told Parviz in Farsi, knowing that Caleb Lewis would understand him, "kill him."

Parviz nodded.

"You can't do this," Lewis began. "This vehicle—"

"We are doing it." Shirazi reached into the car, unlocked the door, then yanked it open. Javed was out of the van now, moving to join him, and together they took Chace by the arms, pulling her from the vehicle. She didn't struggle, semiconscious, and once out of the Benz, became dead-weight in their arms. Together with Javed, they moved her to the van, laying her in the back of the vehicle.

Shirazi climbed in after her, Javed returning to his place behind the wheel.

"That's it," Shirazi called out to Zahabzeh. "We're done."

Zahabzeh, Parviz, and Kamal all began backing towards him, their weapons still held on the Benz and its remaining occupants. One by one the men climbed into the van, and then Javed had them moving again, even before Zahabzeh could close the doors. Shirazi sat down beside Chace, put his fingers to her throat, feeling for her pulse. She was staring up at nothing, her eyes unfocused, glazing, and her chest was rising and falling rapidly beneath the blanket she wore as a shirt.

"How bad is she?" Zahabzeh made the question sound like curiosity, rather than the vital matter it was. "Will she live?"

Bending his head to her mouth, Shirazi felt the woman's breath brushing his cheek. He could hear her over the sound of the engine, the rapid wheeze as she inhaled, exhaled, struggling for air, and he frowned, slipped his hands beneath her blanket, running them over her torso. Her skin was cold, clammy, but he could feel no wound.

"Help me," Shirazi told Zahabzeh. "Hold her head, we need to roll her."

With Zahabzeh's help he rolled Chace onto her right side, again slipped a hand beneath the blanket, now feeling his way along her back, her bare skin, her bra, and then something slippery and wet. He pulled his hand back, saw blood shining black on his fingers, wiped them on the blanket and then lifted it, revealing a tattered and bloody square of plastic stuck to her skin, the tape peeled back, exposing a narrow entry wound.

"The kit," Shirazi ordered. "Oxygen and an occlusion dressing. Quickly."

Kamal moved, staggering as the van made a turn, dropped to his knees between Shirazi and Zahabzeh. He dug in the medical bag, handed over a wrapped dressing.

"Get a mask on her." Shirazi ripped the bandage open, pulling free a thin sheet of shiny foil and gauze. He pulled the plastic from Chace's back, tossing it away, then lay the new bandage over the wound, pressing it firmly to her skin with his palm. "Quickly."

The small canister of oxygen was already out, Kamal moving with surprising speed, and in the back of his mind, Shirazi imagined that the young man thought this a potential redemption, a possible absolution for the murder of Hossein. Oxygen began to flow, and Shirazi took the mask from Kamal, pressed it to Chace's mouth and nose, pulled the strap around the woman's head to hold it in place.

"Lay her down. Gently."

Zahabzeh complied, and together they returned Chace to her back, and Shirazi spread her eyes open wider, looking at each of them closely, then took her pulse again. It was still racing, but stronger than before. The rapid movement of her chest had subsided, her breathing still shallow, but nowhere as labored.

"Tell Javed there's a change to the plan," Shirazi told Zahabzeh. "We have to go by ground."

"It's almost two hundred kilometers," Zahabzeh said. "The helicopter—"

"We put her on a helicopter, she will die, Farzan."

Kamal had shifted, preparing an IV, and now had Chace's left arm in his lap, searching for a vein. Zahabzeh turned to watch, his expression flat as the catheter went into the woman's arm. Her eyes were still open, and she blinked, but made no noise. Kamal handed the IV bag to Parviz, telling him to hold it up.

"By road, then," Zahabzeh said. "It's funny, though."

"What is funny?" Shirazi asked.

"We're working so hard to save her life when we're just going to kill her later."

Shirazi looked down at the woman on the floor of the van. The makeshift *maqna'e* had come loose, the blond hair it had concealed now spilling around her head. Shirazi saw that she was looking at him, and for a moment there was comprehension in her eyes, understanding, even pain. But there was no fear.

"First we will take what we need," Shirazi told Zahabzeh.

CHAPTER TWENTY-FOUR

LONDON—VAUXHALL CROSS, OFFICE OF D-OPS
11 DECEMBER 1756 HOURS (GMT)

The red circuit had opportunity to ring only once before Paul Crocker had the phone to his ear. "D-Ops."

"Duty Ops Officer, sir, flash traffic from Tehran Station, Immediate and Urgent. Rescue attempt intercepted en route stop. Minder One taken by VEVAK forces and in custody stop. Number Two minor injuries stop. Require instruction as to how to proceed stop. Message ends."

"I'm . . ."

"Sir?"

Crocker coughed, feeling as if his head was beginning to spin, as if the room had suddenly lost its balance.

"Sir?"

He drew a breath, slowly, felt his heart pounding hard in his chest. "Send to Tehran Station, immediate and urgent, as follows: imperative you determine location where Minder One detained. Authorized to use all available means, including activation of network assets. Message ends. And Ron?"

"Yes, sir?"

"Tell MCO to get an open line to the Station, and bring in Minder Two, get him up to speed."

"Right away, sir."

Crocker set the handset back in its cradle, stared at it for a moment, and was about to key his intercom when the door opened, Kate standing there.

"She's at the embassy?"

"No." Crocker got up, took his suit coat from the stand, began slipping into it. "VEVAK hit the car before they made it in. Is C still in the building?"

"In her office," Kate said quietly. "She was waiting on . . . she was waiting for the good news."

"Tell her I'm coming up," Crocker said.

For several seconds after Crocker was done speaking, C sat in silence, her face set in stone, impossible to read. Then it cracked, an overwhelming sadness settling on her, and she sighed.

"It's over, then," she said. "Certainly, if they have her in custody, it's over."

Crocker shook his head, refusing the analysis. "I've directed Tehran Station to try to determine where Chace is being held. Minder Two is on his way into the Ops Room, I can have him briefed and on his way to Iran tonight if I can get MOD transport."

"And what is he supposed to do when he gets there? Attempt a rescue? Attempt a *second* rescue?"

"If feasible, yes. Poole is ex-SAS, as well as a Minder. We have time. D-Int confirmed that the Iranians released the news of Falcon's death earlier today, but attributed it only to 'foreign agents.' They'll try to fit her for it, and that certainly means a trial, most likely a very public one. We have some time."

She shook her head, her expression softening, almost affectionate. "I applaud your loyalty to your people, Paul, but the proposition is absurd. Even if Barnett were to locate Chace, it's too late, the damage is done. It's over."

"Poole—"

"Poole will never leave England, Paul!" She got up from behind her desk, exasperated, frustrated. "Have you stopped to consider what you're asking? Even if, by some grace of God, Tehran is actually able to verify where Chace is being detained, even if the location isn't, for some absurd reason, a maximum-security site, it will never happen. The risk of a rescue attempt going wrong is simply too great. Bad enough they've got one of our agents alive, one that they'll undoubtedly put on trial for murder, you would send them a second one?"

"If we find the location, a rescue attempt becomes viable. If we go through MOD, with Poole as lead, if we can get an SAS brick in support, we can get her out of the country."

"You're not listening to me, Paul. It's not going to happen, the PM will never allow it."

"We owe her a rescue. We can't just abandon her."

C's voice turned cold. "We owed her the effort, and we made it as best we could."

"There's more we can do."

"It doesn't matter. The Prime Minister will never authorize an incursion into Iran to save the life of one SIS agent, you know that, certainly not after the failure of Coldwitch. And certainly not in the face of Minder One being the lead story on the morning news. Chace is lost to us, Paul. Our priority now must be determining how we will respond to the Iranians when they put her in front of the cameras, how we can mitigate the damage."

Crocker stared at her, knowing that everything she was saying was true, knowing the logic, feeling it boiling, foul, inside of him. "We have to try."

"We have done," C said. "To the best of our abilities, we have done."

"It's not enough."

She considered him, and he realized what he was seeing from her was very close to pity.

"I don't know any other way to put this that you'll understand," C said. "So I'll say it like this: if you send Poole to Iran, I shall recall him, and then fire you. If you order Tehran Station to do anything other than the most routine intelligence-gathering, I will countermand your directive, and I will fire you. If you do *anything* at all that could further exacerbate the situation as it stands right now, I will reverse its course, and fire you. Iran is now off-limits to the Ops Directorate until I say otherwise. The priority now is damage control, nothing else, and I cannot—I will not—permit you to make things worse."

Crocker said nothing. C pressed the button on her intercom, summoning her PA, and as soon as the door to her office cracked open, spoke to the unseen assistant, saying, "My car, please. And inform Downing Street that I'm coming over with an update on the Iran situation."

The door closed silently.

"What *am* I permitted to do?" Crocker asked.

She looked at him sadly. "Go home, Paul."

Poole was waiting when Crocker returned to his office, and from the look on Minder Two's face, Crocker knew he had already heard the news.

"Got tired of waiting in the Ops Room," Poole said. "When do I leave?"

"You don't." Crocker reached for the red phone, punching a key, and when Ron answered, said, "Inform Tehran Station to stand down, repeat, stand down. Require full report soonest, otherwise Station to resume normal operations."

He hung up before he heard Ron's confirmation of the order, turned back to Poole, to see the man standing, hands clenched, glaring at him.

"We're not doing anything?"

"There's nothing we can do, Nicky."

"You can bloody send me to go and get her!"

"Alone? Really?"

"Lankford's still in Mosul, he can meet me in Basra, we deploy from there—"

"It's not going to happen, Nicky." Crocker dug a thumb against his temple, feeling his head throb. "I couldn't even if I wanted to. C has declared Iran off-limits. No operations, no action, nothing."

"God-dammit, Boss!" Poole's voice exploded in the tiny office. "We owe her!"

"I know."

"Then fuck C and fuck the rest of them and send me to Iran to get her!"

"Knock it off."

"Go to the CIA, then!"

"It'll be the same response. They've already written off Coldwitch."

"She's in some goddamn VEVAK interrogation room right now, they're using rubber hoses on her or needles or whatever the hell's the method of the month over there, and they're going to get *everything* she knows, you realize that? Never mind that she's my friend, and that maybe, maybe, you even think of her as yours. She's a fucking intelligence gold mine for them!"

"You think I don't know that?" Crocker asked. "You think C doesn't know, the CIA doesn't know? If there were even a chance of getting her out of there, you think I'd let C stop me? But there isn't, Nicky. There just isn't."

Poole stared at him for several seconds, struggling, warring with himself, until finally swearing, turning away. His fists tightened, then relaxed, and with it his posture slackened.

"They'll take good care of her." The consolation sounded hollow and false, even to Crocker's own ears. "Reasonably good care. A doctor for her, at least, the medical attention she needs. They'll want her healthy for the cameras."

"Well, that makes it so much better, now, doesn't it?"

Crocker had no response.

"So they'll put her on trial, and then what? Prison for five years before we get her back?"

"The assumption is that she'll be tried for the murder of Hossein Khamenei," Crocker said. "In which case they'll execute her once she's found guilty."

"Lovely."

"Not really."

They looked at each other, the antagonism gone.

"So this is everything," Poole said. "This is all we are going to do."

"For now, at least. Once the Iranians reveal they have her we'll know more. They might not take it public."

"Go to the FCO you mean? The Ambassador?"

"It's possible. Depends what they want."

"Maybe we can work an exchange? Trade her for somebody?"

"Maybe."

"You don't sound hopeful."

"We're not holding anyone they would want, certainly no one of equal or greater value." Crocker shook his head. "And I doubt the Foreign Secretary or the Prime Minister would think Chace's life is worth any concessions the Iranians would ask for."

"Bastards," Poole muttered, the one word an indictment, encompassing each and all of them: the Prime Minister and the Foreign Secretary; C and Seale and the CIA; VEVAK and Youness Shirazi; even Crocker and Poole, himself. They'd lost. Chace wasn't dead, but she might as well have been, because she was never coming back. Chace was gone.

Bastards, all of them.

Crocker had to agree.

CHAPTER TWENTY-FIVE

IRAN—ISFAHAN PROVINCE, NATANZ
12 DECEMBER 0221 HOURS (GMT +3.30)

It had been past midnight when Shirazi and the others reached the house in Natanz, some twelve kilometers outside of town, and he went inside with Zahabzeh, Kamal, and Parviz to prepare it, while Javed stayed with their prize in the van. Chace wasn't going anywhere; after stabilizing her, Shirazi had injected her with ketamine, just enough to put her down for the journey.

The house was small, used by VEVAK for long-term interrogation of prisoners, normally politically sensitive ones. Zahabzeh questioned their using it, wondered why they weren't taking Chace directly to one of the hospitals in Tehran, and then to prison.

"Two reasons," Shirazi said. "We don't want her anywhere public, anywhere her people can find her. Second, too many ears, too many people listening who might report back to the Minister. Her confession must be the confession we want, Farzan, remember. Or have you forgotten it was Kamal's bullet that killed Hossein?"

"I haven't forgotten," Zahabzeh said. "We should inform the Minister we have her, at least. Call off the search."

"Not yet. Not until we have the confession."

"I don't like it."

"You don't have to like it, Farzan. I am in charge, and this is what we are going to do. All of us together, remember?"

Zahabzeh had said nothing for a moment, watching while Parviz checked the security camera for the cell, making certain it was working. "We'll need the confession quickly."

"I am aware," Shirazi said, drily. "Once we have her in place,

I'll go back to Tehran, make certain the office knows how to proceed."

"You're going back?" Zahabzeh looked at him curiously. "Why not use the phone?"

"I want to put in an appearance at the office, maintain a presence for the search." Shirazi smiled at him. "You're afraid I will go to the Minister, claim all the credit?"

"He should be informed."

"No, not yet. I told you at the start, we would take the credit together. I gave you my word."

"Yes," Zahabzeh said. "You did."

Kamal stepped out of the small room used as a cell. "We're ready."

"Help Javed move her inside. Be gentle with her, I don't want the wound reopening."

"Yes, sir."

Shirazi and Zahabzeh watched as Chace was moved into the house, followed as she was carried into the cell and laid on the cot. They had cut the blanket she had used as a makeshift manteau away during the drive, to better visualize her wounds, and now Kamal used a new blanket to cover her.

"Her boots," Zahabzeh said.

Kamal nodded, used a knife to cut the laces on Chace's shoes, tugged them free, then took her socks. Shirazi frowned, but didn't say anything; taking her shoes was logical, a means of keeping control over the prisoner, and objecting to it would have only heightened Zahabzeh's already acute suspicions.

Zahabzeh took the boots, and the four men left the cell, Javed closing and locking the door after them. Parviz was seated at the table, watching the monitor, and Shirazi glanced at the screen, saw the woman lying precisely as they had left her.

"Her things," he asked. "Where are they?"

"Here."

Zahabzeh set the boots on the edge of the table, removed the items they had taken from the spy from the pockets of his jacket. There was a satellite phone, a GPS unit, a folding knife, and several wads of rials. Shirazi looked through them all in the light, noting that both the satellite phone and the GPS unit were switched off. He turned each on, checking their respective memories. The phone's battery was nearly dead, its call log holding only one outgoing and one received in memory, each from different numbers within the U.K. Nothing else was stored. He showed the contents of the log to Zahabzeh.

"Calls to headquarters," Shirazi said. "That would explain how Mr. Lewis knew where to find her."

"Useless now."

"Most likely. I suppose we could call and find out." Shirazi gave Zahabzeh a thin smile, received one in turn, then switched the phone off and set it down again, picking up the GPS unit. There were over a half-dozen points logged in memory on the device, but without a map, there was no way to determine where they were, or their purpose. Most of them, Shirazi suspected, were false entries, inputted simply to make things look proper. Which of them would have been the rendezvous point, again, he couldn't know without a map. It was just as likely that the coordinates hadn't been set in the unit at all, that Chace had held them in her memory. He hoped it was the latter.

"Bag these up," Shirazi told Zahabzeh. "We'll need them for the trial."

He left the house at ten minutes past four in the morning, and despite the late hour and the lack of sleep, felt better than he had in months. The nervousness, the tension, both were still with him, but for the first time since taking Hossein, he allowed for a slight optimism. Things had gone wrong, yes, but now, finally, they were proceeding as he had planned all along. There were complications, of course—Chace's injury foremost amongst them—but Shirazi was confident they could be managed. The hard work was done.

He had his prize.

He had Chace.

By ten in the morning, he had completed his work, issuing new directives and narrowing the search corridor for the spy to the area around Tabriz. He returned to his office, closed the door, and after some searching, found the number for Captain Bardsiri.

"Captain? This is Director Shirazi. We spoke yesterday."

"Yes, sir." The captain's nervousness radiated out of the phone.

"Regarding the incident at the checkpoint, you have filed your report?"

"No, not yet, sir. I was preparing it for submission—"

"Good. When you have completed it, I require it sent directly to my office, to me personally, along with any notes or other information about the incident. Do you understand?"

"That's . . . that's quite irregular, sir."

"I am aware of that, as I am also aware that my office took steps last night to capture the spy regardless of her diplomatic cover. I am trying to protect you, Captain, do you understand?"

"Yes, sir. Thank you. I'll . . . I'll have everything sent to you this afternoon."

"Sooner would be better, Captain," Shirazi said, hanging up. He booted up his computer, found his files on Chace, and proceeded to securely delete each one in turn. Then he checked his desk, looking for anything he might have missed or forgotten, but found nothing. The files on Hossein had already been disposed of, as per the Minister's direction, and no hard-copy information existed about Chace that Shirazi was aware of.

It wasn't yet eleven in the morning when he departed, climbing back into his car to make the return trip to Natanz. He was in no hurry and stopped to do some shopping before leaving Tehran, picking out a new manteau for Chace, and a *maqna'e* that matched.

At eleven minutes past one in the afternoon, Shirazi walked back into the house in Natanz, and the first thing he noted was that Zahabzeh was nowhere to be seen. Javed was seated at the table, watching the monitor, and on the screen he could see Chace, lying on her back, the blanket no longer covering her. Parviz and Kamal had each taken a portion of floor as a bed, dozing with their coats bundled beneath their heads.

"Where's Farzan?" Shirazi asked.

Javed turned slightly, still keeping one eye on the monitor. "He went back to Tehran, sir, as you ordered."

The sense of triumph that Shirazi had allowed to rise within him since that morning vanished entirely. "Tell me what happened."

On the floor, Parviz stirred, lifting his head. Javed glanced away from the screen, to Shirazi, puzzled. "She awoke around six this morning. Deputy Director Zahabzeh indicated he wished to question her, he took Parviz and Kamal in with him."

Parviz was up, shaking Kamal's shoulder. "He said you had given permission."

"What did you do to her?" Shirazi demanded. "Did you drug her?"

"Another shot of ketamine," Parviz said. "She wasn't talking, and the Deputy Director was concerned, he said he would have to report to the Minister. He questioned her, wanted her to confess—"

"Did he take her things?" Shirazi demanded. "The evidence we took from the spy, did Zahabzeh take them when he left?"

Javed nodded, his confusion turning to concern. "He said he was operating on your orders, that he was to present our findings to the Minister."

Shirazi moved forward, taking a closer look at the monitor, at Chace, now stirring on the cot. She was clearly still sedated, though beginning to surface. He straightened, looked over the room, then grabbed one of the chairs at the table and set it in the center of the space.

"Bring her out, now," Shirazi ordered, and Parviz and Kamal hastily got to their feet, heading for the cell door. He hadn't wanted to do it this soon, but now Zahabzeh had forced his hand. Now he had no choice.

From where he carried it at the small of his back, Shirazi drew his pistol, and waited for Parviz and Kamal to bring Tara Chace to the execution.

CHAPTER TWENTY-SIX

IRAN—ISFAHAN PROVINCE, NATANZ
12 DECEMBER 0600 HOURS (GMT +3.30)

She was alone when she awoke, the room small, pale yellow walls lit by sunlight slanting through the narrow grate of the window high above her head. Her neck was sore and her chest ached, but it seemed to her that it was less acute than before, more diffused, a muscle pain. The taste in her mouth made her think of rotten fruit.

With great care, Chace tried to sit up, pushing away the blanket covering her, hearing the metal-frame cot creaking as she moved. Her feet were cold, bare, became colder as she set them on the concrete floor. Her boots were gone, and her top, but she was still wearing her bra and jeans. There was a mark near the inside of her elbow on her left arm, a fresh bruise spreading, and she looked around for the IV, but didn't see one. There wasn't much to see, truth to tell, aside from the cot and the blanket and herself. Only a plastic pitcher, set on the floor nearby, and a plastic cup beside it.

There was also a surveillance camera, high in the corner.

Chace reached for the pitcher, making new muscles ache. Along her back, where she'd been shot, she felt a momentary stab of pain, stopped her movement cold, checking her breathing. No change. There was something on her back, a new bandage, perhaps; she could feel it pulling on her skin when she moved. She extended a hand again for the pitcher, more carefully, discovered there was water inside. She drank, ignoring the cup, washing the paste out of her mouth. Metal rasped over metal, and she lowered the pitcher to see the door, painted the same yellow as the walls, swinging open, inward.

Three men entered, two of them younger, clean-shaven Persians, following after the first, slightly older, with a neatly trimmed beard and mustache. The two split, each taking the corners by the door, and the third closed it behind him, then turned back to stare at her. For a moment, no one said anything, Chace looking at them, they looking at her. The scent of soap reached her, slight, and she noticed their clothes were fresh.

The one with the beard, she remembered him, or thought she did, from when Falcon had died. It seemed a distant memory, hazy, weeks old, but she doubted if it had been more than a day, perhaps two since fleeing Noshahr.

"It will save us time, and you distress, if you confess now," the man with the beard said, speaking English. He spoke it with a slight British accent, as if he'd practiced the language using the BBC World Service.

"Je ne vous comprends pas," Chace told him.

"Vous me comprenez très bien." His French, like his English, was practiced, the accent almost perfect.

"Je m'appelle Pia Gadient, je suis professeur à l'université de Fribourg," Chace said earnestly, doing her best to look bewildered. *"On est où? Comment je suis arrivée là?"*

"Non. Vous vous appelez Tara Chace," the man answered. *"Vous êtes une espionne, une espionne britannique. Vous êtes un agent des Opérations Spéciales des Services Secrets, vous êtes même à la tête de cette section. Vous êtes responsable des meurtres de trois hommes: deux policiers à Chalus et Hossein Khamenei, le neveu de notre Leader Suprême, à Noshahr."*

His expression remained placid, even patient, as he let his words sink in. The two men by the door were staring at her, their expressions betraying nothing.

"Je ne comprends pas!" Chace cried, plaintive. *"Je suis Suisse, je suis le professeur Pia Gadient. Je fais de la recherche sur les poissons, j'étudie les esturgeons—"*

The man snapped something in Farsi, and the two others immediately moved towards Chace, reaching for her.

"Laissez-moi!" she shouted.

They didn't, each one taking hold of her by the arms, grasping her at the wrist and elbow, and the man gave them another order. Chace was pulled to her feet, found herself being pressed face-first against the concrete wall, her arms stretched out at her sides.

"You have been shot," she heard the man say, switching back to English.

His fingers touched her back, dug into the skin at the top edge of the bandage. She realized what he was about to do, cried out, struggling, and the men holding her arms slammed her back into the wall, harder this time. A nail scraped her skin, and she felt the adhesive pulling away, and again the pain rushed into her chest, crushing her from within, choking her.

"The bullet is still inside of you," the man told her. "The wound is still open. We can save your life, we would *like* to save your life, but you must give us something first. You must give us your confession. You must admit to the murder of Hossein Khamenei."

Chace shook her head, or tried to, but the pain in her neck made it impossible. She managed a gasp, barely able to draw the air to replace it, her vision already swirling. Panic was rising with the swelling pressure in her chest, and this was different from when she'd had to treat herself, this was worse, infinitely worse, the sadism of it making her feel powerless and weak and ashamed, and she felt that she would tell them anything if they would just make it stop.

Then the agent's voice, the one in the back of her mind, the one that always sounded, to her, like Tom Wallace, asserted itself. *They're not going to let you die,* it told her. *This is only pain. You can endure pain.*

She stopped struggling, sucking at the air instead, feeling her nostrils flaring. Her vision was swimming once more, the lights returning at the edges of her vision, white dots that danced and sparkled. The man was speaking again, but she couldn't hear him.

Then the pressure stabilized, stopped increasing, and she saw the ceiling, felt the rough blanket on the cot beneath her back. The man was shouting at her, then turning away. Movement, someone joining them, another face above hers, and she saw the needle, a proper tool, the tip of the catheter, and fingers pressing along her ribs, then the stabbing pain, making her eyes water. Air hissed out of her chest once more, and she wondered how many more times they would do this to her, how many more times before her lungs would collapse altogether.

The needle withdrew, leaving the catheter in place, and the new face moved out of her vision, and the man was looking down at her again. Something pierced her right arm, near the shoulder, spreading warm lead through her body, and she felt herself cooling, becoming heavy, knew she'd been drugged. The man spoke in Farsi, turned away, and she heard footsteps, the room emptying of everything but echoes. The door rang closed, sang to her as it locked.

Chace lay still, blinking the tears out of her eyes, feeling her breathing slow, the pain rolling through her body becoming fainter.

They would do it again, she realized languidly. They would keep doing it until she confessed, until she confessed to everything.

She didn't know how much of this she would be able to take.

Drowsy half-images and broken conversations snuck back to her, rambling through her head. Crocker and C and Caleb Lewis, arguing about what to do with her, saying they had to inform the Minister in Tehran that she had been taken. It was what was required, yes, they understood, no, no one was to leave, not yet, but it had to be done. There was no rush. She wasn't going anywhere, no one was coming for her.

The door was opening again, and she saw the same two men who had accompanied the one who'd hurt her, but this time only them, alone. Once more, they took her by the arms, brought her to her feet carefully, keeping hold of her, walking her out of the room. She shook her head, trying to clear it, felt the concrete beneath her feet turn to carpet, saw that this room, unlike the other, was not a cell, that she was in a house of some sort. The sunlight had changed, coming through windows opposite where it had before. There was a chair, and there were two more men, one of them young, like the others, but the other one middle-aged, balding, beard and mustache, glasses.

He was holding a pistol in his hand.

They put her in the chair, released her arms, and the man with the glasses spoke to her, speaking English. "Tara Chace, my name is Youness Shirazi. I am the Director of Counterintelligence for VEVAK."

Chace heard the hammer on the pistol lock back, felt the barrel against her temple, and that didn't make sense to her at all. If they needed her alive, why were they going to execute her in this chair, in this room?

Then the barrel swung away from her skull, and Chace flinched as the gun went off, two shots, two more, then three, and the men standing all around her fell, one after the other, their blood soaking quickly into the carpet. She watched as the man with the glasses, Youness Shirazi, stepped forward, moving from body to body, and at each one he fired again, another round, into the brain.

He turned to her, the pistol held at his side, speaking, and Chace stared at him dumbly, the gunshots still echoing in her head. She wondered if she was still hallucinating, hearing voices, seeing things, because she was certain she hadn't heard him correctly.

"What?" Chace asked. "What did you say?"

"I am the Director of Counterintelligence for VEVAK." The man tucked the gun away at his waist, and stepping forward, helped her to stand. He met her eyes, smiled weakly.

"I wish to defect," Youness Shirazi told her.

CHAPTER TWENTY-SEVEN

IRAN—TEHRAN, 198 FERDOWSI AVENUE, BRITISH EMBASSY
12 DECEMBER 1429 HOURS (GMT +3.30)

His head still hurt, and Caleb Lewis knew it wasn't from the knock he'd taken when they'd been ambushed. No, that had been seen to already, Barnett insisting that he and MacIntyre go to the hospital and get X-rayed as soon as Caleb had finished delivering his report the night before, as soon as he'd told his Number One that they had lost Chace.

"Go get checked out, the both of you," Barnett had said, already unlocking the coms cabinet. "I'll handle London."

"I'd rather stay here, sir," Caleb had said.

Barnett had just given him a look, paternal and stern and sad, then gone back to activating the deck, switching on the phone.

Some three hours later, Caleb returned to the office alone, he and MacIntyre having parted company after each receiving their clean bills of health. The coms cabinet was locked and cold, all the office lights off but for the one by Barnett's desk. Barnett himself sat chain-smoking in the near-dark, listening to the State-run radio playing softly on the shelf behind him.

Caleb stood in the center of the tiny office, feeling overheated in his winter coat, at first confused, and then, ultimately, defeated.

"No orders?" he asked.

Barnett's answer was in two forms. The first was to lean out and take one of the mugs from the tea tray, and then to fill it with whiskey from the bottle Barnett kept in his desk. He offered it to Caleb, waited until he took it.

"From D-Ops, to Tehran Station," Barnett said. " 'Action as normal.' "

Caleb smelled the vapor rising from the mug, stared into the alcohol. "Have they announced it?"

"Not yet."

"I had her." He looked from the mug to Barnett. "I had her, I had my arms around her, she was in the car, next to me. And then there they were, and they just . . . I just let them take her."

Barnett crushed out his cigarette, then took a mug for himself, fixed a drink of his own. "You didn't let them do anything, lad."

"I didn't do anything at all."

"You weren't supposed to. They made it so you couldn't."

"I know. I know. I do. They'd have shot us, I recognize that."

"Then don't go beating yourself up over it."

Caleb shook his head, set down his drink long enough to get out of his coat. His arm caught in the sleeve, and he pulled at it, then again, until finally, furious with it, he yanked it free, swearing. He sat at his desk, took the mug in his hands.

Barnett lit another cigarette, blew smoke, watching him. The radio murmured notes, soft music, designed to soothe any rebellious tendencies. "You're angry."

"I am." Caleb said it quickly, glared at Barnett, challenging him to argue, to invalidate what he was feeling.

Barnett sipped at his mug, took another drag from his smoke. "I am, too."

"But I wasn't before."

"What were you, then?"

"I was scared. I was fucking terrified. The whole time I've been here, I've been terrified, just . . . always afraid."

Barnett started to respond, then stopped as a voice came over the radio, marking the hour, giving the news. They both listened. Hossein's death led, followed by word of the search for his killer-slash-killers. Then they heard about tomorrow's weather.

"That's normal, lad," Barnett said.

"Was it?" Caleb asked him. "Then what is it now? I sat, some doctor shining a light in my eyes, and all I could think was how angry I was. How I'd go out and shoot Shirazi now if I could do it. She was supposed to be safe, Lee, I told her she was safe."

Barnett drained his mug, set it down on the desk.

"I told her she was safe."

"No one is ever safe, Caleb," Lee Barnett said. "Especially not in Iran."

He turned the radio on as soon as he returned to his apartment, kept it on while he showered and shaved, listening to it as he stared at himself in the bathroom mirror and peeled the bandage from his forehead. The collision had thrown him against the side of the Benz, bounced his head against the window frame, and now uncovered, he could see the bruise, yellow and green, the skin angry, shining, where it had torn.

Before climbing into bed, Caleb made his checks of the apartment, doing everything they had taught him to do at the School, and more. VEVAK had identified him now, and it was certain he would be at the head of their surveillance list, that he had graduated to being a priority target. They would try to bug the apartment, monitor his movements, document everything he did, everywhere he went, everyone he talked to. He knew it, and that drove his search, and the fact that he found nothing out of place, nothing altered, no signs of tampering or invasion or search was infuriating, and only stoked the anger he was feeling.

He brought the anger with him to bed, still listening to the radio, and it kept him awake in the dark for over an hour longer, despite his enormous fatigue. He heard the news five more times, and not once was Tara Chace mentioned. No word of an arrest.

That would change come the morning, Caleb was sure.

On his way to the embassy the next morning, Caleb stopped for his usual cup of coffee at the café near the Tehran Bazaar, then stepped next door to pick up copies of the day's newspapers. It was nearly noon, and the streets were busy, despite a new, cold rain that had begun falling sometime after he'd finally managed to go to sleep. He bought copies of the *Iran Daily,* as well as the hard-line *Kayhan International,* and the government mouthpiece *Tehran Times*. Then, instead of turning north, towards the embassy, he continued heading west, to the Park-e Shahr.

There were no signals marked at the entrance, and Caleb continued on, walking steadily, the bundle of papers tucked under his arm. It was too cold and too wet for a lunchtime in the park, and there were very few people around. He made his circuit, trying new turns, and it was on his way out of the park again that it struck him as odd, very odd, that he had seen nothing at all to indicate he was being followed. While he didn't hold great faith in his own skills as an agent, he was certain that he wasn't that incompetent, that useless.

Either whoever Shirazi had put on him was very, very good, or there was no one on him at all.

Of the two possible conclusions, only the first made sense. What had they called it at the School, the system the CIA claimed they had created? The Moscow Rules? Number One, Assume Nothing; but it was Number Four that Caleb kept thinking of as he started towards the embassy: Don't Look Back, You Are Never Completely Alone.

Fair enough, then, but shouldn't he have seen *something* by now?

MacIntyre was on duty at the door into the Security wing when Caleb arrived, greeted him with a noncommittal, "Good afternoon, sir." Caleb asked how he was feeling.

"Sore," MacIntyre replied, and Caleb didn't think the man meant physically.

In the office, Barnett was at paperwork, the coms cabinet closed.

Caleb greeted him, dropped the newspapers on his desk, took his seat.

"Anything?"

"Nothing," Barnett said. "Not a crumb."

"I'd have thought they'd have said something by now. Made some announcement."

"As would I. Given the state she was in, I can't imagine she'd be able to hold out for long."

Caleb looked at him, Barnett head-down to his work. It wasn't something he had wanted to think about, what VEVAK might do to Chace to get her to talk, and he felt a jagged, sudden anger at his Number One for making such a mention so casually. Misplaced anger, he admitted, turning his attention to the papers. He gave them the better part of an hour, reading each one carefully, and there were the expected stories about Hossein's murder and the ongoing search for his killer, including a long quote from the Supreme Leader himself about the outrage, the injustice, of the crime. But nothing else, nothing substantive, and even the details in the *Tehran Times,* which by all logic should have had the most accurate information, were vague.

He closed the papers, slid them off his desk and into his trashcan. His head hurt, the same headache that had nagged him since the crash, and Caleb put his face in his hands, closed his eyes, gingerly rubbed at his bruised temple with a fingertip.

Maybe, just maybe, he was right, Caleb thought. Maybe the reason that he had seen no signs that he was under surveillance was because there were no signs to be found. But why? Why would Youness Shirazi, having positively identified him as SIS in Iran, leave him room to run? Was he baiting another trap, the way Caleb now understood he had done with Falcon? To what end?

It made no sense, none at all, unless Shirazi *wanted* SIS to have room to run.

Caleb lowered his hands, opened his eyes, entirely uncomfortable with his conclusion. "Sir?"

"Caleb?" Barnett answered.

"What if Falcon never intended to defect?"

"Think that's given, at this point."

"No, that's not what I mean. If he was the *wrong* defector. If Falcon was just bait, to get us to put everything right, to put the operation in motion."

"You mean Minder One was meant to take someone else at the last minute? London would've told us, even if not in the first instance, once it all went tits, they'd have said."

"I don't think they knew," Caleb said. "I think it was Shirazi."

Barnett's cigarette, stuck in the corner of his mouth, jerked towards the ceiling as the man grinned. "You think Youness Shirazi set Falcon up to run, planning to take his place at the last minute?"

"Yes."

The grin got bigger, became a laugh.

"I think that knock to your head did more hurt than we thought," Barnett told him.

Caleb frowned, embarrassed, then nodded. *That must be it,* he thought, *I'm just not thinking straight.* Then the telephone by his elbow rang, jarring him, and Caleb fumbled the handset to his ear. The embassy switchboard, there was a call for him, asking for him by name.

"This is Lewis," he said.

"Caleb," Tara Chace said. *"I need you to get a message to London."*

CHAPTER TWENTY-EIGHT

LONDON—HYDE PARK, LOVERS WALK, PARK LANE ENTRANCE
12 DECEMBER 1111 HOURS (GMT)

Crocker found Seale waiting in the usual place, by the statue of Achilles that had been cast from captured cannons won by Wellington from the French. The day was dreary, cold and damp, not quite committed to rain, and the CIA Station Chief stood in his overcoat and gloves, a watch cap on his head. He tracked Crocker's approach, moving to meet him, and together the two men began walking deeper into the park.

They stayed in silence, each of them paying careful attention to their surroundings, more out of habit than necessity. Once upon a time, a walk in the park had been a very safe way to share information, and then had come the age of laser directional ears and parabolic microphones and Internet firewalls and secure phone lines, and it was thought that such rendezvous were passé. But, as with so many things, the wheel had turned, and face-to-face meetings had come, once again, to be recognized for their value. Information shared in person between two men, after all, could not be intercepted, even if there was a risk it would be overheard.

"No news?" Seale asked after a minute.

"Nothing." It was a question asked out of politeness, rather than curiosity, Crocker thought. Seale damn well knew that there'd been nothing out of Tehran since the previous evening.

"You guys formulated your response yet?"

Crocker shook his head. "C's still at Downing Street. According to Rayburn, there's an argument in the Cabinet as to what the response should be."

"I'd think a flat denial."

"The problem with that is there's no way to know what Chace has given them. If they have a confession, and they air it after the Government issues a denial, it'll make us look even worse."

Seale grunted in agreement, fell silent, and they continued walking, listening to nothing but the traffic running past in the distance, the crunch of their shoes on the gravel. After another minute, Crocker realized that Seale wasn't going to ask, and so he reached into his overcoat and withdrew a sheaf of papers, clipped at the corner and folded lengthwise, and handed them over without a word. They walked for almost another fifty yards as Seale went through them, sheet by sheet, then again, before slowing to stop. Crocker continued another couple feet, steeling himself, then turned back to face him. Seale looked genuinely stunned.

"Tell me this is wrong."

"I can't," Crocker said.

"Jesus Christ, Paul, this *has* to be wrong!"

"It's not."

"This is everything she had access to?"

Crocker shook his head. "That's the preliminary list. D-Int is still compiling a master document, but I wanted to get that into your hands as soon as possible. She had nine years as a Minder, five as Head of Section. There's no telling how much operational data she's retained."

"Jesus Christ," Seale repeated.

Crocker said nothing. That Chace would be interrogated, was being interrogated even as they spoke, was assumed, just as it was assumed that, eventually, she'd break. It wasn't held as a reflection of the woman she was, or the spy, and it wasn't viewed as a failing; it was simply true. Everyone, eventually, broke, and she would, too. When that happened, she'd begin talking, and when *that* happened, there was every reason to believe she wouldn't stop until there was nothing left. She would give them everything she had, or, more correctly, they would take everything she had.

Which meant that steps needed to be made now to protect what could be lost. Hence the list, a frighteningly long list of names and operations and networks and contacts and protocols and secrets, so many secrets, most of them belonging to SIS, but not all. Some of them were marked "US-UK EYES ONLY," information shared with or learned from the CIA. That was what Seale held now, the itemization of how Tara Chace could hurt them.

She could hurt them quite badly.

"You showed this to C?" Seale asked, after a second. "She knows?"

"It was on her desk this morning, before she returned to Downing Street."

Seale looked at the papers in his hand, then offered them back to Crocker. "I haven't seen this."

"Julian, you can't do that."

"Paul, if I report this to Langley, there'll be hell to pay. And if I have to bring them a second list, of the things you guys might've missed in the first one, it'll only make matters worse. Take it back, sit on it for twenty-four hours, at least. Give me the master document. If you're going to cut the throat of the Special Relationship, at least do it in one slice."

"Twenty-four hours." Crocker scowled, then reached out and took the papers, adding, "It won't help."

"Maybe, but it won't hurt, not at this point."

There was more to it, Crocker knew, but Seale had the good grace, unlike C, not to say it. If Chace died, she wouldn't be able to tell the Iranians anything, after all.

"You had lunch?" Seale asked. "Let the Company buy you lunch."

"I should get back to the office. I appreciate the offer, however."

"You know where I am."

"If we hear anything, I'll let you know."

"Do something about that list, Paul. You're going to kill us with that list."

Seale turned away, heading northeast, towards Grosvenor Square.

It started to rain.

"Where the hell have you been?" Kate demanded when Crocker stepped into the outer office. He was wet and cold and depressed, and from her words, he immediately assumed the worst, that the news about Chace had broken while he'd been talking with Seale.

Then Kate shoved a signal into his hand, from Tehran Station, flash precedence, immediate for D-Ops.

STATION NUMBER TWO REPORTS CONTACT WITH MINDER ONE VIA TELEPHONE AT 1449 LOCAL, DURATION OF CALL 87 SECONDS . . .

Crocker read the rest of the signal in a rush, then almost threw the paper back at her, sprinting into his office, for the red phone, shouting, "Find C! Get D-Int and DC, tell them I need them to meet me in her office."

"She's still at Downing Street!"

"Then tell DC to get her out of the meeting, we need her here." He stabbed at his phone, wedging the handset between his neck and shoulder as he tried to remove his sodden overcoat.

"Duty Ops Officer."

"D-Ops, for MCO, get me the Tehran Number Two, secure voice, immediately. I'm coming down."

Crocker used a finger to kill the connection, jabbed another key, transferring the phone to his opposite shoulder, letting the coat dump onto his chair, where it then slid to the floor. He kicked it out of his way, looked up as Kate stuck her head into the office.

"DC needs a reason to pull C from the Cabinet meeting. What can I tell him?"

"The first part, that Minder One's in the open again."

"That should do it."

"I'd fucking well hope so."

"Minder Two," Poole said in his ear.

"Ops Room, I'll explain when I get there," Crocker said, then hung up and rounded his desk, heading for the door. He stopped at Kate's desk long enough to point back to his overcoat, lying on the floor. "The list for Seale is still in my pocket."

"What should I do with it?"

"Destroy it," Crocker said, and then he was out of the office, racing down the halls, making for the Ops Room. Hoping that he hadn't been premature; praying that he wouldn't need a new copy of the list to hand to Seale anyway.

"I need a name and an operation," Crocker shouted, as soon as he hit the Ops Room floor, on a straight line for the MCO Desk. Poole had just beat him in, was at Duty Ops with Arthur Grey, and grabbed the clipboard before Grey himself could.

"Name: Cougar," Poole called back. "Operation: Icecrown."

"It's a Special Op, put it up on the board, Minder Two allocated, and bring in a control." Crocker reached the MCO Desk, took the headset Lex was offering him, closed his fist around the mike. "And find out the status on Bagboy, if Lankford is free to move."

"Yes, sir," Grey said.

Crocker pulled on the headset, his eyes checking the clocks on the wall. "Caleb, D-Ops. Confirm, please, time elapsed since contact, sixty-seven minutes."

There was a pause, the static chatter of the scrambler filling the void, before Caleb Lewis answered, *"I have sixty-seven minutes, yes, sir."*

"Her location was south of Natanz at that time." Crocker snapped his fingers, pointing at the map, and someone knew what he meant, because almost immediately a callout appeared on the Iran map, marking Natanz, some one hundred and twenty miles southeast of Tehran. "Heading which direction, did she say?"

"No, she didn't, sir."

"We are designating her package as Cougar, do you understand?"

"Cougar, yes, sir."

"Do the locals know that Cougar has gone walkabout?"

"Think so, yes, sir."

"Explain."

"Station Number One has been making inquiries, sir, he's out of the office at the moment, still pursuing, but he called in twenty minutes ago to say that there's been a hell of a lot of Sepah activity

around the MOIS. Mission Security is reporting active surveillance of the embassy, as well."

Crocker swore. He'd hoped for more of a lead, but if the embassy was being watched, then there was no question that VEVAK knew what was up. If the pursuit of Chace prior to her capture had been intense in the face of Hossein Khamenei's death, the effort to keep her leaving the country with the now-former Chief of Counter-intelligence would be monstrous. In the first, it had been an issue of political value; this time, the value was far more concrete, a target with direct strategic and tactical knowledge that the Iranians could, under no account, allow to escape.

For a moment, Crocker wondered who would have to prepare the list of operations compromised by the defection of Youness Shirazi. He shut down the thought as grossly premature.

"Sir?"

"Just thinking, Caleb. There was nothing in your signal about her health."

"She said, and I quote, 'no exfil by air.'"

"And Cougar didn't have an exfil plan of his own?"

"My impression was that he had been relying on us to provide one, that he had believed the Caspian route was still viable."

"It isn't," Crocker said.

"No, sir, Minder One had already determined that. She didn't say which way they were headed. I think she was concerned the call might be intercepted."

"It probably was. All right, inform immediately if anything else develops. We'll be in touch."

"Yes, sir."

Crocker pulled the headset free, tossed it back to Lex, staring up at the board. Poole came in at his shoulder, mimicking his pose, both of them staring at Iran.

"So who's Cougar when he's at home?" Poole asked.

"Right now?" Crocker said. "He's the man who's saved Chace's life."

Gordon-Palmer, Rayburn, and Szurko were all in their regular seats in the sitting area of C's office, and each of them stared at Crocker as if he had dropped, naked, from the womb, in front of them.

Then Szurko began to laugh, a hearty, gleeful roar that had the merciful effect of pulling both C's and the DC's attention from Crocker to D-Int for the moment. "Oh, that's brilliant," Szurko managed. "That's just—that's bloody brilliant, that's what it is."

C glared at him for a second longer, then pulled her attention away, placing it on Crocker. "Clearly Daniel sees something I don't."

"It worked, though," Szurko said, trying to control himself. "The problem was she was *too* good, don't you see? If she'd been worse, if she'd been slower or stupider, if she hadn't realized Falcon was wrong, it'd have come off perfectly!"

"I still don't—"

Crocker opened his mouth, but Szurko beat him to it, leaning forward on the couch, holding out his hands, index fingers pointing at C as a visual aid. He wiggled the left one, said, "Falcon," then the right, "Shirazi," and then crossed their positions, saying, "Just say Shirazi everywhere you would say Falcon, makes perfect sense."

"We thought we were lifting Hossein Khamenei," Rayburn said. "When in reality we were lifting Youness Shirazi."

"That must have been his initial plan," Crocker said. "It went wrong in Noshahr, when the shooting started. My suspicion is that Shirazi had intended for Chace to be captured unharmed, at which point he would have freed her and taken Falcon's place in the RHIB for the rendezvous."

"But it went wrong," C insisted.

"Bullets," Szurko supplied, unhelpfully.

"Chace was shot, and she did what she was trained to do," Crocker said. "She ran, and she ran exceptionally well, well enough that Shirazi had to hit the embassy car. Even if he had only been considering defection before that point, as soon as Hossein died, he had to know it was all or nothing, that he wouldn't be able to stay."

"Did Chace actually kill Falcon?" C asked.

"I doubt it, but we've no way to be certain," Crocker told her. "I suspect it was accidental. It certainly would have been the last thing Shirazi would have wanted, because it would have drawn attention to the operation. Again, if everything had gone to plan, he'd have been on board a Coast Guard ship before his own people even began to suspect he'd left the country. He could've been at the Farm, being debriefed, before they'd been able to confirm it."

"Clever for another reason." Szurko was smiling, eyes closed, as if admiring the plan in his mind's eye the way a jeweler examined a particularly well-cut diamond. "Dangling Falcon guaranteed CIA support, it guaranteed that we would send our best possible agent to execute the lift, it guaranteed that we would give that agent the best possible cover and exfil possible, and that we would do everything within our power to support the operation should something go wrong. Which we did."

The room went silent again, broken only by another giggle from Szurko, who then opened his eyes, and seemed surprised to find he wasn't alone. C sank back in her chair, clearly sorting her thoughts, and Rayburn likewise was lost in his own, the tip of his tongue just visible between his lips.

"I have to ask this," C said, finally. "Is it possible this is just another dangle, a means of getting us to further expose ourselves in Iran?"

"No," Crocker said, firmly. "Tehran Station confirms that VEVAK has pulled out the stops, they've actually put surveillance on the embassy itself at this point. I'm certain the next report we get from Barnett or Lewis will tell us that the Republican Guards are out in force, and that there's a nationwide manhunt under way. Pursuing Chace was one thing—if she got away, they materially lost nothing, because all she was to them was a gain. But losing Shirazi, that would be devastating. They will do everything they can to prevent that. They'll mobilize every asset, they'll put up jets, they'll roll tanks if they need to. They absolutely cannot allow him to leave the country alive."

"And by that same logic, there's no going back for Shirazi? He won't turn around and betray Chace?"

"It would be suicide."

She nodded. "Then the real question is this: can we get them out of the country?"

Crocker tried very hard not to smile.

"With your permission, ma'am, I think I can manage it."

CHAPTER TWENTY-NINE

IRAN—YAZD PROVINCE, 34 KM WSW OF TAFT

13 DECEMBER 2109 HOURS (GMT +3.30)

They had been driving ever since leaving Natanz, even when Chace had used one of the three cell phones Shirazi had taken from the dead men to call the embassy, to make contact with Caleb Lewis. She was wearing a new manteau, this one black, and a new scarf to hide her hair, also black, both provided by Shirazi.

They had taken the dead men's weapons and their ammunition, and all of the bottles of water in the refrigerator, four of them, and some of the food, mostly dried fruit, but some bread, and a wedge of very pleasantly sour cheese. Then, just before they stepped out of the house, Shirazi remembered the surveillance monitor, and stepped back inside long enough to put two bullets into the hard drive that had recorded the video of Chace in the cell.

Then they were in the car, Shirazi climbing behind the wheel of his own Mercedes-Benz, a new E-Class model this time, as far removed from the embassy car Chace had been pulled from as was possible. It was only then, when they were pulling out, that he did anything that might've betrayed his own excitement and fear, accelerating so sharply that the wheels cried, spinning uselessly before catching pavement. Then they were speeding along the road.

"Not that I don't appreciate everything you've done," Chace said, "but where are we going?"

"North, again," he told her. "The Caspian."

"You've got a boat?"

"No, we'll use your route."

"My route's fucked in the ear, mate," Chace said. "There is no route."

He'd slammed the brakes, bringing them to a halt as quickly as they had pulled out. "You had a fallback?"

"Tabriz, and it wasn't prepared," she said. "We're not getting out to the north."

"Your people must have another route." Shirazi looked at her, incredulous. "There must be another route!"

"My people have written me off. Because *your* people shot me, then arrested me."

Shirazi swore in Farsi, the car idling on the side of the road, and Chace realized he didn't know what to do.

"Turn around," she told him. "Take us south, just keep us moving south."

"There is nothing to the south," Shirazi said, but he put the car back in gear, spun them around. "Only the ocean is south."

"Can you swim?" she asked.

He glanced at her sharply, saw that she was smiling, and then burst out laughing.

"I was right about you," Shirazi told her. "You were the one I wanted all along."

After the first call to Caleb, she'd turned off the phone and then rolled down the window, flinging it out of the car. It was useless now, compromised, and as all of the phones were the same model, identical in all respects, she didn't want to confuse herself and use it again by accident. She let the window remain open for a few minutes after that, breathing the cold air, feeling the steady throb of her chest with each inhale, each exhale, but there'd been no real difficulty in breathing, certainly nothing like what she'd experienced previously. Then she'd rolled the window back up, readjusted the scarf around her hair.

"How long until they know what you've done?" Chace asked him.

"They may know already," Shirazi said. "My deputy, Zahabzeh, he went back to Tehran early this morning, against my orders, and with your things. I am sure he told our Minister that you were in custody."

"Tall guy? Beard and mustache? Youngish?"

"Thirty, and yes, beard and mustache and tall."

"He questioned me."

Shirazi glanced at her, hearing something in the tone, then back to the road. "My apologies."

"Yes," Chace said. "He was rather insistent."

"You are all right?"

"I'm bloody aces right now, my friend. I've got a bullet lodged somewhere in my chest, an occlusion bandage covering a hole in my back, and a one-way valve sticking out above my left tit. What could be better?"

"I can think of three things, immediately."

Despite herself, Chace laughed, then wished she hadn't. Laughing made the pain in her chest worse.

"Zahabzeh," Shirazi said. "He is a hard-liner, you would say. Always suspicious, always . . . self-serving."

"You think he suspected what you were doing?"

"He knew something was not right. We had opportunities to take you before Noshahr, and I told him no, and that certainly made him suspicious. It was only Hossein's death that kept him beside me for so long, his fear that he would be held responsible for it. Now, of course, I have freed him from that, because he will blame me."

"He smart?"

"Smart enough."

"Does he know you well? Well enough to guess what you're thinking?"

"No. He doesn't know me at all."

Now it was his tone that caught, made Chace look at him again, more closely. "How long have you been planning this?"

"For years, Miss Chace."

"You can call me Tara."

"Then you must call me Youness."

"Years?"

"Ten years now, I should think. Once the reforms began rolling back. But it was only in my mind to do it, an idea, not a plan, then. After the Green Revolution, that was what made me realize it was time to act. The election, you know, was a complete fraud. I am still somewhat surprised that anyone thought it would be otherwise. We are a police state, Miss Chace, not an Islamic Republic. There is no rule of law, only a rule of power."

"I'm not sure I understand."

"Ah, well, I am not sure I am explaining myself very well." His shoulders lifted, dropped again in an exaggerated shrug. "It is the difference between the reality and the promise. The promise brought people into the streets, particularly our women, you see, because they believed what they had been told. But the reality brought the Basij into the streets, with their sticks and their batons, with the Republican Guards holding their leash, and the two could not coexist. They cannot coexist. Until the promise is realized, I cannot, before God, serve the reality."

Chace nodded, not speaking. They were racing along the road, and if it had been any other country, she would have suggested Shirazi slow down, to try and not draw attention to the vehicle. But it was his country, and he knew it, and if nothing else, she couldn't argue with wanting to put as much distance between themselves and Natanz as possible. The landscape was radically different from what she had seen in the north, along the Alborz, much more like the deserts of the American Southwest, bare and hard, bathed in gold by the setting sun.

"Do you believe in God?" Shirazi asked her.

Chace thought of Tamsin. Then she thought of Tom Wallace, and the way he had died in Saudi Arabia.

"I want to," she answered.

Chace called the embassy again just past five-thirty in the evening, thinking that enough time had surely passed by now for Caleb to have relayed her initial message to London, and for London to have responded, to have prepared an exfil plan for her and Shirazi. She debated with herself before making the call, however, worried about the exposure, afraid that she was being too hasty. If Shirazi was correct, the search for them was certainly on by now, and there was a good chance that any conversation would be overheard. Having to call a third time would only create greater risk.

She dialed the number from memory, asking again for Caleb Lewis, and the call went through much more quickly than it had the first time, which she took as a good sign. That Lewis answered before the phone had finished its first ring she took as even better.

"It's me," Chace said.

"Your father called," Caleb Lewis said. *"He has the following message for you: delighted you have acquired rare cougar. Stand by to record the following."*

Chace swore silently, with her free hand began searching around her in the car, yanking open the glove box, then the compartment in the armrest beside her. Shirazi shot a worried glance her way, and she saw that he had a pen clipped to his breast pocket, reached out and plucked it free, clicking its end. She bared her arm, wedging the phone.

"Proceed."

"First sequence, F-T-R-E-A-F-L-T. Second sequence, E-Y-E-I-E-Y-R-A. Third sequence, R-R-E-L tomorrow. Confirm."

"Confirmed."

"Dad says you know it like you know yourself."

She grinned. "Understood."

The line went dead, and Chace switched off the phone, lowered the window, and winged the mobile out of the car. She closed the window again, examined her arm, began decoding the message with the pen, still writing on her skin. It was dark enough in the car now that halfway through the process she was forced to turn on the interior light, but once she did, the work was completed quickly enough.

Chace stared at what she'd written on her arm, then clicked the light off again, offering the pen back to Shirazi, who shook his head, vaguely amused by the gesture.

"They have a plan?"

"Yes," Chace said. "Exfil location and a time. Do we have GPS?"

"I had hoped to use yours, but Zahabzeh took it."

"The car doesn't have one, the sat nav?"

"See for yourself."

Chace leaned forward, grimacing as she did so, fiddling with the control dial for the display on the center of the dashboard. She brought up the map screen, and instead of seeing a display of Iran, instead found a message in Farsi.

"Translation?"

" 'That feature has been disabled in this vehicle,' " Shirazi told her. "But we're near Yazd, and I was thinking it was time we switched vehicles there. We should be able to find an Internet café, or, at the least, a store with a map. The coordinates, what are they?"

"To the west of here, near the border with Iraq, I think." Chace read the numbers off her arm in the weak light. "Know where that is?"

"Not precisely. You are correct, though, it would be near the border. They'll take us overland?"

"Possibly."

"That does not give me comfort. The border is well guarded since the war, will be even more so with Zahabzeh looking for us."

"I can call them back if you like," Chace said. "Tell them it's not going to work for us."

Shirazi's laugh, this time, was more forced. "No, no. That would be even less wise."

They dumped the car outside of Yazd fifty-six minutes later, Chace standing watch while Shirazi removed the plates, locking them away in the trunk. He had a satchel, a shoulder bag, and he put the water and food and two of the pistols inside of it, he and Chace each carrying another, concealed. When she saw the bag, Chace had a good idea what it carried, and a glimpse inside while Shirazi was loading it confirmed it; it was his go-bag, stacks of rials and American dollars, some clothes, and several reams of paper. A rainbow flash of light caught her eye, the refraction from a CD.

"What's on the disk?" she asked.

"Disks," Shirazi said, zipping the satchel closed and slinging it over his shoulder. "And every personnel file I could lay my hands on. This way. Keep your eyes down, try to conceal your face, and do not speak. I will do the talking."

Chace lowered her eyes as much as she dared, Shirazi taking her by the elbow, and together they walked along the streets of Yazd, bustling with dinner-hour traffic. The further south in Iran one went, the more conservative the country became, and here, wherever she looked, Chace saw women wearing the chador, hiding everything but their eyes, and even with her manteau and *maqna'e,* she felt underdressed and exposed. Shirazi set a brisk pace and, shuffling to keep up, despite her long legs, Chace felt a burn in her chest, joining the ever-present background ache.

There were soldiers at the corner ahead of them, nearly a dozen that she could see, milling around a vehicle, and Shirazi turned them left, heading east along a narrow street, past ancient mud-brick buildings. The lane twisted, wandering, and she was having trouble catching her breath now, was about to tell Shirazi they had to stop, to slow down at the least, when they emerged suddenly into a newer part of the desert city, hearing music, bright lights shining from windows opposite them. Shirazi halted.

"This will do." He pointed, and she followed the line from his hand, almost laughed when she read the sign painted over the door of the building opposite them. Farsi and English, and the English told her it was an Internet café, THE FRIENDLY CAFÉ, and the irony was practically absurd. Shirazi glanced about the street, then looked at her. "You must wait outside, here. Stay in the shadows."

She nodded, stepped back into the alley from which they'd emerged. Shirazi darted across the street, then slowed, entering the building. She saw him through the window, raising a hand to someone out of sight, and then he crossed the room, disappeared behind the line of heads and monitors. Chace put a hand to her chest, the burning sensation gone, her breathing still pained, but regular. She could feel the butt of the pistol tucked at her waist, digging into her skin. She checked her watch, saw that it was almost seven in the evening, three-thirty or so back in London. Tamsin would be finished with school, would be coming home with Missi, assuming that Tamsin had gone to school at all that day.

Shirazi emerged from the café seven minutes later, turning left as he exited, heading for the corner, and Chace stepped out of her shadows, paralleling him from her side of the street. A police car rolled past, part of the traffic, and she kept her head down, and then Shirazi was crossing to meet her, taking her again by the elbow.

"We have a long way to go before tomorrow night," he told her. "It is near the border, only forty, fifty kilometers from it, in Abadan, a point on the river. I printed the map."

He reached into a pocket, pushed a folded sheet of printer paper into her hand, and Chace tucked it beneath her manteau without opening it. "How far?"

"Seven hundred, perhaps seven hundred and fifty kilometers. It is not as bad as it seems, most of it is across desert, unpopulated areas. If we are discreet, we could make it without being detected."

"We need a car."

"Yes." Shirazi pulled back on her elbow, bringing her to a halt once more. She risked a glance up, saw that they were now just outside the glare of a brightly lit marquee of a movie theater. He pointed at the parking lot, just beyond the edge of the lights. "Do you see one you like?"

Chace looked at the cars, trying to remember how many vehicles she'd stolen already since coming to Iran. She couldn't, and realized with morbid humor that she had truly lost count.

"I like the Renault," she told him.

The Renault, it turned out, was both a good and a bad idea. A good idea because they had no trouble breaking into it, nor in getting it started; bad because, almost as soon as they were out of Yazd, heading southwest along the highway and into the frigid desert night, one of the warning lights on the dashboard came on, telling them that the car needed gas, and would need it soon. Considering how fortunate she'd been with cars thus far, Chace could hardly hold it against the vehicle.

Some twenty kilometers along the road southwest, nestled in a valley, was Taft, and just outside of town Shirazi pulled to the side of the road.

"There should be a service station still open," he told Chace. "It may be watched. Get in the back, pretend to sleep."

She considered the logic, nodded, and changed her position in the car accordingly. Shirazi set them off again, and Chace propped herself gingerly on her right side, face towards the back of the rear seats, feeling the Renault's motion as they descended further, then leveled out. The car slowed, turned, came to a stop, and diffuse light filtered in around her. Shirazi opened the door, and she heard an exchange in Farsi, stayed still, listening hard for anything that might be an indication of trouble. Then the Renault rocked again, and Shirazi was back behind the wheel, and they were leaving the lights behind.

"No trouble?" she asked, turning and sitting up.

She caught his smile in the rearview mirror, thin and uneasy. "No trouble, no."

Chace reached forward, thinking to pull herself back into the front seat, then thought the better of it as her chest and back sent out separate flares of warning. She winced, wondering what was happening inside of her. She was aware that her breathing had once again become incrementally more shallow, wondered if the dressing on her back had slipped, or if this was some further complication.

"We're going to need to stop," she said, finally. "We need to check the dressing on my back, maybe change it."

Now there was no smile in the reflection off the rearview, just concern, and Chace was heartened by its apparent sincerity. Whether or not he actually gave a damn about her as anything more than a means to an end, she didn't know, and it didn't matter; he needed her as much as she needed him, and both of them, she knew, had already realized they would succeed or fail together.

"I left the kit in Natanz," Shirazi said, after a second. He sounded bitter, disappointed in himself.

"We can make do," Chace told him. "Gauze and Vaseline."

"Vaseline?"

"Petroleum jelly."

"Ah, yes, I understand."

Chace drew another breath, this time aware that it was half what it should've been. The back of her mind began to crawl frantic, warning of the need for air.

"We'll need to do it soon," she said.

They climbed out of the valley, back into the desert, and another thirty kilometers or so out of Taft turned into another service area, this one brightly lit in the night, much larger than the one they'd stopped at before. Shirazi parked them away from the pumps, in the shadows near a large building that looked like it had begun its life in the United States, during the fifties, perhaps as part of a drive-in movie theater. The architecture was so absurd that Chace had to keep from laughing at the sight of it, the series of retro-space-age arches that bent over the structure.

"What is that?"

"The Shah," Shirazi said, as if that was all the explanation required. "I will see what they have inside. I should not be long."

He climbed out of the car, and Chace took the opportunity for a last look around the station, seeing it empty, before lying down again as she had in Taft, affecting sleep.

She'd had her head down for long enough to wonder where he was, when she heard the sound of another vehicle entering the lot, the vibration from the engine strong, a diesel, perhaps. Doors slammed, and now there were voices, and Chace moved her hand to the gun at her waist, freeing it so it lay between her and the seat. Light shone in from above, began sweeping the car, and her already diminished breathing grew shorter, and she waited for the beam to hit her.

There was another voice, a shout, and the light cut quickly away. The voices moved rapidly off, and she pushed herself up, peeking through the window, saw that the vehicle looked identical to an old

American Army jeep, hardtop, so much so that she wondered if it wasn't one, or a very precise knockoff. She counted four soldiers, rifles raised and set at their shoulders, and all of them were pointing their weapons at Shirazi, who was standing in a puddle of light from the building, hands raised. In one of them, she saw he held a small, white paper bag.

As she watched, one of the soldiers lowered his weapon, reaching forward, towards Shirazi. Another began reaching for his radio, and Chace knew she couldn't allow that; if the call went out, any call at all, that would be it; even should they escape it wouldn't matter, because more would come, soldiers in trucks and helicopters and tanks if need be, and there was no way they would ever outrun or evade them.

She brought her pistol up in both hands, aimed and fired all together through the window, trying to get up on one knee in the back of the car. The shots were devastatingly loud in the enclosed space, and she didn't hear the window as it shattered, firing twice more, and the third shot caught the soldier with the radio in the neck, made him jerk and drop. She shifted her aim, firing again and again, managed to catch another of them, but all had begun to react, and the returning fire in her direction clattered against the car, broke glass and tore through metal. She tried scrabbling back, screamed as something ripped at her right shoulder. Her arm gave out, and she pitched to the side, off the seat, onto the floor of the car.

There was another cascade of shots, automatic-weapons fire, and then, as abruptly as it had begun, it ended. Chace tried to push herself off the floor, found her right arm useless to the task. She fell back, chest heaving for air, and then the rear door was being torn open, and she saw Shirazi, pistol in one hand, the silly paper bag in his other. He swore in Farsi, reached into the car, not for her but for his go-bag, slinging it quickly, then a second time, now pulling her free, hands under each arm, and Chace screamed again when he did it, despite not wanting to, despite not wanting to waste the air.

"Can you walk?" Shirazi demanded. "Can you walk, Tara?"

She nodded.

"Quickly, this way." He slung an arm beneath hers, supporting her, and she bit back on another cry, managed to turn it into a whimper. Her right arm, she saw, was soaked with blood and dangling uselessly. Some distant voice, objective and all-seeing within, wondered idly if it would have to come off. She hoped not; she wasn't certain how she'd hug Tamsin with only one arm.

He got her to the jeep, dumping her into the passenger seat, then hurried around to the other side, climbing behind the wheel. Chace croaked at him, trying to reach for the top of the manteau with her left, clawing at it. The engine kicked alive, and then they were racing out of the station's lot, into the darkness, just darkness all around, until Shirazi realized and switched the headlights on.

"They didn't call it in," he told her. "You were just in time, they never had a chance to report it, but the station will. We have to get off the main road, we have to put distance between them and us."

Chace's fingers caught the neck of the manteau, and she pulled at it uselessly, feeling the strength in her left arm fleeing, as if trying to imitate her right. She croaked at Shirazi again, trying to say his name, but he was bent over the wheel, eyes fixed ahead, barely sparing a glance to the mirrors.

With the last of her strength, she slapped at his arm, and he looked at her then, and whatever he saw made his expression open in alarm. She motioned to the manteau, unable to speak, her fingers pawing lamely at the buttons on her front. He looked back to the road, then to her, reached out with his free hand, and she put hers on it, trying to guide his palm over her chest, trying to press it to the catheter. His hand slipped out from beneath hers, moved to her back, pushed her forward in the seat until Chace's head was against the dashboard. She felt his hand on her back, then beneath the manteau, and then there was an incredible pain as his finger plugged the hole in her back.

She wheezed, inhaled with a sob, exhaled, repeated, this time taking air deeper.

"Tara?" Shirazi said. "Tara? What can I do?"

She ground her teeth together, the pain from the wound in her back enough to eclipse the trauma from her shoulder. "Don't . . .

move your . . . finger," she managed to say. "Catheter . . . has a one-way . . . valve. . . ."

From the corner of her eye, she saw him nod, still driving with one hand on the wheel, the other on her back. With the entry wound blocked, the catheter was allowing the air trapped in her chest to escape, but the problem, quite obviously, was that as soon as he moved his finger, it would happen all over again. She was dimly aware that the new wound was a problem as well, but wasn't quite sure why.

"You're losing blood," Shirazi said.

That was it, she was losing blood. "Kit," Chace whispered. "First-aid kit?"

"We'll need to stop."

"Don't. Not. Yet."

He glanced at her, back to the road again, then shook his head. "No, we have to stop."

She tried to protest again, but the pain was simply too intense then. The jeep slewed to a side, barely slowing, and they came off paved road onto dirt, the transition rattling them both, and the movement of his finger wedged in her back made her cry out again. She bit into her lip, trying to ignore it, to feel past it, felt her teeth pop skin, tasted blood.

Then the jeep stopped, and Shirazi was shifting carefully around, hand still anchored to her.

"Tara, listen to me. I have to move my hand now. The kit, this is a Guard's jeep, they have a good kit. Pressure bandages, occlusion dressings, they have all of it. But I have to have both hands."

Chace nodded feebly.

"Try to remain calm. Try to stay calm."

The pain in her back exploded, fresh and renewed, as soon as his finger slipped from the wound. She was barely aware of his movement, of him straining around beside her, reaching into the back of the jeep. Her breathing went again, this time disappearing with terrifying speed, and Chace was aware that she couldn't make a sound now, even if she wanted to. His hands were on her back, on her skin, and she felt something tear, a distant vibration through her flesh, and in the silence of the jeep and the night, she heard the air hissing out of her chest, from somewhere below her chin. He gently pulled her back from the dashboard, sat her upright in the seat. She heard his door open, then, a moment later, hers, and he was working at her shoulder, now.

"Clean wound," he was saying. "It went straight through. You saved my life, Tara. Thank you."

She opened her mouth, then closed it again. It suddenly seemed like too much effort to speak. When he was finished doing whatever it was he was doing to her shoulder, he slipped his hands around her, pulled her out of the jeep. She tried walking, but her legs went boneless, and he had to drag her around to the rear of the vehicle. With some effort, he got her inside, laying her on her back. He tore the left sleeve of the manteau, exposing her arm to the elbow, and there was an almost insignificant pain, and she saw that Shirazi was now hanging an IV bag from a hook on the side of the jeep.

"We've got to keep going, Tara," he told her. "We've a long way to go still."

She nodded at him, and he turned to climb back into the driver's seat.

"Youness?" Chace asked softly.

He stopped. "Yes, Tara?"

"Why do they keep shooting me?" she asked.

She didn't understand why he laughed.

CHAPTER THIRTY

LONDON—VAUXHALL CROSS, OPS ROOM
13 DECEMBER 0418 HOURS (GMT)

"You're either a fucking lunatic, or you're a genius," Julian Seale said. "I still haven't decided which."

"Let's find out." Crocker adjusted his headset, nodded to Lex. "Go alive."

"Going live," she said, fingers flying on her keyboard.

On the plasma wall, in the upper-right quadrant, taking over a quarter of the screen in total, static lines appeared, then steadied, resolving into an image, black and white. Poole filled the screen, pulled back, adjusting the camera from his end, then his headset, and then Crocker could see Lankford seated past him in the command post, and Colonel Moss beside them both.

"Icecrown, standing by," Poole said.

"Status?"

Moss leaned forward. He was wearing his commando blacks, and the resolution from the satellite feed made his mustache look like a ragged smear of ink across his upper lip. *"SPT stands ready. Waiting on your order, sir."*

"Make it bleed," Crocker said.

"They can't come out via air," Crocker had told Poole ten hours earlier. "And they can't take the Caspian route, that would never work twice."

Poole looked up from the map spread on Crocker's desk,

frowned. "Then the northwest routes are out for the same reason. Turkey, northern Iraq, etc."

"That's what I'm thinking."

Poole moved his finger on the map, drawing a line east. "Afghanistan's out, too."

"Right."

"Doesn't leave much room."

"It leaves the south."

"That's the Persian Gulf, Boss."

Crocker tapped the map, southeast Iran. "Abadan."

"You're sitting on the Iraqi border there, same problem," Poole said.

"If you go west, which is what they'll think we're doing. Instead, we take them south . . ." Crocker's index finger followed one of the two blue lines bracing Abadan to the east and west, rivers running down into the Persian Gulf. ". . . by boat, have them met at the foot of the delta—say, by the SBS—transfer them to a RHIB, and then from the RHIB to a naval vessel in the Gulf."

"I like it," Poole said, after a moment. "But I foresee problems, namely getting the Admiralty to commit to bringing any of its precious toy boats in that close to Iranian waters. They'll cry 'Silkworm' and argue that the danger of a missile strike against the vessel is too great a risk; they'll tell the PM that one defector and one spy versus two hundred sailors isn't an equitable trade, and they'll be right."

Crocker scowled, looked up as there was a knock at the open door, Daniel Szurko sticking his head into the office, a blue file folder in one hand. "Paul?"

"Something I can do for you, Daniel?"

Szurko stepped in, smiling awkwardly at Poole. "Minder Two."

"D-Int."

"Something I can do for you, Daniel?" Crocker repeated.

"Hmm?" Szurko canted his head, looking down at the map on the desk. "Figured it out yet?"

"Working on it at the moment," Poole said.

"You have to get them out via the Gulf, you know." Szurko looked from Poole to Crocker. "It's the only possible route."

"Yes, we've just been discussing that," Crocker said. "The question is, how to give the exfil room to run."

"I've been wondering that, too." Szurko smiled at them both, then remembered the file in his hand, offered it abruptly to Crocker. "Meet *Hadi*."

"Hadi?"

"I think she can help. Let me know if there's more I can do."

He left the office, humming to himself. Poole watched him go. After a second, he said, "That's called eccentric, yes?"

"That's called brilliant," Crocker said, and showed Poole what was in the file.

"We *have device launch,"* Moss said. *"Seventeen minutes, forty-six seconds to target."*

"You know where to put it, Colonel?" Crocker asked.

"We're your Special Projects Team, sir. It's our job to know where to put it."

Crocker, for the first time in ages, felt himself smile. "Keep the channel open."

"Confirmed."

The screen flickered, changed, showing an exploded close-up of the northern edge of the Persian Gulf, satellite image overlaid upon the graphic. A small green dot appeared, moving from a position south, marked HMS *Illustrious,* tracking quickly north, towards southeastern Iran, the large, deep delta south of Bandar-e Khomenei, the largest oil refinery in the region. A timer appeared beside the moving dot, a countdown, seconds quickly ticking past.

Crocker watched for a moment, then turned to Seale, who was leaning forward, elbows on his knees, chin held in a hand. He slid his eyes to Crocker, grinned.

"Special Projects Team happy to be let out of their box to play?" he asked.

"More than you can imagine," Crocker said.

It took thirty-six minutes exactly from the time Daniel Szurko stepped out of Crocker's office to the time that Colonel Richard Moss, the head of the Special Projects Team, stepped into it. He arrived the way he always did when asked to report to D-Ops, snapping to attention and offering a crisp salute, even though, technically, there was no need for it. SIS fell outside of the Ministry of Defense, and thus was not a military institution.

That said, the SPT existed in the gray area between the two, the unit primarily comprised of combat engineers and military-trained technical specialists in a variety of fields. Theoretically, the unit existed to supplement D-Ops' operational capabilities, to take on those jobs or mission-related aspects that required specialized knowledge. If an operation required a dam breached, or a bridge blown, or power to a certain section of a certain city in a certain country cut at exactly the right time, it was the SPT that would make it happen. Moss was proud of his team's abilities, but as jealous of his men as Crocker was of his Minders.

"Paul," Moss said.

"You know Nicky Poole," Crocker said.

"Of course, good to see you, Nick."

"And you, Colonel."

Moss nodded, looked from one man to the other, then settled, as appropriate, on Crocker. "And what can the SPT do for you today, sir?"

"You're going to put a hole in a boat," Crocker said. "A reasonably sized hole, in a very big boat."

Moss's military bearing cracked as he smiled with pleasure.

"Live for it, sir," he said.

At two minutes, Crocker put his headset back on, signaling to Lex. The screen flickered, the satellite transmission resuming. On the screen, Poole, Lankford, and Moss were all in profile, watching a separate monitor, and past them, Crocker could see at least two other members of the SPT who were aboard HMS *Illustrious* in the

Persian Gulf. He slid his eyes up the clock, saw that it was less than ten minutes to eight in the morning in Iran.

"Closing to target," Moss said, glancing to the camera. *"Awaiting the order to arm, sir."*

"Arm," Crocker said.

"Arm, arm, arm," Moss repeated, turning away, and the command echoed again, distant. *"Would you like to see it, sir? We've got a nice visual on her."*

"Safe?"

"As houses, sir."

"By all means."

One of the SPT technicians moved, sliding back in his chair, and the screen flickered, went dark, then lit again, displaying the live feed from the torpedo speeding through the water. Another flicker, and now a new image, morning sunlight shining off the Gulf water, and the image magnified once, twice, again, bringing the view of a massive oil tanker closer and closer to the camera. Two pilot boats were running alongside it, escorting it out of the delta channel.

"One minute to impact, standing by."

"Hello, *Hadi,*" Seale said from behind Crocker. "Good-bye, *Hadi.*"

"She's the same tanker the Somalis tried to hijack back in '07," Crocker told C. "Iranian Navy managed to arrive in time before she could be boarded. It is conceivable that an action against it could be taken as the Somalis seeking revenge."

"The Somalis hijack ships, they don't sink them, Paul." She looked up from the photographs that Szurko had supplied to Crocker, staring at him as if not entirely certain he was joking. "You want to blow it up?"

"Not precisely," Crocker replied. "The problem is that both Chace and Cougar are being actively hunted. We have to find a way to clear a route for them, to open a passage through which they can make their exfil. Nothing overland is viable, and Chace can't fly. The water is the only option left to us, but we still need a distraction."

"Meaning you want to spill oil into the Persian Gulf."

"The Iranians are practiced at cleaning up their spills," Crocker said, quickly, trying to diminish the indictment. "They'll respond immediately, and the damage will be relatively minimal. But it will justify foreign interest, bringing ships in closer. And it will divide their attention—no matter how badly they want to find Cougar, they won't be able to ignore this."

Gordon-Palmer frowned, studied the photographs again. "It'll have to go to the Prime Minister for approval, and the only way I can see him allowing it is if he can maintain deniability."

"I'll take responsibility."

"Of course you will."

"I'm sending Poole with the SPT to Iraq within the hour," Crocker said. "Lankford will rendezvous with them, but they'll need to proceed to one of our ships in the Gulf for this to work."

"The Admiralty has agreed to the plan?"

"Provisionally. If we can get permission to hit the tanker, they'll bring in HMS *Illustrious* to stage from, and they're offering SBS support for the exfil, as long as we can get Minder One and Cougar out onto the open water."

"They won't go inland?"

"They have expressed reservations. Something about armed soldiers and foreign soil, I believe."

"Ah, yes, I'm told that's called 'an act of war.' " She actually smiled before asking, "And they can make it onto the open water?"

"Working on that part now. But if we're going to use the *Hadi* as a distraction, we'll have to do it by morning tomorrow in zone. Any later and instead of a distraction, we'll have confusion, and that will hinder as much as help."

"Yes, agreed. Very well, Paul, I'll sell it to the Prime Minister. But I know what he'll say."

"He'll say that if we don't pull this off, it's my job."

"Ah, at long last, Paul," C said. "You're learning."

On the plasma wall, the *Hadi* floated placid and stable, beginning to steam forward, into the Persian Gulf. On the headset, Crocker listened to the countdown.

"Impact, impact, impact," Moss said. *"Good impact."*

Nothing visibly changed on the screen.

"Not seeing anything," Seale murmured.

"Confirm impact," Crocker said into the mike. "No visual."

"Above the waterline, you'll not see anything yet," Moss said, and Crocker thought the man was decidedly pleased. *"Triple-D device, sir, directed charge low to the hull. She's bleeding now, sir, trust me."*

As if in response, *Hadi* began to turn to port, and on the screen Crocker could now discern motion on the deck of the ship, antlike figures moving aboard the massive oil tanker. Crocker wasn't certain, but on the surface of the water he thought he was seeing the first striations of color, the rainbow refraction of oil on water.

"Congratulations, sir," Moss said in his ears. *"It's a bouncing baby environmental disaster."*

CHAPTER THIRTY-ONE

IRAN—HORMOZGAN PROVINCE, ABADAN
13 DECEMBER 1658 HOURS (GMT +3.30)

TO: HEAD OF STATION, TEHRAN—BARNETT, L.

FROM: DIRECTOR OPERATIONS—CROCKER, P.

OPERATION: ICECROWN

MESSAGE BEGINS_

REQUIRE YOU DISPATCH STATION NUMBER TWO TO ABADAN. SECURITY DIVISION TO PROVIDE BACKUP DURING TRANSIT AND ON GROUND. STATION NUMBER TWO DIRECTED TO SECURE TRANSPORT DOWNRIVER ABADAN BY WHATEVER MEANS NECESSARY. VITAL TO REACH RZ ALPHA WITH MINDER ONE AND PACKAGE: COUGAR AT 2245 LOCAL, NO LATER, THEN PROCEED RZ BRAVO ALL SPEED FOR EXFIL.

STATION NUMBER TWO DIRECTED TO CLOSE BUSINESS OUTSTANDING PRIOR TO DEPARTURE.

STATION NUMBER TWO AUTHORIZED TO DRAW ANY MATERIEL IN SUPPORT OF ACTION.

STATION NUMBER TWO AND SECURITY ESCORT ORDERED TO DRAW ARMS.

_MESSAGE ENDS

It wasn't until Barnett had handed him the Beretta compact from the gun safe in the office, along with a box of ammunition, that Caleb realized, whatever happened next, he was finished in Iran.

"Hope to God you don't have to use it, Caleb," Barnett said around his cigarette. "And hope even more that if you do, you kill whatever bastard is aiming at you."

Caleb stared at the pistol in his hand, alien and ugly and entirely unfamiliar to him. He had performed dismally on his pistol drills at the School, had barely qualified, in fact. It seemed to him absurd that he should be trusted with such a thing, especially now, especially with what was at stake. He tucked the weapon into his backpack, along with the box of bullets, setting them beside his sat phone and GPS unit, then took the stack of rials Barnett was now offering him. He split them up amongst the backpack and his pockets.

"Medical supplies, you think?" Barnett asked him.

"MacIntyre's already taking care of it," Caleb said. "He's bringing a full kit, think it's even got a bottle of oxygen in it."

"Wise. No telling the state she'll be in when you get her."

Caleb appreciated that Barnett hadn't said "*if* you get her."

"VEVAK'll be on you the moment you step outside, you know that," Barnett said. "They'll be on the car to the airport, and they'll have the flight plan before you're in the air, and they'll be waiting for you when you touch down. Even with the confusion on the ground, all this running about because of the *Hadi,* you're still going to have a hell of a job losing them, and you're damn well going to have to do it if you're to pull this off."

"I was trying not to think about that, actually."

"That's enough of that. You're a better agent than you give yourself credit for being, Caleb. Doubt is good, it keeps us honest. But too much of it is a poison." Barnett put a hand on Caleb's shoulder for a moment, the paternal manner manifest once more. "You were a good Two, lad, and I'll make certain that goes in the permanent file."

"Thank you, sir."

They shook hands.

"You're a hell of a spy, Caleb," Barnett said.

The surveillance was blatant on the way from the embassy to the airport. Two cars, front and back, and only when they rolled out onto the field, to the airplane kept and piloted by the British mission in Iran, did the other vehicles back off, parking within twenty meters. Caleb lent MacIntyre a hand moving their few bags from the car onto the plane, and once everything was aboard, he looked back, saw that men had emerged from the cars. One of them, he was sure, was Zahabzeh, but at this distance it was impossible to read the man's expression, what he was thinking.

Caleb couldn't imagine his thoughts were kind ones, and for a moment he felt an absurd kinship with the man. He didn't know him, in truth didn't want to, but both of them, he recognized, were subordinates, both of them followers, now asked to lead, and he had to wonder if it sat as uncomfortably on Farzan Zahabzeh as it did on himself.

MacIntyre, like Caleb, had brought a go-bag. Or so Caleb thought. Until they were in the air and the man opened it, withdrawing a rifle with a folding stock. Caleb turned his attention from the map he had spread open before him, watched as MacIntyre checked the weapon, breaking it down and then reassembling it before stowing the long gun away once more. Then MacIntyre pulled a pistol from the bag, a Browning, and repeated the procedure.

"You're loaded?" MacIntyre asked.

"Not yet."

The man looked over at him with brown sleepy eyes. "Think you'll have a better time to do it, then?"

"I suppose not." Caleb folded the map away, unzipped the flap on his backpack, took out the Beretta and the ammunition. He loaded the clip slowly, struggling to get the last bullet locked into place, aware that MacIntyre was observing him the entire time. When he finished, he dropped the pistol into his pocket and looked at MacIntyre, not certain if, or even what, he should say.

"Don't think of it as killing," MacIntyre told him. "Think of it as saying 'Stop that' in a very clear, very permanent voice."

It was warmer in Abadan than it had been in Tehran, in the low sixties Fahrenheit, clear and without humidity. Caleb went to pick up the car from the rental station within the decrepit terminal. He had the keys in his hand and was headed to the vehicle itself before he caught the first hint of local attention. It wasn't at all surprising, but for an instant he felt near-panic, wondering what he might do or say if he was stopped with the gun in his pocket.

But it wasn't going to happen, and he knew that. To Zahabzeh, Caleb was secondary, a consolation prize at best; and for exactly the same reason that they hadn't been stopped upon leaving the embassy, heading to the airport, they weren't going to be stopped in Abadan. At least not yet. Zahabzeh had to let them run. They were his only possible leads to Chace, to Shirazi. They were his bird dogs.

Knowing that didn't particularly make him feel much better.

The car was a Khodro, an old one, and Caleb brought it around, waited until MacIntyre had loaded the vehicle and hopped in before pulling out onto Route 37, heading south, then east, into the heart of Abadan. The sun was just beginning to set as they drove past the refinery fields. The massive storage containers loomed along both sides of the road for five, six kilometers before giving way to the city itself. On the outskirts, they passed old houses crowned with *badgirs,* the ingenious natural air conditioners that had been invented centuries earlier, which relied on convection to pull hot air out, to pull even the slightest breeze in and down.

Traffic was thicker near the heart of the city, end-of-the-day commuters, one shift returning from the refineries as another went out to continue feeding the petrobeast. Caleb kept his eyes open for a place to stop, somewhere he and MacIntyre could get a meal. He finally parked outside a café just south of downtown. They exited the car, and while Caleb went inside to buy them each a cup of chay, MacIntyre stayed behind and searched the Khodro.

When Caleb returned, MacIntyre was holding a small, black square in his hand. "What should I do with it?"

Caleb set his tea on the roof of the Khodro, took the tiny tracking device, then tossed it underhand into the road. Traffic had crushed it to bits before he'd had a chance to pick up his tea again.

"You hungry?" Caleb asked. "I'm hungry. Let's get something to eat."

They found a downscale food stand another two kilometers south, closer to the forest of palm trees that grew all along the banks of the river. Water flowed past Abadan to the east and the west, river channels that had been artificially deepened and widened to accommodate the loading of pure light crude. The soil closest to the banks was lush and, even now, in winter, green. They ate outside, MacIntyre keeping one eye on their car, Caleb watching the people around him. For the first time since reaching Iran, for reasons he could not explain, he felt relaxed, and chatted cheerfully with the vendor who made their dinner.

Then MacIntyre said, "Mr. Lewis," and Caleb turned to see a black van pulling up, double-parking beside their Khodro, two jeeps with soldiers accompanying it. The soldiers stayed put, but out of the van came Farzan Zahabzeh, followed by two others. Zahabzeh turned back to them, spoke something Caleb couldn't hear, but its meaning was clear enough, and when he reached their picnic table, he was alone.

"Mr. Lewis," Zahabzeh said, in English. "I wish to speak with you."

"Have you eaten?" Caleb indicated the bench opposite him. "The *chelo mahi* is outstanding."

Zahabzeh shook his head, dismissing the offer and the pleasantry together. He looked meaningfully at MacIntyre, then back to Caleb. "I should like to speak with you alone."

Caleb shrugged, and MacIntyre got to his feet, went back to where the car was parked, leaning against it, watching them.

"We want Youness Shirazi," Zahabzeh said, after a moment. "You want your agent back. Let's make a deal."

Caleb didn't answer, looking at the man opposite him. While he'd seen him before, could remember him perfectly from the night in Noshahr when he'd tried to enter the safehouse, he didn't look quite the same. Caleb suspected it was mutual, and not solely because of the bruise he was now sporting at the side of his head. But the weight of what had transpired in the last two days—God, was it only two days?—clearly sat much more heavily on the man opposite him.

"You are planning to rendezvous with her," Zahabzeh said. "That is obvious; that is the only reason you can be here."

"I'm here to monitor the cleanup of the *Hadi,*" Caleb said.

"We are past playing games. I am offering you a deal. We take our man, you take yours, and that will be the end of things. We will reset the board. We will forget everything. Even Hossein."

"I really don't know what you're talking about," Caleb said. "I'm here to report on the oil spill in the Gulf. That's all."

Zahabzeh made a noise, anger breaking free of its confines, and Caleb saw the man's body tense before Zahabzeh was able to force himself to relax again. He got to his feet.

"Youness Shirazi is a traitor," Zahabzeh told him. "He will be executed for what he has done. Anyone assisting him is either a traitor or an enemy of Iran. If the former, they will be shot. If the latter . . . we will do what we must to protect ourselves."

He turned, returning to the van, not bothering to look at MacIntyre, not bothering to look back.

Caleb watched as Zahabzeh and his men loaded up once more, pulled away. One of the jeeps went with them, but the other one drove halfway down the block before stopping. The soldiers within remained seated, but he could see them watching him.

He thought about that for a bit, then decided he wanted to finish his dinner.

It was full dark by the time he was finished, and when they headed to the car, he told MacIntyre it was time for him to drive. They settled into their seats. MacIntyre started up the Khodro, driving easily, heading northward again. The jeep that had remained parked, watching them, pulled out to follow.

"We're going to have to get a boat," Caleb said. "And we're going to have to lose them before we do it."

"How lost do we want them to be?"

"Whatever it takes," Caleb said.

MacIntyre nodded slightly, downshifting. Caleb checked the mirrors, then the windows. He didn't see the van, and he didn't see the second jeep anywhere. It was possible that Zahabzeh had backed off, had even turned his attention elsewhere, but Caleb doubted that, particularly the latter. Yes, they were close to the border with Iraq, so close, in fact, that the river flowing past the western side of the city served to mark it, but Zahabzeh was still counting on them to lead him to Shirazi and Chace. If he'd backed off at all, it was only to make them think it was safe to run.

Caleb checked his watch, saw that it was forty-eight minutes past eight in the evening. Less than two hours until the rendezvous. An hour at most to get the boat, another hour to reach the pickup. There wasn't a lot of time.

They had entered a traffic circle, and Caleb realized that MacIntyre was now beginning his second loop, accelerating. A horn blared. In the mirror, he saw the jeep coming up behind them, trying to keep pace. They went around a third time, fast enough that the tires protested, and then a fourth, the squeal from the wheels louder, the grin on MacIntyre's face making him look like a boy deep in mischief. Cars ahead of them, behind them, were pounding their horns, and the Khodro was bleating at them in return, and they rounded the circle a fifth time. Now the jeep was ahead of them, not behind.

MacIntyre wrenched the wheel hard, right, and the rear of the car broke free, tires smoking even more furiously than before, and they shot west, accelerating, and turned, turned again, and again. Caleb saw the speedometer brush past a hundred and twenty kilometers an hour, swiveled in his seat to look back, and they were braking again, hard, turning again, and the jeep was nowhere to be seen.

They headed east, towards the river, driving quickly, and then the road narrowed as they passed into thick palms growing deep alongside the banks. MacIntyre turned them south, skirting the shore, killing their headlamps and slowing, and they could see boats moored along the water. Caleb reached for his backpack, pulled the GPS unit out and switched it on, taking a reading.

"Keep going south."

"We'll need a boat."

Caleb shook his head. "Not yet. Keep going south."

They continued following the river. Somewhere above them, they heard a helicopter drone, rotor pitch fading as it moved away, west.

"Mr. Lewis, we need to stop, find someone who'll sell us his boat."

"We're not going to buy a boat," Caleb said. "We buy a boat, there's nothing to keep the guy who sells it from taking our money and then calling Zahabzeh."

"Steal one, then."

"Can you pilot a boat?"

"No, sir."

"Neither can I." Caleb leaned forward in his seat, catching lights shining on the water. "Stop here. Get our things."

MacIntyre did as ordered, Caleb following, slinging his backpack over his shoulders. He felt for the pistol, still in his pocket, took it out and chambered the first round.

"Follow my lead," he told MacIntyre. "Don't shoot unless you have to."

"Never do, sir," MacIntyre responded, pulling out the Browning.

They made their way along the bank, then down to the small jetty, towards the boat with the lights burning inside. Caleb could hear strains of music, a radio playing, perhaps. The boat was a small one, maybe twelve feet, no longer, with the wheelhouse above the sunken cabin. He saw a shadow against the light, waited a few seconds for signs of other movement, other occupants, and not seeing any, stepped aboard.

He reached into his coat, pulled out one of the stacks of rials, holding it in his left hand. With his right, he raised the pistol.

"Excuse me," he said in Farsi, stepping down into the cabin.

The occupant, possibly the owner, was fixing a glass of tea from a small, single-coil burner, and he jumped in surprise, spinning around, then froze at the sight of Caleb, the money, the gun. He was a small man, mid-fifties perhaps, with a weather-beaten face coated in gray-and-black stubble.

"What—what is this?"

"We need to use your boat," Caleb said. He lowered the pistol, held up the rials, then tossed them forward, to the man, who caught the bundle, more out of reflex than intention. "We need you to take us down to the Gulf. We'll be making a stop along the way."

The man stared at him, then at the thick sheaf of bills in his hands. He ran a thumb against their edge, looked up again, this time past Caleb's shoulder, to where MacIntyre was standing behind him.

"I say no you will kill me?"

Caleb took a second bundle of rials out of his coat, this one from the inside pocket, tossed them as he had the first. The man was ready this time, caught them easily.

"Don't say no," Caleb told him.

CHAPTER THIRTY-TWO

IRAN—30.241350 BY 48.464821

13 DECEMBER 2245 HOURS (GMT +3.30)

The jeep, Chace decided raggedly, had probably saved their lives, despite the price she had paid in acquiring it. A military vehicle, it had allowed them to drive almost entirely unmolested, speeding out of the desert through the night, down from the plateau towards the Gulf.

But the price for it, she was beginning to think, might have been a little too high. She was starting to believe she wasn't going to make it.

There'd been three bags of Ringers, or its Iranian equivalent, in the kit, and Shirazi had fed all of them through her IV between that first panicked stop and sunrise. She was certain that was the only reason she was still around. The pain in her chest was constant and almost unbearable now, and it wasn't until he'd hit her with the morphine that she realized she must've been screaming. When the sun rose she understood that it hadn't been the night making her so cold. Through the narcotic haze she knew she was in shock, and falling deeper, the way she knew that while the morphine had stolen her pain, it probably hadn't done her respiratory system any favors. At some point, she'd begun coughing, and there was the taste of blood in her mouth.

Now it was dark again, and she thought her eyes were open and that it was night, but she really wasn't sure.

"Tara?"

She blinked, blinked again, saw Youness Shirazi looking down at her. She croaked at him, mouth coated in copper dust.

"We're here," he was saying. "I think we're here. Come, I will help you stand."

He reached for her, pulling her by her ankles, then wrapped an arm around her waist, and then she was upright, wobbling, clinging to him with her left arm. There was a river in front of her, water flowing quickly past, and the smell of it hit her, strong with oil. She coughed, felt blood in her mouth, tried to spit it out, but instead it ran down, over her chin. She couldn't even spit right.

"The pickup," Shirazi said. "By boat?"

She shook her head, not disagreeing, simply not knowing. Shirazi was walking with her carefully, and then he was lowering her, propping her against something as cold as she was, and Chace looked up, saw that they were beneath a bridge, the jeep parked perhaps ten meters away. Shirazi set his satchel down beside her, then checked her pupils, one eye, then the other. Then he checked his watch, frowned.

"I am going to look for them," he said. "I will not be long."

He started to straighten up. Chace grabbed for him with her left hand, the only one that was still working.

"Gun," she whispered, and even that hurt like hell, just the effort to say the single syllable.

He looked at her, confused, then nodded and pressed a pistol in her hand. She tightened her grip around the butt, barely felt the sensation of the weapon in her grip. With effort, she got her finger through the guard, onto the trigger, watched as Shirazi made his way through the shadows, then into the comparative light of the night, turning out of sight. He was going to check the road, she realized, just to be sure they weren't coming by car.

She closed her eyes, opened them again, saw a boat on the river, two figures silhouetted at the wheel. She heard voices, distant and dreamlike. She closed her eyes again.

When she opened them this time, there was someone coming towards her. She thought it was Caleb, started to say his name, and then he was on her, and she saw that she had been wrong. It wasn't Caleb.

She was looking at Zahabzeh.

For a second Chace was certain she was hallucinating, the morphine still playing tricks with her mind. She'd seen wonderful, horrible things with the morphine. Tom in her arms and Tom torn apart and Tamsin burning alive with fever, and this was horrible, the end of a nightmare, his hand coming at her out of the darkness, and her mind flashed on that hand tearing at her back, opening her chest to the air, and she tried to kick, bring the gun up, scream, all at once. The only thing that worked was the kick, ineffectual, and then one hand was over her mouth, the other hand tearing the pistol out of her grip, and the back of her head hit concrete, and the world went bright before swirling into shadow again.

She was being moved, pulled to her feet, the hand still silencing her. Chace saw the boat on the water, bobbing steadily, felt her feet dragging over the grass on the bank, out of the shadows. There was more light now—not much, but she thought she saw three figures on the boat.

Zahabzeh pushed her down to her knees. There was a van parked nearby, just off the road, and two other men coming towards them, but Zahabzeh wasn't paying any attention to them. He was focused entirely on the boat. He ran the slide back on the pistol he'd taken from her, pointed it at her head, much the way Shirazi had done only the day before.

Somehow, she didn't think this would end with Zahabzeh declaring his desire to defect.

"I'll kill her!" Zahabzeh shouted at the boat. "I will shoot her here and now!"

Chace wobbled on her knees, barely able to stay upright. There was movement on the boat, she saw one of the figures with a rifle. She didn't think it was Caleb, too large, maybe the other one, MacIntyre. That gave her hope, for an instant an almost indescribable feeling of triumph despite all her pain.

If they had Shirazi on the boat and MacIntyre had a rifle, she knew who he was aiming it at.

It wasn't Zahabzeh.

"My people are coming!" he shouted. "They are on their way! Give him up! Give us back Shirazi and you can still escape, you can take her with you!"

Something Tom had told her, when she had first joined the Section, came back to Chace. There were only three ways a Minder ever left, he'd said. They were promoted, they quit, or they died. Most of them took option number three.

"They won't," she whispered, surprised at the weakness of her own voice, unsure even if Zahabzeh could hear her. "He's gone."

Zahabzeh shouted something in Farsi, and the two men took hold of her, brought her to her feet, and she cried out at the pain in her shattered arm, then laughed when he put the pistol against her head.

"Give him back!"

"Shoot me," Chace whispered.

In her ear, she heard the gun go off.

She had just enough time to be honestly surprised that it was Zahabzeh who pitched forward, and not herself, when there was a flash of fire from the boat, the crack of a high-powered rifle. The man holding her right arm twirled away, and almost instantly she heard another shot, and the one at her left fell forward, as well. For a second, Chace thought she was going to fall herself, wobbling unsteadily on her feet.

Then there was an arm around her waist, and Caleb Lewis was holding her up, pistol in his other hand.

"You're safe," he told her.

CHAPTER THIRTY-THREE

LONDON—VAUXHALL CROSS, OFFICE OF THE CHIEF OF SERVICE, "C"
14 DECEMBER 1022 HOURS (GMT)

C leaned forward in her chair, pouring for herself what Crocker thought was a self-congratulatory second cup of tea from the china pot, before sitting back and looking at him with a slight smile. Rayburn, in his chair, and Szurko, beside him on the couch, were likewise jubilant, all of them in their proper place for the traditional morning meeting.

"She'll be all right, then?" C asked.

"They operated on Chace as soon as she was aboard *Illustrious,*" Crocker said. "As of an hour ago, she was stable, and had regained consciousness, though only for a short while. Her shoulder was badly damaged by a rifle round; will most likely require reconstructive surgery."

"And Shirazi?"

"Minders Two and Three took him out via RAF from Kuwait as of oh-four-hundred," Crocker said. "They should have him at the Farm before nightfall. Minder Two reports that Shirazi brought a goodie bag out with him: a list of all VEVAK agents working abroad, including within the U.K."

C moved her cup of tea to her mouth, but not before Crocker saw the smile. "That should earn us some favors from Box."

"I'd hope so," Crocker said.

She took a sip from her cup, set it back on the saucer, then set both on the side table and regarded him. "The Prime Minister phoned me this morning, Paul, once he'd received word of the successful completion of Icecrown. He made a point of saying to me, specifically, that I was to pass on his compliments to you for executing such a successful reversal of fortune. You not only spared the Government a humiliation, you handed them a triumph."

"The Prime Minister is being generous."

"If that's everything?" C asked.

"There is one more thing . . . ," Crocker said.

CHAPTER THIRTY-FOUR

LONDON—VAUXHALL CROSS, OFFICE OF D-OPS
25 JANUARY 0848 HOURS (GMT)

The phone on the desk rang, the red one, bleating once, twice, then a third time, before Kate stuck her head through the open doorway, asking, "You're going to get that?"

Very gingerly, right arm still aching at the shoulder, the muscles still relearning their role, Tara Chace picked up the handset.

"D-Ops," she said.

ACKNOWLEDGMENTS

I am indebted to the following for their assistance in the creation of this novel. While much of the action is clearly anchored in fact, this is a work of fiction entirely, and any verisimilitude is due, in no small part, to the help of the following individuals.

To Lee "Budgie" Barnett, a hypothetical spy, who went above and beyond to answer several questions of the FCO. If you're still under surveillance, feel free to give them my number. I'd love to talk to them.

To Alisdair Watson and Antony Johnston both, for fielding my absurd cultural queries promptly and thoroughly. To Arnaud Savry, for late-night translation work. My French is rusty; yours, sir, is clearly not.

Special thanks to Gerard "Jerry" Hennelly, who continues to be an endless font of information regarding what exactly goes in the black bag, how it's used, and when to use it. Your help on this book was enormous and essential, and I am, as always, grateful.

To those who asked not to be named: thank you.

And finally, to my wife and children, for once again enduring my departure into a world far removed, and for welcoming me back when I returned.

ABOUT THE AUTHOR

GREG RUCKA resides in Portland, Oregon, with his wife and two children. He is the author of ten previous thrillers, as well as numerous graphic novels, including the Eisner Award–winning Whiteout series, also a major motion picture starring Kate Beckinsale.